Rescued by a Runaway Angel

The stranger's eyes opened and, in the waning light, Bella found herself staring down into cobalt blue eyes.

"I never thought I was bound for heaven," the stranger said, his voice a hoarse whisper.

"You have had an accident, sir," she said. "It would be better if you remained quiet. You were set upon by a highwayman. He shot you, but I do not think it is much of an injury."

"Much you know, my girl," the man said. "I have the devil's own headache." In the clear morning light, he surveyed his rescuer with total amazement. She looked so like a fairy sprite that he blinked his eyes to see if she would disappear. His glance flicked across to her horse, the portmanteau, and the bag of supplies and immediately he suspected that his woodland sprite was a runaway. "And where are you bound for on this fine spring day?"

"I am on my way to London," she said.

"Let me guess. You are going to London to be married."

"Oh, no, sir. I am never going to marry."

Berkley Books by Martha Powers

DOUBLE MASQUERADE
THE RUNAWAY HEART

The Runaway Heart

Martha Powers

BERKLEY BOOKS, NEW YORK

To Jean Powers, Jeanne De Vita and Ann Marie De Vita for sharing secrets, laughter and tears, and for bringing out the best in each other. Your friendship is a joy to behold.

THE RUNAWAY HEART

A Berkley Book / published by arrangement with the author

PRINTING HISTORY
Berkley edition / May 1990

ISBN: 0-425-12102-X

A BERKLEY BOOK® TM 757,375
Berkley Books are published by The Berkley Publishing Group, 200 Madison Avenue, New York, New York 10016.
The name "Berkley" and the "B" logo are trademarks belonging to Berkley Publishing Corporation.

PRINTED IN THE UNITED STATES OF AMERICA

10 9 8 7 6 5 4 3 2 1

Chapter One

"First bed her, then wed her, is what I say."

The coarse words and gruff rumble of laughter halted Arabella Mallory as she walked along the path beneath the open windows of the library. It was Derwent Granger's unaccustomed humor that made her pause. She could not recall ever hearing her uncle laugh. Fascinated, she pushed her way into the bushes until she stood below the tall windows and waited to discover the source of his amusement.

"I cannot believe you would joke about such a situation."

Bella smiled at the confusion in her cousin's voice. She could imagine Woodie's round face puckered in bewilderment. His large brown eyes would be slightly glassy as they always were when he failed to understand a joke. She cocked her head so she would miss nothing of this impromptu entertainment. It wasn't eavesdropping, she rationalized, only curiosity.

"Think on it, Woodruff. The girl is fond of you, but you will have to let her know you are interested in marrying her." Derwent's voice boomed in disgust. "You've got to be more forceful in your approach."

Now Bella's interest was truly piqued. She hadn't known that Woodie was contemplating marriage, but liked her cousin well enough to wish him luck in his suit. She wondered if it was a local girl, but couldn't think of anyone in whom he had shown any interest. But then they only saw others on Sunday when they went into the village for church services. No one called at the hall, at least not since Uncle Derwent had taken over on the death of her father seven years earlier.

"I haven't an idea how to go on, Father. She does not see me in the light of a suitor."

Poor Woodie, Bella thought. She wished she could see into the library, but she could imagine her cousin staring down at the Aubusson carpet in an agony of embarrassment. He was four years older than she, but at times Bella felt they were the same age. For all that he had been in London for the past several years, he was no more sophisticated than she who had been isolated on the estate. It was apparent from his voice that her cousin had little idea how to conduct a courtship.

"You've been in the bloody girl's pocket for the past two weeks and have made absolutely no discernible progress." Derwent's voice was scornfully biting.

"I was laying groundwork," Woodie defended sulkily.

"You should have been laying the girl instead."

"Derwent, there is no need for such coarse language in my presence." Bella heard the quiver of agitation in Aunt Emma's soft voice.

"Begone, woman," Derwent snapped. "This has naught to do with you."

"I wish to r—remain," Emma stammered. "Matters of the family are my concern, too."

Bella was amazed at her aunt's temerity in speaking so plainly. The poor woman rarely stood up to her husband, preferring the invisibility of silence to anything that might bring attention to herself. Bella felt a curious satisfaction now that her relatives were all present. The cast was complete, and she leaned against the rough brick wall waiting for the scene to continue.

"Woodruff is not your son, madam," Derwent sneered. "If his mother were alive, I would not be saddled with such a wife as you. If you must remain, do so, but keep your tongue firmly between your teeth. Now, Woodruff," he continued, "have you mentioned marriage to the girl?"

"Not exactly." Bella smiled at Woodie's hesitancy. "I've brought up the subject many times, but she has never shown much interest."

"Much interest!" Derwent exploded. "I told you last week to offer for her."

"I tried to, sir, but she kept changing the subject."

Bella's shoulders shook as she was overcome with amusement. Even at twenty-five, her cousin still needed a great deal of direction. It wasn't that Woodie was stupid, just that he was not a particularly quick thinker. A bumbler, if the truth were told. Whoever his sweetheart was, the poor girl would hardly swoon with delight at his hesitant declaration.

"God give me patience!" There was the sound of a crash, as if Derwent had swept something from the desk in his exasperation with his heir. "Before the week is out, you will offer for the chit."

"What do I do if she refuses me?"

"Bella cannot refuse, you idiot!" Derwent roared.

Her legs unable to hold her up, Bella slowly slid to the ground until she was sitting with the wall of the house supporting her back. Only her stunned surprise at her uncle's statement kept a cry from bursting from her lips. Inwardly she was torn by a hysterical urge to laugh and an even stronger feeling of outrage.

Marry Woodie? It was not that she wasn't fond of him. When he wasn't away at school, he was a good companion. They did not have much in common except their isolation on the estate. He was not kin; he was Aunt Emma's stepson. Thankfully he was not much like his father. Woodie was rather slow-witted, but there was a kindness in him that Derwent lacked. Although she liked her cousin, she did not wish to spend her life with him. The thought was ludicrous. Why on earth had her uncle even considered such a preposterous idea? As though in answer to her unspoken question, the conversation continued.

"Bella has no other option than to marry you. She has been kept isolated here at Mallory for the past seven years. She has seen virtually no one in society because we have told the neighbors that their visits were unwelcome. You have seen for yourself that she has no one to talk to. When I took over here, I dismissed all the old servants, and each year I replace them so that none will find their loyalties tested."

Now Bella understood why her home which had hummed with the activity of contented servants had become a place of gloom and resentment. Her father would have been furious to discover that all the servants who had served him so faithfully had been dismissed. The replacements wore dour expressions, outward symbols of their inner discontent with the bone-wearying duties and penny-pinching pay. Her mouth tightened as Derwent's harsh voice continued.

"You will marry Bella because it is my wish. I and your step-mother are her legal guardians, and she will do as we say. Look at how she has obeyed us in these seven years. She has rarely questioned any of our decisions. She firmly believes that we are doing the best we can to save Mallory. For that alone, she will be grateful to accept your offer."

"Then the estate is safe from her father's creditors?" Woodie's voice was incredulous.

"Don't be a nodcock, boy. Mallory was never in jeopardy. When Bella's father died, the estate and all his investments were in fine shape. All set down in trust to the girl. Luckily, she was overcome with grief at the time of his death. If she had been able to come to the reading of the will, all this would have been impossible."

A spasm of pain crossed Bella's face, leaving it white and pinched in the afternoon sunlight. Wearily, she leaned her head against the bricks, finding the answers to some of her unconscious questions in Derwent's harsh voice. She winced at the thought of her own stupidity at never questioning him. Granted she had been only fourteen at the time, but surely she might have known that her father could not have been the spendthrift Derwent had charged him. How could she have been so easily fooled?

She remembered her devastation after the death of her father and with what happiness she greeted Aunt Emma's arrival. Motherless since birth, Bella had welcomed her aunt's soft voice and quiet demeanor, thinking to replace some of the love she had lost. It was only when her uncle arrived that she sensed the weakness in Emma's character.

Derwent Granger had arrived on a rainy Sunday, and since then her life had been overcast and gloomy. With little emotion her uncle had told her that her father was deeply in debt and that only through his intervention were they able to stave off the creditors who were crying for payment. She had been so brokenhearted at the death of her father that she had accepted his words without question.

"You mean, all these cheese-paring economies were merely

to convince Bella that she was a pauper?" Woodie's voice brought her out of her reverie. His words were slow, as if he had difficulty taking in the duplicity of his father.

"Of course they were," Derwent blustered. "What does a young girl know about business matters? I was her guardian, and I was protecting her interests. I have managed Bella's investments all these years and her holdings have increased to a very tidy sum. She is a wealthy young lady. What did she need with a large household? She was adequately fed and clothed."

Bella stared down at the brown bombazine dress that she had made over this spring. It had little shape, hanging limply to her ankles, the only trim an inch of lace beneath her breasts. A single tear slid down her cheek, not for the lack of pretty clothes, but for how hard she had tried to save money. She had been proud of her sacrifices, knowing that every economy must be employed to preserve her ancestral home. And all her paltry efforts had been totally unnecessary.

"Really, Woodie," Derwent said. "I could not have the child running through her money. And now I see little point in letting the estate fall into the hands of an outsider. I have planned for a long time that you would marry the girl. She is of a proper age now, so there is no need to wait. Thinking she has no dowry to offer a possible husband, she should be more than willing to accept your suit. But it must be done soon. In two years time she will be twenty-three, and then she will come into her inheritance. Once she marries you, Woodie, everything will be in our control," Derwent explained slowly, as though to some lackwit.

"But I don't want to marry Bella," Woodie burst out, his voice aggrieved. "She is pretty enough with her curly hair and wide brown eyes, but with her hoydenish ways she would make me a laughingstock in the *beau monde.* She is far more at home in the woods than she would be in a drawing room. Naturally, sir, I am fond of her, but I do not wish to marry her."

"I am not interested in whether you wish it or not. You *will* marry her, Woodie." Derwent's words were soft, but there was a hint of steel that usually presaged a temper tantrum. It was never wise to cross the man. "She need be little bother. Once you marry her she will remain here at Mallory, and you can return to your life in London. I will make it my business to care for Bella."

There was a heavy silence within the library. Bella pressed her back against the brick, the rough surface a physical reminder of the reality of the overheard conversation.

"What do you mean, Derwent?" Emma asked.

"The girl needs schooling." Bella shuddered at the streak of menace in the voice of her uncle. "I have been gentle with her thus far, but she is far from docile. Ever since that unfortunate episode concerning her bloody horse, there have been occasions when she has not jumped to obedience. Once she marries, there is no longer a need to treat her so—so carefully. No need to look astonished, Emma. It can't have escaped you, madam, that if the chit dies unmarried her money reverts to some charitable organization that benefits unwed mothers or some other group of layabouts."

"I will not permit anything to happen to Bella," Emma declared, her voice shaking but determined.

"You will not permit, madam?"

"Nor will I allow Bella to be hurt in any way," Woodie said, for once unafraid to challenge his father's authority.

Once more silence invaded the study. Outside, cowering beneath the window, Bella could feel the pulsing tension in the room.

"Surely, you two mistake me," Derwent said unctuously. "I have no intention of harming Bella. I want only what is good for the girl. She will marry you, Woodruff, and that will be the end of all this nonsense."

Perhaps the conversation continued, but Bella's mind went blank, unable to cope with any more information. It was some time later when she again became aware of her surroundings. There was no sound from the library, and all around her the grounds were silent.

It was strange that she felt no real surprise at all that she had heard. Ever since her father's death in the carriage accident, she had watched the changes at Mallory with a certain puzzlement. Her father had always told her that if anything happened to him she would be well taken care of, so she hadn't understood why the estate was in jeopardy. Now she felt guilty that she had ever questioned the character of her father.

Her mother having died in childbirth, Bella had been particularly close to her father. Sir Robert was a scholarly man and delighted at the quick mind and insatiable curiosity of his daughter. His hobby was tracing the early trade routes to the Orient, but he would leave his books to entertain Bella with stories and games, many a night keeping her past her bedtime, much to the disapproval of her nanny. He had taught her to read and helped her learn the countries on the freestanding globe in the library.

Bella had adored her father and was hurt by Derwent's accusations that he had been a rake and a spendthrift. With the knowledge of her uncle's duplicity, her father's reputation had been restored and he stood before her again in untarnished glory.

A sense of outrage that she had been so easily gulled came to her, and she debated her best course of action. For seven years she had let a ruthless man control her destiny, but she was determined that she would not continue in such a vein. She must act if she intended to save herself.

With determination she rose to her feet and brushed off her dress. She checked to be sure there was no one on the path before she sped off to the stable. Slipping inside, she crept to Violet's stall, jumping when the mare whickered in greeting.

"Softly, sweetheart," Bella said.

She reached up to stroke the velvety nose and leaned her forehead against her old friend's neck. She had raised Violet from birth, and the horse had been her only consolation after the death of her father.

Reaching up beside the box, she took down the lead rope, then tied it to Violet's halter. She opened the door of the stall and led the mare out the back door of the stable to the path that led toward the home wood. She moved briskly, mindful of Violet's condition. Unbeknown to Derwent, Bella had bred the mare with one of the tenants' stallions. Violet was close to term, due to drop her foal within the month.

Bella felt more secure once they were inside the woods but moved steadily along the path until she reached one of the far pastures. She undid the lead rope and scratched between Violet's ears. The mare brushed her face down the front of her dress, blowing in contentment. Bella petted her for a moment, then pushed her away and dropped to the grass to watch Violet graze.

Time slipped back seven years as she remembered how close she had come to losing her four-legged friend when Derwent announced that most of the horses would have to be sold. Though she had wept, Bella believed her uncle when he told her that such stringent measures were necessary to save the estate. He told her they would keep only a few of the carriage horses; all the others would be put on the block.

She assumed that her own horse Violet would remain, but Derwent said they could make no exceptions. Bella had refused to consider parting with the mare. She knew Violet would not bring in a substantial sum, and she told her uncle that she would write her father's solicitor to explain the situation.

Bella laughed, the sound sharp in the silent pasture. It was clear why Derwent had given in and let her keep Violet. At the time, she assumed he was showing a moment of compassion. She realized now that it was only her mention of contacting the solicitor that had saved her mare.

Anger burned away some of the heartache that she felt over Derwent's betrayal. He had lied to her for seven years and now was planning to force her into a marriage with Woodie in order to gain complete control of her inheritance. Never! Bella vowed.

The mere thought of marriage sent a tremor of fear through her body. She would never marry. She had decided that many years earlier, and nothing would convince her to change her attitude.

Aunt Emma had explained most succinctly what she could look forward to in marriage. Once wed, she would become the chattel of her husband who would be free to abuse her, dominating every part of her life. Her aunt had told her of the pain and humiliation she would discover in the marriage bed, and for that alone Bella had vowed never to put herself into the hands of any man.

Even before Aunt Emma had spoken, Bella had seen the kind of life her aunt endured. She was afraid of her husband, moving like a shadow in his presence so as not to incur his easily aroused anger. Many times Bella had seen bruises on her aunt that spoke of a brutality in their relationship that repelled her.

Remembering back to Derwent's words in the library, Bella shuddered at her uncle's promise to care for her. She had always been afraid of him. Even at an early age she had realized that he took delight in meting out punishment. He had caned her several times, and she had been more terrified of the way he had handled her than she had been of the beating itself. She had never considered that he was being gentle with her because he did not have full control of her inheritance. If she married Woodie, she suspected that Derwent would take pleasure in taming her to his idea of obedience.

Just the thought of being in Derwent's power sent a shaft of weakness through her. What could she do to protect herself from such a fate?

She could contact her father's solicitor, she decided in rising excitement. On further thought, her shoulders drooped with the realization that the man could really do little to protect her. Derwent was her guardian, named in her father's will, and the solicitor might pity her conditions but in the final analysis could do nothing to mitigate her circumstances.

The only hope she had of avoiding Derwent's total domination was to run away.

Just the thought sent her stomach plummeting in fear. She rose to her feet and whistled to Violet. The mare raised her head, whickering softly in response, before she picked her way through the grass to Bella.

"Oh, Violet. Whatever am I going to do?"

The mare stared at her with great doelike eyes, as if she were considering the words.

Bella chuckled. "You're right, old friend, there is little to choose from in this case. If I stay, I shall be trapped in a loveless marriage under Derwent's control. What could happen to me that would be worse? Being shut up in a convent would be preferable to remaining at Mallory!"

That idea held a certain appeal, she thought as she resumed her seat on the ground. She had read about the rich women who had become abbesses in ancient times. After she gained her inheritance she might consider such a plan. She could read and do good works and live free from the domination of men.

Once she began to consider the idea of leaving Mallory, she felt a slight glow of excitement. In the past seven years, the books in the library had become companions in her loneliness. She had read about exotic places and had traveled far in her imagination. She had never thought that someday she might visit the places that she had dreamed about. This was her chance, but did she have the courage to take it?

Yes, she decided without further hesitation.

She needed to get away from Mallory and find a place where she would not be discovered by her uncle. Basingstoke was the closest village of any size. Her father had taken her there once, not long before he died. It was not too far, but unfortunately it was precisely where Derwent would expect her to go. Even though it would be more difficult to get to, London was the obvious choice. In such a large city she would be able to find work and remain hidden for two years, until she could claim her inheritance.

She would have to move quickly. Woodie, under his father's pressure, would offer for her immediately. If she accepted him, Derwent would see that they were married with all speed. If she refused him, she suspected that her uncle would find some way to force her into the relationship.

In two days' time, Uncle Derwent would be meeting with some of his cronies at the pub in the village. They met every Friday, much to Aunt Emma's approval, for it meant one night that she was free to do as she pleased. Bella was not sure what besides drinking and gambling went on, but she knew that Saturday morning her uncle never rose before noon. With him out of the house, Friday would be the perfect time for her escape. Once Aunt Emma was in bed, she could let herself out the kitchen door. The servants were accustomed to her comings and goings, and she had no personal maid to note her absence. With any luck Derwent would not discover her disappearance until late on Saturday, and by then she would already be well on her way to London.

Having picked the time, Bella reviewed the things she would need in order to escape. She would definitely need money for such a venture. She would have to pay for food during her journey, and then of course she would need money to maintain her until she could find a position in London.

Uncle Derwent made no secret of the fact that he kept coins in the desk in the library. He had often indicated the hoarded pile as proof of his diligent economies that preserved the roof over her head. On Friday night, she would take whatever money was there. It was not actually stealing, she thought, raising her chin in defiance, since the money belonged to her.

She was only sorry that she would not be present to see Derwent's face when he discovered the empty strongbox.

Her stomach lurched at the thought of her uncle's anger. She knew him well enough to realize that he would find some way to vent his fury. And with a sinking feeling she suspected he would take out his vengeance on Violet.

The only solution was to take Violet with her when she left. Although she would have to be careful not to overtire the mare, it would be wonderful to have a companion. It would be like taking a piece of Mallory along with her.

Satisfied that she had considered all exigencies, Bella stood up and prepared to return to the house. If Woodie proposed, she would appear to be demurely surprised by his offer. She would act flustered and ask for time to think it over. On Saturday, her disappearance would be answer enough.

Chapter Two

The earl of Wyndham placed his elegant hands over the backs of his playing cards and rose to his feet. One black brow rose in arrogant hauteur, but there was a twinkle of amusement in his dark blue eyes. He stared around the table, shaking his head sadly at the group of grinning nobles.

"Gentlemen, I cry craven. I fear I must end this evening of high stakes before I lose not only my reputation as a gamester but every last farthing to my name," he said.

" 'Tis not your farthings that interest us, Tristram," Merriweather drawled, " 'tis the pound sterling."

"I stand corrected, old man," Tristram replied. Then despite the good-natured suggestions to continue, he demurred and made his farewells. "I have to make an early start of it in the morning. Without my proper rest, I shall look exceedingly hagged."

With easy grace, he left the table, strolling through Watier's toward the door. He waited for his multi-caped greatcoat which he whirled carelessly around his shoulders and then, saluting the footman with his silver-headed walking stick, left the club. He sniffed the June air, grateful for the early morning freshness of the breeze. His face was a study in concentration as he stopped outside. His thoughts were so deep that, when he moved, he failed to notice the man just exiting the club and slammed into him.

"Devil take it, sir!" The assaulted gentleman sputtered and

thrashed about ineffectually, blinded as he was by the brim of his hat which had fallen forward.

Tristram recognized the voice immediately and a grin cut across the grimness of his features. Bowing clear to the waist, he spoke, his voice trembling with dismay. "Dreadful sorry I is, gov. I didn't bloody well see your trim and agile figure."

A growl of anger rumbled from the man. He snatched off his hat and his full head of straw-colored hair above a good-natured face gleamed in the lamplight. "Are you having me on, sir?" he growled.

"Dinna fash yerself, darlin'," Tristram crooned, peeking through his thatch of black hair as he bowed elegantly before the enraged figure.

"Tristram! By all that's wonderful!" Edward Heathrow-Finchley threw back his head in full enjoyment of the joke. "I must have missed you inside. Devil take it, it's good to see you."

"And you, Neddy." Tristram rose to his full height, where he towered over his stocky friend. "In town for long?"

"A sennight. Millicent is here to purchase gowns for the fall season. That is something I will never understand. A man may wear his clothes for several years, but his wife must be freshly decked out each new season." His voice held a doleful tone, indicating his awareness of the inroads made on his pocketbook by such extravagance. "Enough said, Tristram. Millicent will demand you join us for dinner tomorrow. I hope you're free."

"Unfortunately I'm off to Dragon's Keep tomorrow."

"But I've only just arrived, old boy. Couldn't you put it off?" Neddy asked. "It's been too long since I've seen you."

Tristram's features settled back into the grim cast it had worn earlier, and he shook his head. "I'm truly sorry, but my visit cannot wait. However, if you can take me up, I shall offer you a brandy on your way home."

"Good Lord, man. You can't mean you're walking!"

There was such horror in his friend's voice that Tristram could not contain his amusement. The deep sound of his laughter echoed back from the buildings on the street as the coach drew up at the curb. Neddy was much affronted and with a sniff he waved the still chuckling Tristram up the steps as he gave directions to the coachman.

"If you weren't such a great towering fellow," Neddy said as the carriage started, "the footpads would fleece you with the ease of a greedy mistress. There is something quite daunting about the breadth of your shoulders, even to those of us who know you."

Tristram merely smiled at his friend's grumbling. He had known Edward Heathrow-Finchley since they had been up at Cambridge together. Despite their disparate sizes they had become friends and had invaded London together, managing to work their way through a great quantity of brandy, gambling hells and opera dancers. Neddy always said traveling in Tristram's company was to his advantage. According to him, women were drawn to the taller, handsomer nobleman, but by the time Tristram made his choice they had fallen under the spell of Neddy's charm and good nature.

They both had married the same year. Neddy had been swept off his feet by Millicent Dunwoody, a bustling dynamo in her first season. Neddy loved playing the hen-pecked, exasperated husband but Tristram knew that his friend adored his wife and was almost disgustingly happy. Unfortunately Tristram had not been so lucky. His eyes were bleak when they arrived at his town house.

"Glad to see you have such a well-stocked cellar," Neddy said, appreciatively sipping the fine liquor. "I've had to make do with the occasional smuggled bottle. Damn Napoleon!"

"Agreed," Tristram said.

They drank in companionable silence, but finally Neddy placed his snifter on the table and stared across at his friend. Despite the fact that he lived a short distance from Tristram's country estate, Neddy had seen little of him in the last several years. Ever since Tristram's wife died in childbirth, there had been an estrangement that he much regretted.

Looking at him now, he did not like the lines of discontent etched in Tristram's face. His hair was still midnight black, but now there were wings of white at his temples. He had heard from friends that Tristram's temper was explosive and that his wit contained more sting than it had in their early days. There appeared to be a wariness in his bearing, as if he had retreated to the sidelines of life and was looking on, a semi-interested observer of the foibles of human nature. The carefree companion was gone, replaced by an austere stranger.

"Is Colin here in London?" Neddy asked, pleased to note the softened expression at the mention of Tristram's son.

"Yes. The bantling is champing at the bit to examine the entire city while he is here. He is not content with an occasional trip to Astley's."

"I have not seen the lad in quite a while, but Millicent says he visits the children with great regularity. She fair dotes on him, as you know."

"He is a good lad. Tends to be far more sober than I was in my youth, but perhaps that is just as well. At my advanced age, I doubt I could handle a child who was the scourge of the countryside." Despite his words, Tristram sounded slightly baffled that this should be the case. "He always has his nose in some heavy tome. Of course he is alone a great deal, but has had excellent tutors and seems to have an endless curiosity."

"Not unlike his father," Neddy interjected. "How is his seat?"

Tristram grinned, knowing Neddy's passion was hunting. He was forever chiding Tristram for not being more available during the hunting season. "You will be pleased to know he is eager to join the hunt. He's a natural rider and has a real feel for a horse. He walks about a great deal so his legs are strong. Not a flashy rider, mind you, but eminently solid."

"What more could one ask? It will make him a capital hunter."

"Just what I have been thinking. I've been looking around at Tattersall's for a horse for his next birthday. Although his hands are strong, I don't want to get one that will be too much to handle."

"What age is he now?"

"He's just turned nine."

"Devil, you say." Neddy shook his head in wonder. "I forget he is so much older than Carolyn. She is only six."

"As lovely as her mother?"

"Perhaps not," he said, grinning fatuously. "But the chit does have rather a winning way. She has Millicent's ability to go after what she wants and will turn London on its ear in ten or more years."

"And the rest of your brood? I fear I have lost count. You

may have been a late starter, Neddy, but you have made up for the delay in the amount of your progeny."

"It seems I have discovered a real talent. If only I could find a way to make such an accomplishment put gold in the coffers. Unfortunately I have produced a colony of females, which is a decidedly costly affair. The expense of ribbons and other folderols threatens to make me a pauper." He ruffled his straw-colored hair in exasperation, but there was pride evident in every line of his face. "After Carolyn, we had Jennifer, then Letitia, and last of course the twins, Bethanne and Amy."

"Good Lord, Neddy!" Tristram got to his feet, chuckling appreciatively. He strolled to the mantel and stared gravely down at his friend. "Have you considered taking up a hobby? Or long walks? By this time, Millicent must have suggested a mistress."

Neddy shifted in his chair and a flush rose to his round face. "Well as a matter of fact, she did mention some such thing just recently. I assured her I would consider it, if this latest addition turns out to be a boy."

At this news, Tristram threw his head back in laughter. To Neddy it was as though he were seeing his old friend again. He smiled contentedly as he let Tristram enjoy his amusement.

"I'm glad I've had this chance to see you again, Neddy. And as soon as I get back we'll get together. I'd love to see Millicent," Tristram said. "I wish I didn't have to tear off in the morning."

"Why such a rush to partake of the bucolic pleasures of the countryside?" Neddy asked. "Have you become jaded with the delights of the city?"

Tristram snorted in amusement. "Questions like that impune my carefully cultivated reputation as a man about town. I have to make a quick trip to Dragon's Keep on estate business. Hopefully not above a day or two. I don't like to be gone overlong, as I'm concerned about Lady Wyndham."

"Your grandmother? Is she unwell?"

There was a slight hesitation before the answer. "In a way. She's been living here since Christmas. Rarely out and about. She did not even enter into the season." Tristram set his glass on the mantel and stared glumly into the fire. When he looked up, his eyes were troubled. "Damn it all, Neddy! The woman is dwindling away before my very eyes."

"I saw her but a year ago and she was still bristling with energy. Is it consumption or some wasting disease?"

"In my opinion it is sheer spite."

"I say, old thing, isn't that rather harsh?" Neddy eyed his friend with concern, uncomfortable with the anger he saw in the snapping blue eyes. "The old girl is getting on in years. Must be all of seventy, so it ain't surprising she should be slowing down. Although I did have the feeling, she had held the choir of angels at bay through their fear of her sharp tongue."

Tristram snorted. He was silent for a minute and when he spoke his voice was contemplative, as if he were working through his own thoughts. "It started right after Christmas. We had a particularly sharp exchange, but I thought we had reconciled. Eventually I began to notice that she was not going out in society much. She didn't take to her bed, mind, but she might just as well have for all that she hung close to the fire. She seemed to have lost her zest for living. Daily, she became quieter and more amenable. Since this was so unlike her, I called in the local doctor. He said there was nothing physically wrong with her. He suggested a fever of the brain."

Neddy shifted in his chair, stretching his short legs toward the fire. His good-natured face was wrinkled with concern as he considered his friend's words. Tristram had always been close to his grandmother who had raised him after his parents died while he was still in short coats. That they remained close was even more mystifying in the face of the fact that the dowager countess had been at loggerheads with Tristram since the day he came out of his mourning period. Although others might think it, Lady Wyndham was the only one who had the temerity to suggest that he remarry.

Remembering the old tartar, Neddy laughed. He'd always had a soft spot for the dowager countess and hated to think of her diminished by ill health. "Is it possible that she does have some—uh—inflammation of the brain?" he asked.

"No," Tristram answered sharply. "She is playacting. I am convinced of it. The woman hopes to force me to her wishes and, despite my love for her, I cannot agree. It would be laughable if it weren't so frustrating. It's as though she has given up on life. And she's just stubborn enough to stick her spoon in the wall rather than give in to reason."

"I suppose she still wants you to remarry," Neddy ventured,

wincing at the black-browed glower on his friend's face. "Even though you bite my head off, I must say I have always thought that would be a good idea."

"No!" For an instant, a spasm of pain crossed Tristram's features before his eyes closed and all expression was wiped from his face. "Sorry, Neddy. It's just that I have been married once and have promised myself I will not repeat the experience." He held up his hand as his friend started to speak. "I know you are content, nay enthralled, with Millicent, but we are not all so lucky. In your enthusiasm for parson's mousetrap, you would wish it on your friends. Believe me, I am adamant that I will not marry."

It was clear to Neddy that the subject was closed. He remained for a while and they conversed on noncontroversial subjects, but he was sad to note the bitter quality that edged much of Tristram's words. Eventually the topics dwindled and he took his leave.

Tristram banked the fire, smiling as he thought about Neddy's burgeoning family. The man would overpopulate the countryside at the rate he was going. He and Neddy had been so close once, before their lives had taken different paths. He missed the frequent visits with his old friend and promised when next he was at Dragon's Keep for any length of time that he would not hold himself apart from Neddy and Millicent.

His grandmother would be delighted, for she would surely think that association with the Heathrow-Finchleys would remind him of the joys of married life and convince him of the necessity to remarry. As he should know, she never gave up that particular crusade, though her current campaign might likely kill her.

She had always been a domineering, vigorous woman wanting nothing better than to meddle in the lives of others and most especially the affairs of her grandson. Since Johanna's death she had attempted to pair him with every marriageable woman in London. It was only when Tristram had adamantly announced that no matter what ploy she used he would not marry that she had moved into his London town house and had fallen into a fit of the sullens.

At first he had paid little attention to her sulks. Eventually he began to notice a change in the dowager countess.

Lady Elizabeth Wyndham was shrinking. His grandmother

had always been a large-boned woman with a majestic presence, but now she appeared to be smaller. Scrutinizing her more closely, he realized it was more a matter of attitude than any change in her appearance. It was as if the old woman had withdrawn from life and the very withdrawal was sucking the life out of her, leaving nothing behind but a shell.

Her sharp tongue, renowned through London for its lightning thrusts, had lost its edge. Occasionally he had gotten a rise out of her, but only when he had provoked her outrageously. To Tristram's despair, the dowager countess, who had left princes and paupers trembling in the wake of her biting setdowns, was becoming a sweet-tempered old lady.

Despite his suspicion that his grandmother was acting out of pique, he was genuinely concerned for her. He had searched the London shops for a present that might intrigue her but came away empty-handed. He knew it would take more than a trinket to pique her curiosity and renew her zest for life.

Knowing he had to leave early in the morning, he quitted the library and climbed the stairs. He let his valet prepare him for bed but after the man left, stood at the window looking out over the square. He was not particularly tired. The visit with Neddy had stirred up memories of his early days in London, and he was reluctant to retire to his bed. There were too many ghosts waiting to people his dreams.

He tried to push away the memories but the face of his wife appeared clearly in the darkness. Johanna had died giving birth to Colin. She had cursed Tristram at the end, swearing she would have her revenge. He had accepted her words because, although the cause of her death was the baby, he felt guilty that his own arrogance and stupidity had played a strong role in her death.

What a miserable journey, Tristram thought as he shifted on the unfamiliar saddle. The stallion was no better than a job horse and he would be lucky to reach the Golden Cockerel by sundown. He supposed he shouldn't complain but instead be grateful that he hadn't been thrown when his curricle lost the wheel.

He had finished his business at Dragon's Keep quickly and had been making excellent time on his return to London when he feathered a bend in the road a little too tightly. When the wheel had spun off, he had managed to keep his seat by sheer strength; if not, his grays might have been permanently injured. As it was they had gotten off with only a few cuts and bruises. He had left them at a nearby inn and continued on to London on the rented horse, an ornery, hard-mouthed beast if ever he'd seen one.

A sharp bark made him aware of the need to stop. His eyebrows lowered over his eyes as he glared down at the wicker basket tied to his saddle. He should have left the puppy with the innkeeper, but the thought of Colin's disappointment had spurred him to improvise a method of bringing the blasted beast along. A brown head poked over the rim of the basket, then lifted a pair of wide eyes to Tristram in silent entreaty.

"A winsome trick, old son, but most effective," Tristram said, sighing in resignation as he reined in the stallion. Dismounting, he plucked the pup out of the basket and set it on the ground. He frowned as it seemed far more interested in investigating the long grass than in accomplishing anything more productive. "Cut line, Beau. We haven't got all day."

Leading the stallion, he followed the wriggling brown body along the road. He hoped Colin would appreciate the sacrifice he was making in wet-nursing the dog. He could just imagine the boy's face lighting up at the story and chuckled in anticipation. If it hadn't been for Colin and the joy he found in the boy's existence, he would wish he had never married. His marriage to Johanna had been a mistake from the moment the bishop pronounced them husband and wife.

Johanna Lindsey had been acknowledged as an Incomparable at her come out ball. Tristram had first seen her, surrounded by a circle of dandies, looking like an exotic rose in a field of wildflowers. There was a radiance about her that he found intoxicating and from that moment he was blinded to any of her faults. With the totally committed enthusiasm of a twenty-two-year-old, he had fallen in love. He courted her amid the exciting entertainments of London and married her in a dazzling ceremony at the end of the season.

He knew now that he had been mesmerized by her elegant beauty and the sensual excitement that emanated from her. He had assumed that her outward loveliness was a reflection of her soul, not a shiny patina to cover the shallowness of her character. He had not known the real Johanna. He had clothed her with the virtues and qualities he desired; he realized now that the woman he loved had been a figment of his imagination.

Peace had been declared and she'd begged him to take her to Paris. Their honeymoon was the extension of a dream. They danced through society by day, and at night indulged in an erotic whirlwind beyond Tristram's wildest imaginings.

Their return to England and Dragon's Keep rang the death knell to their relationship. While he was contented to be at home with the woman he loved, Johanna hated being away from London and her legion of friends. She detested the boring details of day-to-day life on Tristram's estate, dubbing Dragon's Keep, "The Heap". She had no care for the historic beauty of the place; she thought it was old-fashioned and grim.

Far from the glamour and entertainments, Tristram discovered that they had virtually nothing in common. He loved books, and she sneered at his idea of reading as a form of entertainment. He loved the countryside, but she pined for the frivolous amusements and excitements of the city. He tried to engage her in conversation but discovered that beyond fashion and gossip she had little desire for discourse. She rejected all of his values and pleasures with one exception. Johanna needed his lovemaking.

Each night she sought his bed, seducing him anew in the dark hours of the night. For Tristram who desired a more complete relationship, this aspect of their lives filled him with despair because, despite the disaster of their daily lives, he found the nights sensuously intoxicating. Each morning he cursed himself for his weakness.

Perhaps if he had been older and more mature he might have handled things better. Admittedly he had been hurt by her rejection of him in any other terms than sexual. He had no idea how to deal with his selfish, pleasure-loving wife. When she sulked, he rode out his ill temper. She filled the Keep with loose-screws and dandies invited down from London for her endless house parties. And he, in his confusion, spent more time away, occupied with the business of his estate. He hoped that by ignoring the problem, in time things would improve. He left her more to herself only to discover that what little relationship they had established in their first months together was irreparably lost and, worse yet, he had no desire to rebuild it.

The remainder of their short marriage was a kaleidoscope

of house parties and arguments, culminating in Johanna running off with Henry Addison, a love-struck baronet from the next county. Tristram debated divorcing her, but his pride would not permit such a move. He pursued her out of anger, rather than desire or love. He killed her lover in a duel, then dragged her back to Dragon's Keep. He tried to convince her that they could rebuild their marriage but it was too little, too late. Johanna died giving birth to Colin, and to his eternal guilt, Tristram felt only relief.

A low growl interrupted Tristram's musings, and he stopped walking and looked down at the puppy. Beau's floppy ears hung close to his small head and his body was motionless as he stared at the woods lining the road. Rustling noises could be heard in the brush, and the puppy bristled at the unfamiliar sounds. He looked up at Tristram for reassurance and then returned his attention to the intriguing noises. He trotted a few steps away, then cocked his head to the side as if to hear more clearly.

"My guess would be a rabbit," Tristram said to the dog who was clearly puzzled by the situation.

Beau lifted each foot, held the pose for a moment and then carefully set it in front of him. Finally he could contain his curiosity no longer and bounded forward. He was almost to the trees when a particularly loud crash sent him scuttling back to the safety of the road.

Tristram snorted as he reached down to scratch between the floppy ears. The puppy was delighted with the attention and leaned against his Hessians, contented for the moment. Tristram scooped him up, stroking his soft coat before setting him back in the basket. He looked up at the waning sunlight and calculated how much farther he had to go. It would be close, but they should make the Golden Cockerel before dark. He mounted and, after giving Beau a final reassuring pat on the head, kicked the stallion along the road.

He had only traveled a short distance when suddenly the stallion sidestepped, almost jerking the reins out of Tristram's hands. He heard the gunshot but, before he could react, he felt a blinding pain on the side of his head. Abruptly, the light began to dim. The darkness swirled around him as he slid sideways toward the ground.

* * *

Bella's feet hurt. She had been walking on and off since sunup and now it was late in the day. She tried to ignore the discomfort but she found her entire concentration focused on her feet. Promising she would rest when she got to one hundred, she began to count her steps. By eighty, she was limping and it was only with the strongest resolve that she continued to the end. Gratefully she dropped Violet's reins, sat down on a fallen log, and stretched her legs out in front of her.

She looked up at the sunlight filtering through the trees and wondered how far she had come. By the slant of the sun, she estimated that it was getting close to sundown but she could have guessed that from the nagging hollowness in the pit of her stomach. She had been gone from Mallory for nearly a day. She knew that her uncle would be furious when he discovered her missing and would search until he found some clue to her whereabouts. Although she had tried to cover her tracks, she had not come far enough to feel secure.

She ought to look for a spot for the night. She couldn't risk going to an inn and sighed at the thought of another night spent in the woods. Aside from missing the comfort of a soft bed, she was reasonably pleased with how her escape had gone. Except the next time she ran away, she would consider proper footgear.

Her half boots had seemed the logical choice. She should have realized that she could not ride Violet for long, especially since the mare was so close to term. Her boots were not very comfortable for long walks. They rubbed her heels and pinched her toes but much as she would prefer it, she could not walk barefoot.

Violet nuzzled her shoulder as if to apologize for her condition. Bella reached up to stroke the satiny neck. "It's not your fault, old girl. Father always said timing was crucial to all campaigns."

Tonight she must start earlier to find a place to camp. She chuckled at the thought, wondering if her father would be surprised that his liberal education of his daughter had resulted in an ability to run away.

Sir Robert had not raised her as the pampered lady of the house. He had encouraged her to visit the tenants, feeling that their native common sense would leaven the arrogance natural to the aristocratic world she would be entering. She had worked and played alongside the tenants' children, learning the secrets of the land that would eventually be hers. She had learned the skills to survive out of doors and, although she had never had an opportunity to depend solely on herself, felt competent enough to make good her escape.

Bella yawned, rolling her shoulders to ease their stiffness. She was really tired since she had only permitted herself a short rest the night she left. She had quitted Mallory just after midnight and had wanted to get as far away as possible. She alternated between walking briskly along the moonlit road and riding on Violet. Since she kept Violet's pace slow, she was not sure that walking wasn't faster but at least it did give her sorely abused feet a rest.

When she had stopped for the night, she knew she could not risk a fire so close to the road. The June night was chill, and a hot cup of tea would have been most welcome. Instead she had snuggled beneath her blanket, her head pillowed on her portmanteau.

She dozed during the remainder of the night, waking at every unusual sound, to lay with heart pounding until she could decide if the noise represented any threat. Seeing the first streaks of sunlight, she quickly made a small fire and brewed herself a mug of tea with water from a nearby stream. After the tea and some bread and cheese she was still cold and stiff and began to walk just to get warm. Her spirits were at a low ebb, but she remembered what waited for her back at Mallory and her resolve to escape returned. Now that it was daylight, she kept to the woods, making use of the footpaths and animal trails, keeping one eye on the sun for direction.

Bella's stomach grumbled, reminding her that she needed to hurry before it got dark. After wriggling her toes experimentally, she once more struggled to her feet. She had not gone far before she heard the tinkling music of moving water. The thought of soaking her throbbing feet spurred her onward until she came to a small clearing. Water, too shallow to be called a stream, trickled over moss covered rocks.

She led Violet to the water, unpacking her bundles as the mare lapped thirstily. After removing her bonnet, she set about making camp and gathered branches and twigs for a small fire. Suddenly the sound of a shot rang out and she quickly hurried to Violet's side to soothe the startled animal. Her heart pounded as she strained her ears in the silent woods.

The shot had been fired closeby, and now Bella could hear the sounds of a horse moving along a road, apparently just beyond the trees. A second horse approached. There was a furtive quality to the movement that sent a wave a fear trembling through her body. She held Violet's muzzle so the mare would not whicker, and waited in growing suspense. A second shot was fired. A horse screamed and thrashed in the brush, then once again silence clamped down over the woods. After several minutes, the sound of hoofbeats retreated on the hard-packed trail.

All this activity seemed to take a long time but Bella guessed, all told, it had not taken more than five minutes. It was terrifying being able to hear so much but not see what was happening. Her imagination was afire with possible dangers. All she could do was guess. But no matter what she guessed, she knew she would have to investigate before she would feel safe again.

She left Violet beside the stream and walked quietly down the trail toward the area where she had heard the gunfire. The woods began to thin and eventually she could see that her path would intersect the road. She cut into the woods, moving as silently as she could and stopping every few feet to listen. All was silent.

Breaking through the trees, she looked both ways but the road was empty. She stepped away from the comfort of the woods and saw a horse lying beside the road.

The fully tacked black was dead. Bella felt her stomach lurch at the sight of his bloodied head. She backed away, knowing there was nothing she could do for the poor animal. A soft cry stopped her in her tracks.

She waited for the sound to be repeated, hoping she would hear it over the pounding of her heart. When it came again, she relaxed, recognizing the sharp little bark. She approached the horse, circling it until she spied the wicker basket attached to the saddle. It was upside down and, from the angry rustle, it appeared that something was trapped inside. She hurried forward and lifted the basket to discover a small brown puppy.

"Why, you're only a baby," she crooned as she picked it up.

The puppy wriggled in her hands, licking at her cheeks while emitting sharp little cries of welcome. She cuddled it to her as she walked back to the road. Beneath her fingers, she could feel the tiny heart racing, and she whispered soft words until the beat slowed to a more reasonable rhythm, then set the dog on the ground. He sniffed along the edges of the hard-packed surface and then stopped, standing motionless for a moment before bounding into the tall grass.

The puppy was invisible, but Bella could follow the sound of his thin whining. As she moved toward him, her heart pounded and a presentiment of what she would find prickled along her nerve endings. The pup was standing beside the body of a man whose face and shirt were covered with blood.

Bella hurried to his side but at first glance could see no reason for hope. She knelt down beside him, reaching out to place her shaking fingers against his neck. A cry burst from her lips as she felt the heartbeat, weak but steady, beneath her hand. The man was alive.

Chapter Three

Although the wounded man was alive, unless he was cared for immediately Bella suspected he would not be in that condition long. Remembering the sound of the two gunshots, she felt an urgency to remove him from the area. She had no way of knowing whether the highwayman would return, but she had no intention of letting him find the injured man and finish his work. He was much too heavy for her to carry; for that she would need help.

Leaving the puppy beside the injured man, she hurried back into the woods. She gathered up her blanket and knife, then, leading the mare, returned to the road. Once more she knelt beside the man. Grateful for her experiences in caring for the tenants at Mallory, she checked his limbs for any sign of broken bones. Finding none, she spread the blanket and, trying her best not to jostle him too much, rolled him onto the blanket. She could not hope to lift his deadweight onto Violet's back, so she would have to improvise a way for the mare to pull the blanket.

Going to the dead stallion, she unbuckled the bridle and, with hands shrinking from the blood on the leather, pulled it off. She tied the reins to two corners of the blanket, then fastened the bridle to Violet's saddle. She led the mare, pulling her awkward burden, back along the path to the clearing. She was grateful that the man was unconscious for despite the slow pace, his body jerked over the ruts and dents on the trail. She did not know whether the movement would kill him, but she felt certain if she left him where he was he would die.

Bella was damp with perspiration by the time they reached the clearing. She untied the blanket, leaving the horse and man beside the stream as she returned to the road. There was no way she could unsaddle the dead horse, so she cut the girth with her knife and retrieved the saddle, saddlebags, and the saddle pad. After taking them to the clearing, she again returned to the road.

She cut a leafy branch and brushed the road free of tracks. If the highwayman returned, she did not intend to lead him to the clearing. She cut brush and piled it at the entrance to the trail. From the road, the path should be invisible. Finished at last, she hurried back to the stream.

Kneeling down, she once more felt the man's throat, praying that her rough usage had not completed the task that the robber had begun. His heart beat steadily beneath her fingers.

She moved quickly now, rummaging in the man's saddlebags until she found a fine lawn shirt. Saving a wide piece for a bandage, she ripped the shirt into strips and dipped them into the stream. She bathed the man's face, relieved to see that despite the amount of blood, there was only a thin cut just above his ear.

"I'd say the gentleman is very lucky," she said to the puppy, an interested observer of her ministrations.

Taking a fresh wet pad, she washed the cut slowly, watching in concern as bright red welled up in the wound. The man moaned and his body moved restlessly, but he did not regain consciousness. Deciding the cut was clean enough, she pressed the fresh bandage against his scalp and tied it firmly across his forehead. Night was descending fast, and Bella hurriedly wrapped the blanket around him and pillowed his head on the saddle pad.

She sat back on her heels, debating what to do next. The puppy nudged her arm with his cold, wet nose, and she picked him up and cuddled him in her lap. She stroked his soft coat, and the rhythm had a soothing effect. So much had happened that she had not realized how shaken she had been, until she felt the relaxation of her tensed muscles. She would love to make a fire, but was too afraid of giving away their presence to anyone in the vicinity. Although it was a little cooler, the man was covered enough so that he wouldn't take a chill. She could do nothing more for him until he regained consciousness, except prepare for night and wait for morning.

With a final pat for the dog, she rose to her feet and took the stranger's bridle off Violet's saddle, washed the blood off the leather, and placed it beside his saddle. She removed Violet's bridle and saddle and, knowing she would not stray, let her graze around the edge of the clearing.

The puppy frisked about her feet while she worked, yipping sharply as she dug into the food bag. She hand fed him some ham scraps, smiling at the tiny body, wriggling in enthusiasm for such a treat. Just watching him recalled her own hunger, and she took out some bread and cheese, dipping a mug into the stream before she returned to her patient. She placed her hand on his forehead, grateful that the skin was cool. She smiled when the puppy curled up on the blanket, adding his contribution to keeping the gentleman warm. From the quality and cut of his clothes, Bella had already ascertained that he was probably a nobleman.

While she ate, she studied the man. She liked the aesthetic lines of his face. She took note of the patrician nose, broad forehead, and stubborn chin that hinted at the arrogance of the man when he was awake. The black hair with wings of white at the temples lent a devilish quality to the handsome face. He was very tall with broad shoulders and long, lithely muscled legs. Bella suspected he might be quite intimidating, especially if he were angered, but the lines at the corners of his eyes indicated he also was quite familiar with humor. She leaned closer, studying the stranger's face as she wondered what color his eyes were.

The stranger's eyes opened and, in the waning light, Bella found herself staring down into cobalt blue eyes.

"I never thought I was bound for heaven," the stranger said, his voice a hoarse whisper.

"Oh," Bella cried, embarrassed to be discovered staring so intently.

"What happened?"

"You have had an accident, sir," she said. She placed her hand on his shoulder, holding him still when he tried to sit up. "It would be better if you remained quiet."

"I was on my way to the Golden Cockerel," was the next whispered utterance. "There was a shot."

"You were set upon by a highwayman. He shot you, but I do not think it is much of an injury," Bella said, trying to encourage him.

"Much you know, my girl," the man said. His conversation seemed to waver between confusion and an amused awareness. "I have the devil's own headache."

"Don't move. I'll be right back."

Quickly, Bella took one of the damp cloths and wetted it in the stream. She wrung it out, folding it before she placed it on his forehead. The gentleman's sigh of pleasure was answer enough that her ministrations were welcomed.

"My horse?"

"I am sorry to say, sir, that it's dead. I had to leave it. I did rescue most of the tack."

"What an enterprising angel," he commented.

Bella was amused by his sarcasm which she suspected covered a feeling of helplessness. Even injured the man had an air of authority. She would venture to guess that he was seldom at the mercy of others and must chafe at the thought that he was not in command of the situation.

She thought he had drifted off to sleep and remained quietly at his side for fear of waking him. Night was creeping into the clearing, blurring the edges of the trees and hiding them away from intruders. The stranger's voice sounded frail when he spoke again, and she was amused at his attempt to conform to the amenities.

"I am Wyndham. Lord Tristram Wyndham. At your service." His ironic words were followed by a chuckle that Bella felt more than heard.

"I am Arabella," she said. "Try to sleep. You will feel better in the morning."

"I frankly doubt that, my dear," he drawled.

Bella changed the cloth on his forehead, smiling at the repeated sigh. She placed her hand on his shoulder, just to remind him of her presence, and was grateful when she felt his body slowly relaxing. By the time the moon rose, Lord Wyndham's breathing was the steady rhythm of sleep.

Getting to her feet, she retrieved her portmanteau and rummaged inside until she found her cloak. She returned to Lord

Wyndham's side, checking to be sure he was well-covered. She was bone-tired after her short, fitful sleep of the night before and her exertions of the day, but the lingering fear of the return of the highwayman and her patient's troubled sleep kept her awake most of the night.

Bella was grateful when morning came. A smile stretched her mouth as she observed her patient's chest, gently rising and falling in a natural sleep. Stiffly she rose, careful not to wake him, and walked down the path, cutting into the woods as it came close to the road. The road was empty, and she listened intently for several minutes but could hear no one about. In relief she returned to camp, determined to make a small fire after completing her ablutions.

After a necessary trip to the woods, she washed her hands and her face, released her hair from its braid, and brushed it. She tied it back with a ribbon, debating whether she should change to a fresh dress as she ruefully noted the dirt and blood staining her gown. The thought of tea convinced her to wait.

Using the firestone she had brought from Mallory, she soon had a small fire going. Roused by the activity, the puppy trotted into the woods, bounding back after completing his mission. She fed him while she waited for her tea to brew, then cupped her hands around the mug, absorbing the heat from the metal as she raised it to her lips. She closed her eyes and sighed as the warmth crept through her body.

Tristram awakened slowly, lying perfectly still as the memory of the night before returned. In the clear morning light, he surveyed his rescuer with total amazement. Arabella, of the soft voice and gentle hands, was nothing more than a child. She looked so like a fairy sprite that he blinked his eyes to see if she would disappear. Her hair was brown but held streaks of gold which shimmered in the sunlight. With her wide brown eyes and curly hair she looked as adorable as the puppy who was snuffling around the clearing.

He felt a twinge of annoyance that such a child could be so efficient. It did not fit the picture of heroic behavior that he held of himself. By God, the girl had nursed him like a baby.

A frown wrinkled his forehead, and the sudden pain reminded him of his own infirmity. Instead of anger, he could feel a wave of amusement washing over him as he imagined what his friends would say to his current predicament. In particular, Neddy would be delighted at such a turnabout.

"Would you like some tea, Lord Wyndham?"

Tristram had been so involved with his own internal dialogue that he had failed to realize the girl had come to his side. He squinted up at her and she quickly dropped to his side. In the sunlight, he was pleased to see she was as sweet-faced as he remembered.

"I would love some tea," he said, attempting to sit up.

He had to bite back a sharp retort as his petite rescuer moved to help him. His light-headedness reminded him that he must submit to petticoat tyranny for the moment. However, once he regained some strength, he would regain control of the situation. After all, a man was surely more qualified to undertake any rescue mission.

The ministering angel's hands steadied him as he waited for his head to clear. It amused him that she seemed to sense the moment he became restless under her care, for she immediately stood up and brought him the promised drink.

His hands shook and he held the mug against his chest, inhaling the pungent odor. He raised it to his lips, took a swallow, and then several gulps. When he lowered the cup, he raised an eyebrow at the smiling expression of the girl who eyed him with the same approval as his old nanny when he had performed particularly well. Startled, the girl blinked her eyes in embarrassment.

"Is there more?" he asked.

For answer, she leaped to her feet and returned with a small teapot. She poured with the elegance of a formal tea, her face intent with concentration. She waited solemnly while he finished the second cup.

"How does your head feel?" she asked.

Tristram shook it experimentally and was relieved to experience only a dull throb. He grinned. "My father always said I had a thick head, so I should not be surprised that I have taken little injury. I feel weak but otherwise quite fit."

"Once you have had some food, you should be well on the way to a full recovery," Bella said. "Unfortunately I must change the bandage and I doubt if that will be all that is pleasant. I will try to be gentle."

She untied the bandage and soaked the pad covering the

wound to ease its removal. Tristram felt slight discomfort and was amazed at her general efficiency. Her fingers were cool against his skin. Once when she leaned forward, her hair brushed against his cheek. The tumbled curls were silken and smelled of the woods. He inhaled her scent, disappointed when she finished and moved away.

"It is healing beautifully, Lord Wyndham." Her face flushed with triumph as she continued. "It is not bleeding, so I will not put on a new bandage. The air will be good for it. There is no sign of infection."

"Many thanks to a gentle doctor." Tristram nodded his head in gracious salute, smiling as she blushed in confusion. "Now, my girl, where is this food you so blithely mentioned? Despite the luxury of this place, I cannot loll around all day."

Quickly Bella emptied the food bag, laying out the bread, cheese, and ham, then hurried back to the fire to brew a fresh pot of tea. She was flustered when she realized that he was waiting for her and sat down across from him and reached for a slice of the ham.

"Your name is Arabella?" he asked, selecting a thick slice of bread.

Bella's mind seemed frozen as she debated her best course of action. She doubted that he would recognize her name, but she did not intend to take any chances. Her eyes shifted desperately around the clearing as she struggled to invent a suitable name.

"I am called Bella, your lordship. Bella—uh—Waters," she mumbled in sudden inspiration.

"Charmed, Miss Uh—Waters," Lord Wyndham said gravely. "Perhaps you might enlighten me as to how we happen to be in company. There are parts of yesterday that seem rather a blur."

Bella explained what she had heard as she was making camp and how she had found him. She was pleased when he rewarded the puppy's role in his discovery with a shredded pile of ham. After the hungry pup had eaten his fill, he curled up on the edge of Bella's skirt. With a soulful glance from his brown eyes, he dropped his head onto her foot and went to sleep.

"His name is Beau."

"He is a very fine dog, Lord Wyndham," she said, stroking

the silky head. "Beau refused to leave your side until you were bandaged properly."

"He is a present for my son. Despite the fact I was cursing his presence earlier, I think he will be a welcome addition to my household." After a pause, he continued. "You say the stallion had been shot."

He frowned when she described finding the stallion but had to chuckle as she explained how she had brought him back to camp on the blanket. When she finished, she ate in silence, waiting for him to assimilate all the information.

"What a wonderment you are, Miss Waters."

Tristram shook his head in disbelief at all the petite girl had done. He was most impressed by her inventiveness. He did not know anyone who could have done more. The thought of the danger the child would have been in if the highwayman had returned sent a surge of anger pounding up to his head.

He tried not to stare at the girl, but as he watched her beneath half-shuttered lids he became more and more curious about his companion. Her clothes were unfashionable and of poor quality. Her dress, already several years old, apparently had been sewn by an inept seamstress.

Surprisingly, she had the manners and speech of a well-born lady with none of the artificial affectations he usually associated with a debutante. He assumed she must be very young since she had shown no fear at his presence and had nursed him through the night with no awareness of the impropriety of her actions. For a moment he wondered if some one of her relatives had not waylaid him for the express purpose of compromising the girl. He was ashamed at the thought, after all she had done for him. It was a momentary aberration, quickly dismissed after one look at Bella's steady brown eyes. This was no scheming wench.

Now that he had eaten he felt far better, and his brain slipped away from his own difficulties as he considered the puzzle of the girl. His glance flicked across to the horse, the portmanteau, and the bag of supplies and immediately he suspected that his woodland sprite was a runaway.

"And where are you bound for on this fine spring day?"

With a mouthful of cheese, Bella was saved from immediate reply. She stared at him for several minutes, attempting to take his measure. He certainly was handsome, she admitted, and she did like the amusement that occasionally flickered in his eyes. There was a look of honesty and stability in his austere face that convinced her that she might tell him the truth. Or at least part of it.

"I am on my way to London," she said.

"Let me guess," Tristram said. "You are going to London to be married."

"Oh, no, Lord Wyndham. I am never going to marry."

"You don't say." He had been sure she was running away to join her sweetheart, but there could be no mistaking the shock in her voice at the suggestion of marriage. There had also been fear, he noted with surprise. More curious than before, he asked, "Then why are you going to London?"

"I have left my position in the country and must find work. It seemed to me that my best chance of employment would be in a large city. And besides," she added, "I have always wanted to see London."

"An excellent reason," Tristram said. "Although I would suggest it as a fine place to visit, I would not recommend it for one not acquainted with its more sordid aspects. Couldn't your last employers recommend some position not quite so far? Unless, of course, you left under some kind of cloud."

"Oh, no, milord!" Bella cried. "I was not turned out. I just decided it was time to leave. I have thought a great deal about what I wish to do, and it seems to me that only in London will I be able to achieve my goals."

Tristram took a sip of his tea before he spoke. "And to what lofty position do you aspire?"

"I was hoping to become an abbess?"

Caught off-guard by her words, he sucked in his breath, choking on the tea. He coughed until his eyes ran and his head throbbed with pain, all the time goggling at the girl who had so blithely admitted to aspiring to the ranks of the muslin trade. His voice was a mere rasp as he barked out his question. "What did you say?"

"I wish to join a nunnery," Bella said, slightly taken aback by her companion's reaction. "I have read about such women who do good works and I thought it a worthy goal. I do not know exactly how one goes about such a thing, but I think in London I should be able to find out. I don't suppose you know?" she asked.

"Good Lord!" Tristram said. He was torn between hysterical laughter and downright annoyance that the chit should be so unsophisticated. Despite all her expertise in caring for him, he could just imagine this artless child arriving in London, prey to the first unscrupulous person she met. He would have to convince her that she could not continue on a path that would surely lead to her destruction. Noticing the offended expression at his exclamation, he rushed into speech.

"Forgive my words, Miss Waters," he said. "It was only my surprise that you should be set on such a decision with so little thought as to how you might attain such a goal. I myself do not know the particulars, but I feel certain that you might do more harm to your cause by dashing off to London. It would seem to me that you should return to your home and make inquiries from there."

The wide brown eyes dropped, and Tristram was treated to a view of her hair as she shook her head.

"I have no home," came the soft reply. "I am an orphan and quite on my own."

"Surely you have relatives to whom you might apply?"

Once more her head shook in negation.

Tristram was sorry that his grandmother wasn't present. She had always accused him of being the debaucher of all sorts of innocent women, and yet he was actually in the process of trying to convince this stubborn child to return to the safety of her home. The dowager countess would truly appreciate the irony of the situation. Knowing his grandmother's penchant for meddling in the affairs of others, he suspected that she would be plagued by curiosity until she found out who the girl was and restored her to the bosom of her loving relatives.

With a start, Tristram narrowed his eyes and scrutinized the youthful figure of the girl. He had been cudgeling his brains for something that might rekindle the dowager countess's energy, and the puzzle of Miss Bella Waters might just be the answer. Besides, the resourceful child had saved his life.

"Perhaps I may be able to help you, Miss Waters," he said.

Those who knew the earl of Wyndham might well have been suspicious of such a dissembling tone, but Bella was blissfully unacquainted with such subterfuge. She raised her head and smiled trustingly at her new acquaintance.

"I would be most appreciative of any advice you might have for me," she said.

"Excellent. Now, my dear, what exactly was your last position?"

The girl looked startled at the question, but gamely stuttered out an answer. "I w—was a governess."

"Humm," Tristram said, trying not to snort at such an obvious bouncer. The girl's youth alone would refute such a story, but beyond that no woman of sense would bring such a beauty into her home.

The girl was quite adorable with her ingenuous brown eyes and lovely face. For all her efficiency, there was a vulnerability and sadness behind her eyes that touched some cord of compassion in his breast. Weariness was etched in the lines around her eyes and the sweet mouth that smiled as Beau snuffled in his sleep. Although she would never admit it, the girl was clearly exhausted.

"A governess," Tristram continued. "I can well understand your eagerness to get to London. The opportunities and wages will be much greater there than in the smaller towns. And with your references, you probably would be able to secure a new place quite easily."

References! Bella's heart jolted in dismay at the word. She could not believe that she had not considered such an eventuality. Even in the country one needed some kind of recommendation to get a position. Without references she would not be able to get any kind of work.

For a moment, panic threatened to overwhelm her. She had money but knew that it would not last long if she was unable to find work. She pressed her hands together, afraid that their shaking would be obvious to her companion. Slowly her mind began to work again, and she considered the possibility of writing her own recommendation. She would just have to pray that would be sufficient. Lord Wyndham's voice brought her back to a sense of his words.

"It is really a strange coincidence," he said. "You see, Miss Waters, I am at this very moment seeking a governess. And after all, you have done me a very singular service so that it would be only proper to offer you the first opportunity to apply for such a position."

"You are looking for a governess?" she asked.

"For my son, Colin. He is nine and could benefit from the company of a governess. Currently he is staying with me in London and is alone, except for my grandmother who lives with us."

"Your wife?"

"Colin's mother is dead."

As tired as she was, Bella immediately noted the tightness around his mouth and hurried to fill the tense silence that followed his words. "Is your estate closeby?"

"My principle residence is hard by Salisbury. I was there yesterday and was on my way back to London. A wheel came off my curricle, so I had to leave it and my grays at an inn and rent a horse. You recall the rest of my story." Lord Wyndham cocked his head on the side as if he had suddenly had a thought. "If you are set on going to London, would you possibly consider applying for the position as governess for my son?"

Bella blinked at the actual offer. She was quite aware that her present situation was precarious. She must find a way to earn money if she was to hide from her uncle for two years. The thought of arriving in London without friends or some hope of a position was daunting. It had seemed simple when she'd first planned her escape, but now she suspected she had been naive to consider such a venture. Dare she consider this offer?

There was something about Lord Wyndham that had gained her immediate trust from the moment she had stared into his dark blue eyes. She might not be so lucky with her next employer. Besides, she was very tired and still feared that Derwent might find her if she did not get farther away.

Gulping down her apprehension, she asked, "You are not asking me out of charity, are you?"

"I must answer your question with one of my own. Do you think you could handle a boy of nine?"

Bella hesitated, disliking the fact she was forced to lie to such a helpful gentleman. She had never been a very good liar, but she suspected that was because she had so little practice. Her practical nature asserted itself, and she lifted her chin with decision. The thought of arriving in London with some place to go gave her the courage to face the nobleman with some assurance.

"My last charges were not quite so old," she hedged. "I do like children, and I am well schooled in history and maps and even some science. I do not know whether you would require more instructions than that for your son, but I would try my best to fulfill my duties."

"Actually, the boy has a tutor in Salisbury," Tristram said. "I am looking for a governess to act more as a companion than as an instructor. Since that is the case, I do believe you might suit admirably. Will you come?"

Bella could not hold back a sigh of relief at the possible solution to her problems. If she accepted, she would be out of the reach of her uncle. He would assume that she was still close to Mallory and might not wish to broadcast the fact that she had run off. If she could make a success of this opportunity, it might be the very place to remain hidden for the next two years.

"I would like very much to apply for the position as governess," she answered solemnly.

"You're hired, Miss Waters."

Before she could even express her thanks, she noticed the signs of discomfort on her patient's face. She thought at first he might be in some pain from his injury and looked at him in question. At the embarrassment she saw there, she chuckled in enlightenment.

"Can you move about a bit?" she asked delicately. At his startled expression, she moved the puppy off her skirts and stood up. "Then if you will excuse me for a short time, I will change into some fresh clothing while you take care of—uh—things," she finished lamely.

Without a backward glance, she picked up her portmanteau and walked into the woods. She was still smiling at Lord Wyndham's awkwardness as she pulled out a clean dress. It was a light brown wool, suitable for the early June weather. She shook it to remove some of the wrinkles but knew there was little she could do to make it look more than presentable. She changed her clothes quickly, feeling much better now that she wasn't covered in dirt and bloodstains. Giving her patient enough time to complete his ablutions, she eventually strolled back to the clearing.

Lord Wyndham had also attempted to correct his appearance. His saddlebags were open, and he was struggling into a fresh shirt. She was embarrassed at the nudity of his upper body, all too aware of the muscular chest against the whiteness of the shirt. In an instant she took in the pattern of dark hair on his tanned skin, and a flush rose to her cheeks. She was about to slip back into the woods when she saw the whiteness of his face and hurried to his side.

"I am quite all right, Miss Waters," he said through gritted teeth. "Just a little stiff."

She was uncertain whether she should insist, but one look at the determination in his blue eyes convinced her she would be better use making more tea. When she returned with the mug, Lord Wyndham was seated on the ground, his cheeks pale but his expression triumphant.

"Thank you," he said, accepting the tea. He drank slowly and deliberately before he spoke again. "Well, Miss Waters, we must now consider how we are to get to London. If you would lend me your horse, I will ride to the inn and rent some kind of conveyance."

"Is it far?" she asked.

"Several miles, I should think."

"I suppose if you go slowly Violet could manage."

At her words, Tristram looked more closely at the horse and groaned as he took in the resplendent shape of the mare. "When is she due to foal?"

"Some time this month."

"My dear girl, what on earth did you plan to do with the animal?" he asked. "I can imagine the consternation on the face of your new employer when you arrived with Violet in tow."

"Well really, Lord Wyndham, I am not such a green girl." Bella was annoyed at the implied criticism. "I was planning to find some boarding for her in London. After all, she is my horse, and I could not leave her behind."

"Naturally not," Tristram snapped, for some reason angry at the naiveté of a girl who would run away with a horse so close to term. The girl was not stupid, so obviously her situation had been desperate to take such measures. The very fact that he did not know why she had left made him short-tempered, and he took a deep breath to calm himself. "I will take very good care of the mother-to-be," he drawled.

"Thank you, Lord Wyndham," Bella said.

Without further comment, she saddled the horse and led her over. He refused to mount the mare in her presence. He had already lost enough dignity to the ministrations of the efficient Miss Waters. He was now taking over command of the situation, and he preferred to speak to her from the ground rather than from the back of a pregnant animal. She handed him the reins, then pressed her face into the side of the mare's neck. Her actions were so touching that for a moment Tristram could not move. Then he spotted the lost look in the girl's sad brown eyes and impulsively reached out to pat her shoulder.

"I will return as quickly as I can," he said. "For your own safety, I would ask that you remain here. I will leave Beau as your guardian."

Chuckling at the idea of such a protector, the girl picked up the puppy and cuddled it in her arms. Her enormous brown eyes resembled the puppy's as she stared up trustingly at Tristram. He reached out his hand, intending to stroke her cheek, but instead ruffled the hair on Beau's head. As he led the mare along the trail to the road, he took one last look back and saw her standing in the clearing, her hair aglow in the sunlight.

Even after they were out of sight, Bella waited until all sound of their progress had faded in the distance before she moved. For some reason, despite Beau's presence, she felt abandoned, and she fought back the tears that filled her eyes.

How could such a chance encounter with Lord Wyndham have affected her so? Why did she feel bereft now that he was no longer here? No doubt her emotional state was partially because she was tired. She sniffed one last time for good measure, then put the puppy down on the ground. She moved around the camp, packing everything away in preparation for Lord Wyndham's return.

It never occurred to her that he would not return for her. In just the short time she had been with him, she had given him her total trust. Beneath his fashionable clothes and handsome features, she had found a man she knew instinctively was honest and loyal. For all her confidence, it seemed a very long time before she heard the sounds of a carriage approaching. It was all she could do not to race to the road, but she contented herself with remaining in the clearing and greeting Lord Wyndham with a wide smile of welcome.

"I'm delighted to find you here," he said, returning her

smile. "For a while I wondered if I had only imagined your presence and, like a spirit of the trees, you would have disappeared when I returned."

He helped her gather their belongings, and as they walked out to the road, he explained that he had left Violet well cared for at the inn to be picked up when his servants retrieved his curricle and grays.

If the hired coachman was surprised at the sudden appearance of a young lady and a puppy, he made no comment. Bella was slightly dazed by the speed of their departure and, rather breathless, she sank self-consciously against the squabs of the carriage as it took the road toward London.

"Please be at ease, Miss Waters," Lord Wyndham said as if he sensed her apprehension. "I realize that all this must seem rather irregular, but I promise you I mean you no harm."

Bella stared into the dark blue eyes of the virtual stranger across from her. She was caught by the intensity of his gaze and could feel an immediate relaxation of the tension that had filled her momentarily. In his care she would be safe. She knew that with a surety she did not understand and accepted it without thought. Once more Lord Wyndham seemed able to read her thoughts and nodded his head as one of the infrequent smiles stretched his mouth in a flash of white teeth.

For the next several hours, they talked easily as Lord Wyndham answered her questions about London. She had read so much about the city and was anxious to see the many wonders that awaited her. He told her a little about Colin and agreed to make arrangements so that she and his son could investigate the tamer aspects of the city.

Late in the day, they stopped at an inn to change horses and refresh themselves. Once more back in the coach, well satisfied with the luncheon she had consumed, Bella yawned discreetly behind her hand. Her sharp-eyed companion took immediate notice.

"It is a long way to London, Miss Waters. You might be more comfortable if you removed your bonnet and tried to sleep. I suspect Beau would appreciate the company," he said, gesturing to the dog on her lap.

With little argument, Bella followed his suggestion. She was close to exhaustion from her adventures. The moment she had put her trust in Lord Wyndham, her body and mind had relaxed, and she'd felt a numbness creep into every pore. She snuggled beneath the blanket, holding Beau in the circle of her arm, and soon, lulled by the gentle rocking of the carriage, she was fast asleep.

Tristram marveled at the ability of the very young to doze in less than perfect conditions. He stared out the window as the carriage rolled on toward London, but found his eyes drawn continually to the lovely face beneath the tumbled, burnished curls.

Although he knew himself to be a cynic, he could not believe that anyone could be as trusting as the efficient Miss Waters. The thought of the child arriving in London, alone except for the company of a mare due to drop her foal, sent a burst of anger through him. Despite her ability to survive in the woods, she would be as defenseless as Beau in a city that devoured the naive or gullible. From talking to her he knew she was intelligent and that she realized the dangers inherent in such an undertaking as running away, so he was all the more curious as to the situation that had driven her to take such a drastic step.

His high-handed manipulation of the girl did not trouble his conscience. He wasn't sure what he would have done if she had refused to accompany him. The flash of fear in her eyes, when he had mentioned her family, had disturbed him. Now that he had taken responsibility for the child, he intended to discover what had driven her from her home before he consented to her return.

He was much intrigued by the mysterious Miss Waters. Her attitude toward him was even more baffling. He knew from experience that he did not instill trust in the breasts of the women he met. The more sophisticated acknowledged the sensual quality of his nature and either accepted or rejected his unspoken invitation. The young debs were tantalized by his reputation and excited by the hint of danger that fluttered along their nerves at his knowing glances. Most children, with the exception of his own son, were intimidated by his austere expression and tended to give him a wide berth.

Miss Waters's attitude toward him was surely unique. She had given him her trust from the first moment he spoke to her. To his utter bemusement, she did not appear to find him the least bit daunting, and treated him with the hominess reserved for a favorite uncle. Although as far as Tristram was concerned her youthfulness would protect her from any advances, she had no way of knowing that this was true.

Perhaps he was getting old, if a beautiful child such as Miss Waters felt safe in his presence. He glared across at the girl whose very ability to sleep indicated how little she feared him. As the sun set outside the windows, Tristram withdrew into his own thoughts, considering the accident that had resulted in his meeting with the enterprising Miss Waters.

He had been avoiding searching too closely into the circumstances of the shooting until he had more time. The two things that bothered him were that the horse had been killed and that he had not been robbed. He had not been waylaid by a highwayman, but shot and left for dead. He assumed the horse had been shot as well so that it would not run off, signaling the presence of an injured rider along the road. All the indications led to the belief that it had been a deliberate attempt on his life. This conclusion led to another question. Had the wheel come off his curricle by accident or design? Tristram made a mental note to dispatch his head groom, Whitcombe, rather than a groom to retrieve the curricle and the grays. The wily old buzzard would be able to assess the damages for any sign of tampering.

The thought that someone had actually set upon him was decidedly unsettling. He was hardly free of enemies, but offhand he could not come up with anyone who would attack him in so cowardly a fashion. His thoughts were grim as the coach approached the outskirts of London.

When they drew up on the pavement in front of the town house, there was the usual amount of confusion as servants descended on the carriage. Tristram lifted Beau from the nest of blankets that covered the girl. With instructions to walk the puppy, he handed the wriggling body to the astonished footman who opened the door.

The noise of their arrival had roused Bella but, half-asleep, she blinked in the glare of the torchs and shrank against the seat in bewilderment. Tristram spoke softly to her and, when she had recognized him, he scooped her up, blankets and all, and stepped from the carriage. She sighed contentedly, placed her arms around his neck, and lay her head against his chest. He ignored the stunned expression on the faces of the footmen and settled her more comfortably. Looking neither to right nor left, he marched up the short flight of stairs leading to the front door.

Not by a single change of expression did Dillingsworth indicate that there was anything unusual about the earl of Wyndham arriving home with a young girl in his arms and a puppy sniffing at his heels. The butler led the way across the marbled entrance hall, up the staircase, and, with proper ceremony, opened the doors of the salon.

"The earl is arrived, Lady Wyndham," Dillingsworth said, his voice pitched just above a whisper.

Tristram knew that his grandmother had heard the sounds of his arrival and had prepared herself for his entrance. Her head drooped dramatically and her face, beneath a lace-edged cap, was pale and lifeless. She was huddled in a large wing chair, with a fluffy shawl clutched around her shoulders as if for warmth, her ever-present walking stick dangling feebly from one hand. She held the pose for several seconds, before she slowly raised her eyes to his.

Tristram could feel a smile tug at the edges of his mouth at the abrupt change of expression on his grandmother's face as she spied the bundle in his arms.

"Good heavens, Wyndham," she snapped. "Are you so devoid of respect that you would bring your light-o'-loves into your home?"

"Softly, madam," Tristram said as he moved closer. " 'Tis a mere babe."

Ignoring his grandmother, he crossed the room and settled Bella on a sofa near the fireplace. He tensed when the girl stirred, but she only seemed to be changing to a more comfortable position. He fussed with the blankets until they were arranged to his satisfaction, then lifted a silken curl away from her face and tucked it behind her ear. Only then did he turn back toward his grandmother.

Lady Wyndham, eyebrows raised in astonishment, was staring at Beau who had trotted in behind Tristram. The pup was oblivious to the intimidating glare and sniffed his way around the room until he caught sight of the old woman. He trotted across the Aubusson to her feet, his stub of a tail wagging in a frenzy of delight. He plunked his bottom on the carpet and raised his face, cocking his head to the side. A small pink tongue poked from his mouth, giving his pose a rakish air.

"Where did that beast come from?" she said, pointing her stick accusingly at the pup.

Lady Wyndham's voice should have shriveled the animal, but quite unaware that he should be cowed, Beau tried to jump up in her lap. The distance was too great, and he fell back to the carpet, where he lay shaking his head and looking quite startled. Apparently even the dowager countess was not hardened to the appeal of the little brown fellow. In amazement, Tristram watched as his grandmother laid aside her stick, picked up the puppy, and set him on her lap. Beau licked her blue-veined hand and then, content with his lot in life, curled up on the velvet gown.

"His name is Beau," Tristram said as he bent to kiss his grandmother's soft cheek. "I thought Colin might enjoy his company for, as you can plainly see, he has a certain charm." As he straightened up, he said, "I trust I find you well, madam?"

Lady Elizabeth Wyndham's eyes narrowed as she stared up at him. "My health is not in question here. What have you to say for yourself, you scapegrace?"

Tristram took his time, sitting down in a chair across from his grandmother. He was gratified to note an edge of acid in her tone that had been missing for much too long. There was color in her face and a decided spark of temper in her eyes. Pleased with the progress thus far, he crossed his legs, carefully smoothing the material over his knee, before he spoke. "I have completed my business at Dragon's Keep with excellent dispatch."

"Don't be such a gudgeon, Wyndham." The dowager countess sat ramrod straight, and there were spots of bright color on her cheeks as her choler rose. Pointing at the slumbering figure on the sofa, she demanded, "Who is *that?*"

"Miss Waters can hardly be considered a that," Tristram said reasonably. "In actual fact, Grandmama, Miss Waters is a present for you."

Chapter Four

"A present?" Lady Wyndham asked in confusion. "There are times, Tristram, when I begin to wonder if you have more hair than wit. Perhaps you will be good enough to enlighten me as to your most recent activities, paying close attention to anything that might touch on the presence of *that* female"—she gestured with her stick—"in *this* drawing room."

"All in good time, madam," Tristram said.

He was delighted to hear the sarcasm in his grandmother's voice, and grinned at the militant gleam in her eye. There wasn't a trace of the lifeless old woman who had sulked in his presence. After assuring himself that she had already eaten, he rang for a light supper and secured a brandy from the sideboard. Before reseating himself, he knelt beside the girl to check on her condition. Her face was still pale, but the lines of exhaustion had smoothed out in her sleep. He rose as the doors of the salon opened.

Dillingsworth led in a footman bearing a tray of sandwiches. He directed the setting up of a small table near the earl. He never let his eyes wander to the sleeping figure on the sofa, but Tristram knew that he had taken note of everything. Satisfied with the arrangements, the butler withdrew, closing the doors behind him.

Lady Wyndham waited impatiently for Tristram to eat something. She tried to keep a tight rein on her curiosity, but her mind was whirling with conjectures. Her long-fingered hand stroked the puppy in her lap, and the gentle rhythm had a calming effect on her unsettled nerves. Between bites, he filled her in on the affairs of the estate that had forced his absence from London. He spoke in such a calm manner that she thought she might scream.

His hunger appeased for the moment, Tristram wiped his fingers on a linen napkin and set it on the tray. "Colin is well?" he asked.

"As far as I know," Lady Wyndham said. She let the words hang in the air but, when her grandson made no further comment, her hard-won patience came to an end. "The girl?" she prodded.

Tristram explained about the accident with the curricle and how he had been shot, leaving out his suspicions that it was anything more than a highwayman. Nothing would do but that his grandmother examine his head. She was pale after surveying the cut, but thankful that his injury was no worse. Seeing her distress, he poured her a small brandy and stood over her as she took a sip. Her color returned, and he sat down to continue his story.

Lady Wyndham sat forward in her chair, her hands braced on the top of her stick and listened without interruption as he told her how he had been rescued by the resourceful Miss Waters. She was thoroughly stunned at the fact that, but for the young girl asleep on the couch, she might this night be mourning the loss of her grandson. He made a good story of it, laughing as he described being at the mercy of such a petite tyrant, but as he spoke of the girl there was an undercurrent of tenderness that quite intrigued the dowager countess. It was at the end of his tale, when he described the hiring of the runaway girl, that Lady Wyndham was overset.

"Great gods in their heaven, Tristram!" she cried. "While I am sensible to the fact that the girl most probably saved your life, you cannot just pick up the child on some whim. She may have been running away from home, but you cannot aid her in such a folly. Just think of her family."

"I am thinking about her family." His brows drew together as he scowled at the sleeping girl. "There is something havey-cavey about this whole affair. I don't know what it is, but I intend to discover exactly why Miss Waters ran away."

"But they will be frantic! You must have a loose screw if you think to get away with such outrageous behavior,"

"I could not leave the child," Tristram stated in a tone that was firm and unequivocal. "I had no other option."

Although the dowager countess was appalled by his near-abduction of the girl, she was far more stunned by the self-righteous defense of his actions. Since the death of Johanna, Tristram had seemed devoid of any feelings other than anger and bitterness. He had cut himself off from involvement with anyone except Colin and herself. With others, he was aloof and uncaring. Somehow Miss Waters had breached his defenses.

Cognizant of that thought, Lady Wyndham continued more cautiously. "Since you are determined to have her here in London, the least we can do is to notify her family."

"Unfortunately, madam, I fear that may be quite impossible," he said. "I suspect we would find no Waters in the area where I found her. I believe the name was invented on the spur of the moment. In fact, if I am not mistaken, the only truth in Miss Waters's story was that she was heading for London."

"Then who is she? What if she turns out to be of good family? Not to put too fine a point on it, you have spent the night alone with the girl. It will mean nothing that you were in no condition to make advances. Her family will scream that you have compromised the girl." Lady Wyndham was amazed that even that comment drew nothing but a shrug from her grandson.

"From the look of her clothing and her lack of sophistication, I feel there is little chance that she is a runaway debutante. Actually, when she is scrubbed up, I think she will show to advantage. She's a taking little thing."

Tristram's eyes shifted to the sleeping girl. His eyebrows were bunched over his nose, and he looked perplexed as if he were trying to understand what had brought the child into his care. The girl shifted and he tensed, relaxing only when she quieted again. There was a softness to his expression that Lady Wyndham had rarely seen. At least not since the early days when he was courting Johanna.

Lady Wyndham sighed. "Well, Tristram, I see no purpose in trying to solve the mystery of Miss Waters until we have all had a good night's sleep. What plans have you for this disreputable mongrel?" she said, stroking the furry body in her lap.

"I may live to regret that particular addition to the household. Beau seems to have a curious knack for insuring his own comfort. Soon he will have us all pandering to his every whim."

Tristram rang for Dillingsworth. After sending Beau off to the kitchens, he arranged for one of the maids to stay in the room that had been prepared for Miss Waters in case she should wake in the night and become disoriented. He kissed Lady Wyndham good night and then, as if it was the most natural thing in the world, he picked up the sleeping girl and carried her out of the drawing room.

Lady Wyndham remained in her chair, staring after her grandson. She did not know by what alchemy this runaway girl had touched some core of feeling in her grandson, but for her part she would be forever grateful. For nine years she had tried to convince Tristram that Johanna was not a fair representative of the female sex. She had thrust every woman of marriageable age in his path, only to watch him withdraw further into himself. She had tried every ploy, but he was adamant that he would never take another wife.

And she was determined he would remarry.

She was extremely curious about the young runaway. Her grandson spoke of her as if she were no older than Colin. However, from what Lady Wyndham had seen of the girl, she had ascertained that Miss Waters was a young lady, not a child. Perhaps if the girl was presentable, it might be possible to encourage a match, because it was apparent that he was already intrigued with the chit.

Lady Wyndham rose with unaccustomed alacrity. She was relieved to no longer have to play the part of an aging old woman. It was a role that had not become her, and she had chafed under the restrictions of such a spineless character. Besides, as far as Tristram was concerned, it had had little effect. She sought her bed, anxious for the morning when she could evaluate the possibilities for the plan she had already begun to visualize.

Bella came awake slowly. She snuggled beneath the sheets, curling herself into a protective ball as she tried to recapture her dream. She could not remember it, but knew it had been pleasurable. A trace of lavender from the bed linen drifted to her, and her nose wrinkled at the puzzle. The linens of Mallory did not smell of lavender.

On that thought, her eyes flew open. She lay perfectly still, looking around the room in sudden apprehension as a remembrance of her adventures flooded her.

She was lying in a large four-poster bed hung with black silk floral draperies lined with yellow. Strangest of all, the bed was placed on a platform in a recess, set off from the rest of the room by a railing. The railing matched the headboard of the bed, both a very light oak and heavily carved with medieval scenes of battle. The remainder of the space was arranged as a sitting room, the sofa and several side chairs upholstered in black satin edged in gold. The walls were covered in yellow silk, and the same black floral material that adorned the bed draped the windows. Bright sunlight filtered through the sheer yellow curtains and puddled on the carpet.

"Good morning, miss."

Bella squeaked in surprise at the sudden voice and struggled to sit up. An aproned maid was just coming in the door with a tray. At Bella's cry, a flush of color washed up from the neck of her uniform.

"I'm ever so sorry, miss. I didn't mean to startle you," she said. "My name is Sarah, and Mr. Dillingsworth said I was to do for you."

"Mr. Dillingsworth?" Bella did not recognize the name, although she had a vague remembrance of an enormous, stern-faced man in livery. Now that she looked more closely, she remembered that Sarah, who looked to be the same age as Bella, had helped her undress and climb into the tall bed.

"That's Lord Wyndham's butler, miss. He looks ever so starchy, but he's just an old granny with no teeth." The girl chuckled as she set the tray on a table near the windows.

Bella digested this invaluable piece of information as Sarah fussed over her. Before she could ask further questions, she was washed and snugly tucked back under the comforter to receive her breakfast tray. She remembered the hard-faced servants who were hired by Derwent at Mallory and had the feeling her present comfort was merely a dream from which she would eventually awaken. She knew enough to realize that this sort of pampering was most unusual for someone who was being hired as a governess. Practical by nature, she took advantage of the moment and luxuriated against the pillows, drinking her hot chocolate while Sarah chattered her way around the room.

"The dress you arrived in has been washed and pressed, miss," Sarah announced. "Except for the dress with the stains, I've hung up the rest of your things in the wardrobe."

Although the maid offered no comment, Bella was aware that the young servant's clothing was better than her own. The girl was dressed in a simple black dress of merino wool, covered by a crisp white apron with a plain mobcap topping her neatly braided black hair. She was plain of face but had sparkling eyes, and her frequent smiles indicated a sunny nature. Bella liked the look of the girl and hoped they might strike up a friendship.

"As soon as you're finished, miss, Lady Wyndham will see you in the main salon."

At Sarah's words, Bella placed her cup back down on the tray. Nervousness put period to her appetite. "That's Lord Wyndham's grandmother, isn't it?" she asked.

"Yes, miss. A great lady to be sure. We've all been right worried about her ladyship. She's not been herself for some time now. It's just like the poor old dear is plumb wore out. Must be near a hundred." Sarah removed the tray, then returned to fold back the comforter and help Bella down from the bed. "We used to see her only a few times a year when the house would be turned inside out with her visits. Then all of a sudden she moves in with a carriage full of boxes and cases and never a hint of her old self. Used to singe the hair on your head iffen you so much as dropped a dish. Cook said this morning that Lady Wyndham blistered a footman for a button missing from his livery. Mayhap the old girl's taken a turn for the better."

Bella was grateful for the chattering of the maid while she dressed. She was slightly embarrassed to have the girl fussing over her, since as a governess she was little better than a servant herself. When she demurred at Sarah's help, the girl looked so crestfallen that she agreed to let her arrange her hair. She sat quietly while the maid brushed her hair, hoping that her unruly curls might be restrained so she would make a good impression. Finished at last, Bella stared glumly into the mirror over the dressing stand.

Despite its pressing, the light brown gown looked worn and shabby. She had made it from material Derwent had brought her from London several years earlier. She had cut the pattern bigger than needed because she'd assumed she was still growing. Unfortunately she had not. The dress bagged on her, and the sash beneath her breasts did nothing to mitigate the bunching of the excess material. There was a band of black braid at the neck and wrists which had once looked quite fashionable, but now had a purplish cast from many washings.

"The dress makes me look a proper quiz," Bella said glumly.

"It would not be my choice for you," Sarah admitted. "But your hair is truly lovely, miss."

"Thank you, Sarah. For all your help. I suppose I cannot hide away forever. Could you tell me how to find the main salon?"

"Dillingsworth will be downstairs to show you. He keeps to the old ways and would chew me out proper if I used the main staircase."

Bella only caught quick glimpses of rooms as she followed Sarah through the corridor to the staircase that led down to the first floor. Mallory in its prime had been a graceful old country house—nothing in comparison to the elegance of this London town house.

The banister was a lovely sweep of walnut, and the walls were lined with what she assumed were family portraits. She was so entranced with the pictures that she almost bumped into the man at the bottom of the stairs. One look at the grim-featured face told her she must surely be meeting the redoubtable Dillingsworth.

"The countess is waiting," the butler said in clearly admonitory tones. Without a word he led her to the doors of what Bella assumed was the main salon. "Miss Waters, Lady Wyndham."

Bella was far too nervous to look around and, gaze fixed on the patterned carpet, walked straight across to the woman seated in a chair by the fire. Only when she reached her destination and had dipped a curtsy did she dare raise her eyes.

Lady Wyndham sat perfectly straight, leaning slightly forward with both hands atop a carved ebony walking stick. Her dress of black satin had a close-fitting collar of heavy black lace that swept across her high bosom and cascaded off her shoulders in a caped effect. She was a large-boned woman, almost majestic in the way she held her head. Her face was deeply lined, especially around the eyes that, despite being a faded silvery blue, scrutinized Bella sharply.

"Well, miss, what have you to say for yourself?" Lady Wyndham snapped.

"I—I'm pleased to meet you, your l—ladyship," Bella stammered.

"Then obviously you know little about me."

Lady Wyndham snorted, then waved her stick in the direction of the chair across from her. Bella hurried to sit, but was much too nervous to relax and perched on the very edge. She tried to still the shaking of her hands and in desperation took a firm grip on the material of her skirt. Although she cursed herself for a coward, she trembled, knowing that without the old woman's approval she would once more be on the road.

"Now then, my girl, let's have plain dealing with each other." Seeing the fear clearly visible on the young woman's face, the dowager countess softened her tone. "My grandson has told me you were a governess, but after one look at you it is apparent your story is no better than a Banbury Tale. Even in the country, no woman of sense would hire a girl fresh from the schoolroom. Well?"

Bella stared down at her lap. She bit her lip, wondering what story she might tell that Lady Wyndham would believe. When she looked up, the sight of the imposing woman convinced her that only the truth would do.

"You are right, ma'am; I was never a governess." Bella smiled at the startled look on the woman's face in response to her ready honesty. "I did not like lying to your grandson. It was the first thing that popped into my head. It was only later that I realized he probably would not have been interested in hiring me without any experience, and by that time I really wanted the position."

"How old are you?" the dowager asked.

"Twenty-one, milady."

"Fustian!" the old lady snapped. "You do not look much over one and five."

"Your grandson must think so, too, because since his recovery he treats me as if I were a child in need of protection," Bella grumbled. "I do not mean to contradict you, ma'am, but

I really am twenty-one. It must be my size that makes me seem so young."

"Well, now," the dowager said, looking more keenly at the girl. Myriad questions came to mind. Tristram had asked her not to admit she realized the girl was a runaway, but it was natural that she would question a prospective governess. "Your name is Arabella?"

"You are correct, ma'am. My name is Arabella, but my father preferred Bella."

"And your family?" the dowager asked.

"My father died seven years ago." Bella caught back the lump that rose in her throat and continued. "My mother is also dead. I know you must think I am a harum-scarum girl to be running about alone, but I assure you I am a person of very honest character."

"But surely there are others in your family who will be concerned for your welfare, child?"

Lady Wyndham caught a flash of fear in the young woman's glance before she dropped her eyes to her lap. She understood now why Tristram was determined not to send her back. There was definitely something not right in the situation.

"I am quite alone in the world, ma'am," Bella stated, raising her chin in determination.

The dowager countess had had enough years in society to be able to gauge the honesty and character of those around her. In Bella's case, she would bet her sapphire necklace that she was dealing with a young woman of good background. Into the silence that ensued, the doors of the salon were opened and Dillingsworth brought in a tea tray. With her stick, Lady Wyndham pointed to a small table beside Bella.

"Will you pour? My hands are rather stiff today," Lady Wyndham said.

She watched as the young woman fussed over the tray. It was apparent that she was comfortable with the routine, which indicated much concerning her upbringing. Bella was such a study in contrasts. On one hand she lacked the sophistication of a gently bred girl, and her eyes held the naive trust of a child. Yet, she spoke well and was perfectly at home in the elegant setting of a London town house, which would indicate she was used to the trappings of society.

The dowager was most impressed and mightily intrigued.

Tristram had spoken of her as if she were a child, but Lady Wyndham could see beneath the ill-fitting gown that Bella was a grown woman. There was a vulnerability to her that had touched her grandson who had built a wall around his feelings. This mysterious chit had taken his attention when he had permitted none of the more experienced women of his acquaintance to invade his life. Was there a possibility that Tristram might fall in love with the girl?

If it turned out that Bella was a girl of good family, then quite naturally Tristram could be forced to offer for her. Lady Wyndham supposed that the custom was archaic, but she would employ a great deal of pressure to be sure her grandson remarried. However, if things progressed as she hoped they might, perhaps such drastic measures would not be necessary.

Lady Wyndham refrained from rubbing her hands at the thought of such a triumph, but there was a crafty smile on her face as she accepted the tea from Bella.

"For the time being, I will agree to your taking the position as governess." The dowager graciously nodded her head in the face of Bella's cry of delight. "However, you must permit me to outfit you properly, and I encourage you to join in various social activities as if you were a member of the family."

"I have no pretentions to enter society, ma'am," Bella said in alarm.

"It would please me if you would permit me to repay you in some small way for the service you have done in saving my grandson's life." The dowager waved her hand negligently at the girl's protests. "I was not planning to palm you off as a young deb, my dear. Although do you doubt that I have the consequence to pull off such a scheme?"

"Oh, no, Lady Wyndham. I am quite confident that you could take on His Majesty's forces and have them suing for mercy." Bella laughed at the dowager's glare.

"Cheeky, gal," the older woman charged, but there was amusement in the look she bent on Bella.

The two women relaxed in their chairs as they finished their tea. It was evident to Bella that the dowager was taking her measure, and she prayed that she would acquit herself well. Thankfully she had been well schooled by her father, and they talked with much pleasure of books for the better part of an hour. Bella was thoroughly enjoying herself and smiled warmly at Lord Wyndham when he entered the room.

"Good morning, ladies," Tristram said cheerfully. "I trust you slept well, Miss Waters?"

"Very well, Lord Wyndham," Bella answered. "Your hospitality was most welcome."

"I was not certain you would be awake after yesterday's tiring adventures. Besides, I have been told respectable women do not rise much before noon."

"Perhaps that's true of women of fashion, but I have no such illusions as to my place in life. You forget, Lord Wyndham, I am merely a governess and am used to the clean, fresh air of the morning," Bella stated primly.

"If anyone had seen you yesterday, they would not have thought you had been frolicking in the clean, fresh air," Tristram shot back with a grin. "Actually, clean did not come to mind at all."

"For shame, sir," Bella said. "To twit me for such a thing. A gentleman would never mention my disrepair."

"Few who know me call me a gentleman, my dear. I have little use for the flowery phrases required to do the pretty in society," he said.

"How is your head?" she said, searching his face for any sign of pain.

"I am rather stiff, but all in all have taken no permanent injury," Lord Wyndham said. "I was on my way to join Colin, and I thought to introduce you."

"If Lady Wyndham will excuse me, I would be delighted to join you."

Bella turned to the dowager and was surprised at the calculating expression on her face. Almost immediately a smile transformed her features, and she waved her hand toward the door.

"Run along, Bella," the dowager said. "It is obvious Wyndham is anxious to be off. He will no doubt drag you off to the stables in the mews to show you his latest acquisitions. I trust it's not another matched pair. Those high-steppers you won at faro several months ago were short on wind, as I recall."

"It would seem to me, madam," Tristram said, "that if you wish to emulate your contemporaries, it would behoove you to concentrate on being a little more forgetful. Especially when it comes to my ill-advised wagers."

Lady Wyndham snorted. "Contemporaries indeed! Most of my friends are either dead or the next thing to it. Off with you now while I take up my needlework as befits my advanced age."

Bella chuckled as Lord Wyndham ushered her out of the room. He waited while she ran upstairs for her bonnet and a shawl, then led her outside to the garden. She raised her head to sniff greedily at the warm spring air. Suddenly she felt a strong tug on her skirt, and a sharp bark caught her attention.

"What ho, Beau, my ferocious friend," she cried. She dropped to her knees while the puppy leaped up and down, trying to lick her face. She caressed the wriggling little body as she smiled at the young boy standing stiffly on the path.

Somehow Bella had expected a miniature version of Lord Wyndham, but there was no family resemblance between them. The boy was built much stockier than his father, and his hair was a dark brown rather than black. Instead of the dark blue eyes, Colin's were a silvery gray. Even the boy's skin tone was different, tending to be more gold in color than the darker brown tan of his father. For all the differences, Colin would have been a handsome boy if his face was not set in a sullen cast.

"Miss Waters," Lord Wyndham said. "This is my son Colin."

After a quick glance at his father, the boy bowed politely, but there was little friendliness in his manner. It was apparent to Bella that the child was not best pleased by her arrival. From the dark look he shot her, she suspected he was insulted by the sudden appearance of a governess. To cover the awkward silence, Bella gave Beau a final pat and then rose to her feet.

"I am delighted to meet you," she said.

"My pleasure, Miss Waters," Colin said gravely. He was trying hard to hold himself stiffly aloof, but a smile touched his face as the dog bounded to his side.

"I have already grown quite fond of your puppy," Bella said. "He was good company on my trip to London with your father."

"Father has told me Beau must be taught better manners," the boy said with a sidelong glance at his parent who seemed totally immersed in a study of the leaves of a nearby bush. Realizing there would be no help from that quarter, Colin shrugged and turned back to Bella, resigned to further conversation. "Beau seems ever so bright. I am sure I will have no trouble teaching him."

"Perhaps we might stroll through the garden while we chat," Lord Wyndham interjected, earning another glare from his son.

Bella followed along on a tour of the garden, listening as Lord Wyndham questioned his son on his activities while he was away. Colin asked questions about Dragon's Keep, and it was apparent that he knew much about the running of the estate. She was impressed by the maturity of the young boy and wondered why on earth his father thought he needed a governess.

It amused her to watch the play of emotions across the boy's expressive face. It was clear that he resented her position, but there was an ingrained politeness that would not allow him to be rude. She suspected he would prefer not to acknowledge her presence, but he answered her questions with great care in order to give no insult.

"Well, now," Lord Wyndham drawled. "Since you are getting on so swimmingly, I feel my presence is no longer required."

Colin stiffened and glared at the toes of his boots. Bella caught the tug at Lord Wyndham's mouth as he looked down at his son.

"Perhaps a suggestion might be in order here, halfling," Lord Wyndham said. "You might entertain Miss Waters with stories of your adventures in London so that she might have some idea what grisly amusements you would enjoy. Once you are well acquainted, I am sure you will be amazed that you have so much in common. I shall excuse myself for the moment, but be assured, Colin, I will require a report later in the day."

Tristram Wyndham bowed, a quick dip of his shoulders, and turned on his heels. Bella and Colin remained standing, watching as the figure disappeared in the direction of the mews. Beau ran a few steps forward, then stopped, cocking his head as he looked back at his young master. Bella took in the clenched fist and set face of the boy and chuckled.

"There's no need to glare after your father, Colin," she said. "It's all my fault, you see."

Chapter Five

"My presence in your household is not your father's fault, Colin," Bella stated. "It's mine."

Her words seemed to startle the boy, and he swung around to face her. "What do you mean?" he asked.

"I think you're hurt that your father has hired someone to wet nurse you. When I came here, all I knew was that you were nine years old. I did not realize that you would be above the average in maturity. I understand why you are angry at the arrival of a governess. Even I can see you are beyond the age for that sort of thing."

The guilty look on the boy's face was an obvious admission that she had guessed correctly. Bella sat down on the grass, carefully spreading her skirts to cover her ankles. She might as well not have bothered with such ladylike behavior, as Beau immediately pounced on her and tried to nip at the ends of her bonnet strings. By the time she managed to capture him, the puppy had pulled her bonnet onto the side of her head. Colin tried to keep a straight face as he looked at her but failed. The smile transformed his face, and then Bella could see a strong resemblance to Lord Wyndham. There was a wealth of charm in the boyish smile which lit up his gray eyes and softened the lines of his face. Laughing, he bent to rescue her from the ravages of the dog.

"I'm ever so sorry, Miss Waters," Colin said, holding the squirming puppy against his chest.

"Beau definitely wants for better manners," Bella said primly, but then spoiled the effect by laughing. She took off her bonnet to survey the damage. "He is going to be a ferocious hunter, if you can convince the rabbits to wear ribbons."

"I hope he didn't ruin yours. I would be happy to purchase you some new ones if he has done so."

Bella could see that the boy was sincerely concerned and smiled warmly across at him. "This *chapeau* has seen better days, Colin. I fear even without Beau's attentions, it was never very stylish."

"With bright new ribbons it would look—uh—better."

"A very pretty speech, kind sir. You are bound to be a breaker of hearts with such address."

Color rose to Colin's cheeks, reddening even the tips of his ears. The boy buried his face in Beau's soft coat until he could regain his composure. Finally he peeked up at Bella, who was grinning happily at him.

"Now that we are in charity with each other," she said, "let us start over. Although your father has asked me to keep the circumstances of my meeting with him a secret, I believe it is necessary to explain. I think you misunderstand the situation, and in consequence are angry with your father. Besides, I am going to need your advice."

"My advice?" The boy's voice squeaked in surprise.

"Exactly," Bella said. Keeping her narrative brief, she explained how she had found Lord Wyndham. "So despite Beau's deplorable manners, he is quite a hero."

"I should say so, Miss Waters." Colin scratched the puppy between his ears, much to the dog's satisfaction. "But I still do not understand why father thought I needed a governess."

"When I met your father I was on my way to London to find a job. Now as I think on it, it was a great piece of lunacy." Bella shook her head at her own stupidity. "Although I have read a great deal about London, I suspect arriving in the city without friend or advisor would have been quite disastrous. I should have given it more thought, but I did not have the opportunity when I decided to run away from home."

"Cooee!" Colin whistled softly, and there was awe on his face as he stared at the young woman at his side.

"Believe me, it is not such a wonderful experience." Bella reached out to stroke Beau who was curled up between them.

"My feet hurt, and I was close to exhaustion by the time I met your father."

"Did he know you were a runaway?" Colin whispered after looking carefully around to be sure they were not overheard.

"I thought I was very clever, but now I realize he must have known right along." Bella sighed at her gullibility. "You see, I told him I was a governess and was looking for a position. He said he was trying to find one and hired me on the spot. I thought at first it was my great good fortune, but I now see that I was mistaken. It is apparent you have no need of a governess and that your father hired me out of gratitude."

"That does not sound overly like Wyndham," Colin said, a frown perched above his steady gray eyes.

"Perhaps not, but I believe it is so. Governesses are not given lovely bedchambers and waited on by servants. It also would explain why, after only minimal questions, Lady Wyndham accepted me so easily." Bella was still working out some of the mysterious events since she had arrived at the town house. "For some reason she has decided to go along with the fiction, but for the life of me I cannot understand why she should take me up."

"She has nothing better to do," Colin said in a burst of candor. He grinned, and the sulky look disappeared completely. "She came to visit over Christmas and had a great row with Father. I'm not exactly sure what the turnup was about, but ever since she's been in a fit of the sullens. Father and I have been worried about her and thought she might be sickening."

"I'm surprised to hear that," she said. "I did not think Lady Wyndham was in ill health. She seemed particularly sharp for a woman of her age."

Colin looked thoughtful. "Perhaps she is getting better," he ventured.

"In any event," Bella continued, "I cannot stay here and accept such gratitude. I did nothing more than anyone would have done. You see, even though I've never been a governess, I thought I would be able to handle a young child. When I thought I was really filling an empty position, it was all right. But you have no need of a governess, and it would be no better than charity."

"But if you left, Miss Waters, where would you go?" Colin asked in concern.

"I haven't a clue," she said glumly.

Colin stared at the young woman, trying to think what to do for the best. It was true that he had been angry when his father told him that he had hired a governess. He had thought he would dislike the woman heartily, but found that he was enjoying Miss Waters's company. She did not speak to him as if he were a child, but rather as if they were friends. He felt very grown up to have her confide in him, and besides, he had to admit that it would be nice to have someone to talk to.

"Perhaps I do not *need* a governess, Miss Waters," Colin said. "But I think I should *like* to have one."

At the boy's words, Bella searched his face and she immediately recognized the fact that much of Colin's maturity came from the fact that he was a very lonely child. She knew because she had seen that same look in her own mirror over the past seven years. There was something more that she noted, yet could not identify it. There was a deep sadness in the boyish face, and she felt a need to banish such a shadow. A slow smile stretched her mouth.

"I would like very much to be your governess," she replied hesitantly. "But do you think it would be quite honest?"

"My father has always told me that it is important to try to fulfill people's needs." The boy grinned mischievously as he held out his hands and began to tick off his conclusions on his fingers. "First there's Lady Wyndham. She needs something to interest her. Second, Father. Well, for our purposes we must suppose that he needs to administer charity. Third, I need someone to talk with. And—" Here Colin looked triumphant. "Lastly, Miss Waters, Beau needs someone to help him learn his manners."

"You, sir, can be most persuasive." Bella nodded her head in decision. "All right, Colin, I shall stay on for the time. I cannot promise more."

"Good show, Miss Waters!" he crowed.

"Besides I must wait here until my horse Violet is brought to London. Your father wished to return to town with speed, and my poor mare was not up to that. Do you like horses?" Bella asked, aware that she must find some common interests if she was to spend time with him.

"It is my very favorite thing to ride the estate. My father has impressed on me that I must be well acquainted with my tenants, since one day I will inherit Dragon's Keep. Although I have visited some of his other estates, I have spent most of my life there. Did you live in the country?"

"Yes, and I, too, loved it there."

"What was your favorite thing to do?"

"Fish," she answered promptly. "We had an especially good stream, and I spent many a lazy day fishing."

"I have been fishing since I was a child," Colin said, with the advanced wisdom of a nine-year-old. "That is what I miss most about being in town. Father has been invited for a visit to Lord Leanderthorpe's later in the week. He has a wondrous good stream, and I have been there many times. Father promised I could accompany him and as my governess you would naturally accompany me."

"I would like nothing better."

Colin grimaced, looking around the garden. "Since I have been in London, I have memorized this place. Sometimes Father takes me for a ride in the park but it is rather tame sport. I have felt confined here, just knowing there are so many things to see in the city."

"Then we shall see them together," Bella announced. "Naturally I shall have to ask your father's permission, but in truth, I can hardly wait to investigate all the sights."

"Topping, Miss Waters!"

Bella climbed slowly down the bank, making sure to keep her shadow from falling on the water. She crouched low, gathering her skirts in one hand and her rod in the other as she crept closer to the edge of the stream. She slipped to her knees, then reached up to untie the ribbons on her bonnet. The wide-brimmed hat shaded her eyes, but the confining ribbons made her feel hot and sticky. She opened the top buttons of her dress and flapped the material to cool the perspiration at her neck. The noon sun was hot, and there was no shade on this particular stretch of the stream.

Feeling decidedly cooler, she relaxed in the grass and looked along the bank until she spotted Colin. The boy had not been bragging when he said he was an expert angler. Although he had the enthusiasm of a youngster, his concentration was complete, and he used his rod with a cool efficiency that was totally unchildlike. She herself was quite proficient, but Colin had out-fished her early on. Bella was amused that he graciously excused his success by explaining it was his familiarity with the area, but she sensed he would be quite at home on any stream.

Her life had changed immeasurably in just one week. She could not recall a time after her father died when she had been so happy or contented. Since her arrival in London, she had spent most of her time with Colin and found the boy to be delightful company. Their curiosity about the city had drawn them together, and on their early expeditions she would have been hard-pressed to decide who enjoyed the outings more. In no time at all, he was treating her with the teasing camaraderie of an old friend.

Each day she had been called to the salon for a visit with the dowager countess. She listened with delight while the old woman regaled her with the gossiping tales of London society. It amused her that Lady Wyndham tested her at every turn, hoping that Bella would let slip some information that would help to identify her. Although she recognized that it was a game for the dowager, her own fear of discovery kept Bella from confiding in the woman.

She had seen little of Lord Wyndham. He had questioned her several times, obviously pleased that she was getting on well with Colin. She thought back to their night in the woods and wondered if she had dreamed the ease of their dialogue. He treated her now with the avuncular fondness he showed to the puppy.

She was disappointed that Lord Wyndham had not joined them on the stream. He had been closeted with Lord Leanderthorpe since their arrival. She frowned, wondering at her own contrary nature. She had looked forward to today's outing with particular pleasure, but now found that her anticipation had been greater than the reality. The thought that Lord Wyndham's absence had anything to do with her discontent was rather disturbing, though she refused to dwell on it.

Sitting on the bank, she reveled in the warmth of the sun and watched Colin, enjoying the rhythm of his casting motions. The gentle rippling of the stream reminded her that she needed to mind her own business, and she once more flicked her line out over the water, forgetting her surroundings in the joy of the sport.

Tristram sat his horse on the top of the bank, looking down

at the figures along the stream. Colin was standing in the shallow water casting downstream while Beau guarded the bank and eagerly sniffed around the game bag. Tristram was used to the boy's proficiency since they had fished together a great deal, and smiled as Colin pulled a fat trout out of the water.

His eyes moved upstream, searching the bank until he found Bella. It was difficult to think of her as Miss Waters after their night spent in the woods. He constantly found himself reliving that time as if it were some treasured memory. The girl had a magical quality to her that he was quite at a loss to explain.

In one short week she had made a friend of Colin, who had totally resented her arrival. His grandmother seemed to have fully recovered from her reclusive stage and was now out and about in society to a dizzying degree. Tristram suspected that her fondness for Bella was pushing her to inquire discreetly for information about runaway girls. Even the servants had taken the girl to their hearts, including Dillingsworth, who treated her with the protective indulgence of a besotted father.

He refused to consider the fact that he had forcibly absented himself from the house because he found his thoughts turning more often than was healthy to the vision of his woodland rescuer. Shaking his head at his juvenile imaginings, Tristram dismounted. He tied his horse to a low branch before sauntering toward the stream, canvas bag in hand.

When Colin had insisted his governess join them on the visit, Tristram had assumed that she was going along to keep the boy company. Watching her, he was quite amazed at her obvious skill with the rod. He knew very few women anglers; with their missish airs, most were put off by a dread of getting dirty. The little governess looked as natural beside the steam as Colin. She was such a tiny thing that she was nearly hidden in the tall grass, but as he moved nearer, he marveled at the golden brown curls shimmering in the sunlight. She was partially turned toward him, and even at a distance he could see the total concentration on her face as she played her line along the far side of the stream.

He hung back when he saw the sudden movement of the fishing line. He wondered if the girl had felt the pull, then realized she had by the absolute stillness of her body. After several seconds, her dainty fingers pulled the line in slowly and at the next tug, jerked back to set the hook. The fish broke the water and she jumped to her feet, fingers moving efficiently as she once more released the line. She played the fish expertly, letting it tire itself out before she stepped to the shoreline and scooped the wriggling fish into her net.

"Well done, Miss Waters." Tristram applauded as he came to admire her prize.

"Thank you, Lord Wyndham." She smiled proudly as she held up the fish, unfazed by the water that dripped onto her skirts. She did not seem particularly surprised to see him, and her next words confirmed it. "I did not wish to shout a greeting for I was determined to land this one. Oh, look, Colin," she called to the boy galloping across the grass with Beau in hot pursuit.

"Good show!" he cried, examining the fish after greeting his father. "It's a beauty, Bella. I saw you working that spot, and I was sure you'd not come up empty-handed. Did you come to join us, Father?"

"I just came to see how you were getting on. It seems as if you have little need of my expertise." He chuckled when his companions objected. "However I did think you might be thirsty, and Lord Leanderthorpe's cook was good enough to provide an additional treat."

He indicated the canvas bag at his feet, and Colin immediately fell on it. "Wizard, sir!"

"Perhaps we might find a spot of shade. By the looks of it, you both have had enough sun for the moment." Tristram pointed to a stand of trees beneath the high bank.

"Oh, my hat," Bella cried. She ran back to the stream to find her bonnet, taking advantage of the water to freshen up.

The scene gave Tristram a feeling of *déjà vu* as he saw her take out a handkerchief and dab at her face. For a moment he was back in the clearing the morning after he was shot. He had woken up and watched as she washed beside the stream. Then as now she was totally unconscious of her beauty, enhanced by the out-of-doors setting.

By the time Bella returned, Lord Wyndham had produced a jug of chilled cider, metal cups and some meat pasties still warm from the oven. She had been having such a lovely time that she had not realized she was both hungry and thirsty. The cider was ambrosia, and she sighed with pleasure.

"Although it is always a delight to see you, Lord Wyndham," she said, grinning over the rim of the silver cup, "the fact that you have brought such treats makes you especially welcome."

"I should mention, Miss Waters, that I do not always carry food and drink with me," Tristram drawled. "I would hope you would not shun me if I came upon you empty-handed."

"While it is true that I have a very healthy appetite, I would hope my manners would be proof against such insult." She spoke quite seriously, but there was a twinkle in her eyes as she continued. "However perhaps it would be best if you went about with a pocketful of delicacies, just to be on the safe side."

"I think a well-filled hamper would be better," Colin chimed in. "We have had a very pleasant time of it, so I trust your visit has also been enjoyable."

"It has, Colin, although I suspect you think it is tame sport indeed compared to your day." Tristram ruffled the boy's hair. "Lord Leanderthorpe and I were at school together, Miss Waters. Like two old cronies, we have been catching up on each other's news. Well aware of the hunger of growing boys, but not, I suspect, governesses, he suggested this alfresco meal before we return to the city."

"Sounds like the last meal before a hanging," the boy said, grimacing as he reached for another meat pie. He broke off a corner and fed it to Beau, who waited eagerly, tail wagging in anticipation. "You better have another, Father, before they're all gone."

Tristram leaned forward to take a pasty just as a shot rang out and a bullet grazed the tree in front of him. Without hesitation, he jumped to his feet, shouting back over his shoulder as he charged toward the bank.

"Stay here, both of you!"

Bella had seen the bullet hit the tree and quickly realized what had happened. Without appearing to hurry, she rose to her feet, standing between Colin and the bank. Although Lord Wyndham had disappeared, she could hear him crashing up the side of the hill. From the puzzled look on the boy's face, apparently he was not aware of the near disaster.

"What is it, Bella?" Colin asked. "Was that a shot?"

"Yes, I'm afraid so," she said, keeping her voice steady. "Perhaps we might gather things together while we wait for your father."

"I suppose it was a poacher," the boy said as he picked up the cups and the jug replacing them in the bag. "The last time we were here, Lord Leanderthorpe was complaining about them."

Tristram climbed back down the bank and made his way across the grass. Bella swung around at his approach and he noted with approval how she stood between Colin and any danger. He felt a burst of anger that such measures should be necessary. As he reached down to take the canvas bag from his son, he tried to smooth his features, but his fury boiled just beneath the surface.

"Did you catch the poacher?" Colin asked.

"Unfortunately, once he realized there was someone near at hand, he took off," Tristram said. His voice was calm, but his face was pale and his mouth grimly set. "I suppose when he heard me coming he realized his folly."

"Just wait until Lord Leanderthorpe hears," the boy said with decided relish. He hefted the game bag to his shoulder as his father led them back toward the bank.

Tristram held out his hand to help Bella up the last few steps, and then tied the canvas bag to the saddle of his horse. Untying the reins, he led the horse as he joined the two walkers. He intended to keep his companions under his eye until he had a chance to talk to his host. He noticed that Bella had placed Colin in the middle. The muscles in his stomach knotted in anger at the thought that either she or the boy could be at risk, but he was somehow pleased that she would be perceptive enough to recognize the possible danger to Colin. He was in a foul humor by the time they reached the manor house and the waiting Leanderthorpe.

"Good heavens, Colin," Bella said. "We can hardly return to London in such a condition. What would Dillingsworth say?"

The boy laughed as she led him away, and again Tristram was amazed at how readily Bella had seen that he wished to talk to his friend in private. After a brief discussion with his shocked host, Tristram's expression was grimmer than ever.

When Bella returned, she took in the air of tension between the two men and moved Colin quickly through his enthusiastic gratitude for the day on the stream. Adding her own thanks, she ushered the boy into the carriage. Lord Wyndham followed, and they immediately took off for their return to London.

Blessedly, Colin and Beau were tired from their long day and leaned against her to sleep. One look at Lord Wyndham's face convinced her that he was in no mood for conversation. The muscles along his jawline rippled beneath the skin as he glared out the window. His profile seemed carved from granite. She stroked the hair off Colin's forehead, soothed by the soft rhythm of his breathing. She smiled at the sweet picture made by the boy and the dog. Beau was curled up in Colin's lap, his head nestled in the crook of his master's arm. They looked so peaceful, quite unfazed by the unusual ending to the day. For herself, she was grateful that neither Colin nor Lord Wyndham had taken injury from such a dreadful accident.

She had to admit that she was shaken by the incident. She had only known the father and son for a little more than a week, and yet they seemed very important to her. Glancing down at the sleeping boy, she readily accepted the fact that she was incredibly fond of him. He had crept into her heart from the first moment that he glared at her in the garden. There was something about him that reminded her sharply of her own loneliness as a child. He had never spoken of it, but she understood by his joy in her company.

Beneath half-lowered lids, she peered across at Lord Wyndham. She was hard-pressed to understand the moment of fear that had stabbed her when he'd disappeared over the edge of the hill in pursuit of the poacher. She really knew little about the man, and yet she had been frozen with terror, wanting to call him back to insure his safety. She could still recall the relief that had flooded her when he'd returned uninjured. It had taken all her control not to rush at him, wanting him to hold and comfort her and reassure her that he was well.

Chagrin at her ridiculous emotions had held her in place. Lord Wyndham would have been embarrassed at such a display. After all, she was the governess to his son, not an intimate who might have been forgiven for such gaucheness. Her face burned in the darkness of the carriage, and she chastised herself for acting like the veriest schoolgirl.

When they arrived back at the town house, Bella schooled her thoughts to other matters and concentrated on getting through the remainder of the evening with Colin, almost afraid to be alone with her wildly swinging emotions.

Since her arrival, Bella had been taking her evening meal with Colin in a room at the top of the house which had been made into a playroom for him. It was furnished for comfort rather than fashion, and was lined with windows, much like her imaginings of an artist's loft. By day, it was filled with light, even when the weather was gloomy; by night, the lights and the rooftops of the city created a lovely view.

The outdoor exercise had given them both an appetite, and they tucked into the freshly caught trout with considerable enthusiasm. As a special treat, Cook had sent up cherry tarts, which were Colin's favorite.

"Take another fish, Bella," Colin said. "These are absolutely super."

"There's nothing I'd like better, but I'm stuffed."

"Then you won't want your tart," he said. His teeth flashed in a triumphant grin.

"Wretched child," she said. "It just so happens that I have saved just enough room for at least one tart. You, however, will probably burst from such greediness."

"I suppose even I will only have room for one." Colin grimaced in annoyance, but then brightened. "I'll wager that I can convince Cook to make more tomorrow."

"That's a wager I'm not willing to take. She fair dotes on you." Bella checked the watch pinned to her dress. "Will you have time to visit Lady Wyndham this evening?"

"Lady Wyndham?" he asked as if he did not recognize the name. "Whatever for?"

"Well, I assumed, since you've been gone all day, you would want to tell her about your expedition."

Bella was surprised at his reaction to her words. The happiness that had been so apparent all day seemed to dim, and his face returned to the closed expression he had worn when she first arrived. He dropped his eyes and busied himself with his napkin. She wondered what had brought on such a withdrawal, and waited in silence until finally he spoke.

"Father will tell her about our day," he said.

"I'm sure she would much prefer hearing about it from you."

"No, Bella, she would not."

The words were final, said in a tone that left no room for argument. Bella bit her lip in confusion. She thought back over her week with Colin, and her eyebrows lowered at the sudden realization that she had never seen the boy in the dowager's presence. And stranger still, the older woman had never mentioned Colin in any conversation. Now that she thought on it, Bella wondered why Lady Wyndham hadn't asked how she and Colin were getting along. Surely that would have been a natural question.

"I apologize, Colin, if I have brought up a sensitive subject," Bella said, searching for understanding. "I assumed you saw Lady Wyndham during the day when I was otherwise occupied."

"That's all right. You couldn't have known," he said. "You see, Bella, Lady Wyndham never speaks to me."

"Not at all?"

His words had jolted her, but she forced herself to look mildly curious and waited patiently for him to continue. There was a moment of silence, and finally the boy looked up. His face was carefully blank, but there was pain behind the gray eyes. Beneath the table, Bella gripped her hands in her lap; she wanted nothing so much as to reach out to him, but she knew intuitively he would accept no comfort.

"Father has explained that Lady Wyndham is not comfortable around children," he explained. "It has always been this way."

"I see," Bella said, although she did not believe a word of it. It was true that she had only known the old woman for a week, but she considered the explanation nonsense. The dowager might be an old tartar, but she was a woman of warmth and kindness.

"I can remember one time when I was very small," Colin said, a wistful smile on his face. "We were at Dragon's Keep and I ran away from my nanny. I had a wonderful time peeking into all the rooms on the first floor. Lady Wyndham was in the great room when I opened the door. She really looked surprised to see me. We stared at each other for ever such a long time. Then she got up and pulled on the bell rope. I knew she was sending for someone to remove me, and I asked her if I might stay if I was very quiet. She didn't turn around."

Bella felt a lump rise in her throat at the quiet timbre of the boy's voice. The very expressionless quality told her that such treatment still pained him. She tried to think of something to say, but knew her words would be cold comfort.

"I watch her from the windows, and I think how nice it will be when I am older," Colin continued, his tone slightly dreamy. "When I am grown up, she will feel comfortable with me around. There are many questions I would like to ask her, but I will just have to wait. I think she will like me then."

"I am sure that is true," Bella said, hoping it was so. "She will be quite surprised at what a fine boy you are. And I suspect she will be sorry she has missed the chance to know you when you were younger."

Colin's face lit up at the thought, and Bella could have wept for the eagerness of his expression. "Do you think so?"

"How could I possibly be wrong?" Bella said archly, making him giggle as her mouth pursed primly. "After all, Colin, I am an adult. And when have you ever known an adult to be wrong?"

This sent them off into laughter which pushed away the tension that had filled the room at their discussion. Bella kept Colin busy for the rest of the evening with stories and games culled from her own childhood. When she finally returned to her room, she sat for long hours staring out the window in thought.

She did not believe the story that Tristram had told Colin about Lady Wyndham. From everything she had seen, the old woman was not one to mingle only with the older set. She might enjoy her cronies, but she would not prefer them to others. In fact, as Bella recalled, Lady Wyndham had said that it was important to surround oneself with people of all ages in order to remain youthful in one's thinking.

There was some mystery here that surrounded Lady Wyndham's relationship with Colin. It was clear that the boy was unhappy with the situation, and it was surely an unhealthy one. She wondered if she was brave enough to ask Lord Wyndham, for she had no doubt he was aware of everything that concerned his son.

There was another matter that she wanted to explore, and that was the subject of Colin's mother. She found it curious that no one ever mentioned the woman. Usually servants could be counted on for retelling the history of a family, but even Sarah never mentioned the late Lady Wyndham.

Colin had a miniature of his mother, and Bella had been awed by the glorious beauty of her face. The artist had invested the portrait with a shining excitement in the blaze of her eyes and the defiant set of her chin. What woman could compete with such an exquisite predecessor? She could understand why Lord Wyndham had never remarried. No doubt he was disconsolate without her.

Perhaps that was why there was a bitterness to his words and a look of discontent to his handsome face. She had been told it was a love match, and she could understand if he railed against the fates that had borne away his beloved wife.

She realized there was much she did not know about the household. She would wait for a few days to see if some of her questions were answered before she approached Lord Wyndham. There was obviously some mystery here, and as long as she was partially responsible for Colin, it was her duty to investigate.

Chapter Six

Raindrops spattered against the windows of the salon, sounding like small stones hurled at the glass. The dowager countess was impervious to the storm outside. She sat as still as a statue with her blue-veined hands clamped atop her walking stick. Her beaky nose, which usually was softened by the translucence of her skin, appeared even sharper beneath the lowered brows of her frown. Her silvery blue eyes were unfocused as her mind wrestled with annoyance at what she considered the thwarting of her plans.

She had decided that Tristram would marry the mysterious Miss Waters. She had liked the look of Bella from the first moment she had laid eyes on her. But more to the point, she had realized immediately that her grandson was drawn to the chit as he had not been to the myriad females she had thrust in his path. Faces paraded through her mind representing all the ages, from the artless debs to the jaded widows, she had trotted out for Tristram's approval. All to no avail. And now she possessed the very woman who had intrigued the stubborn man enough for him to bring her into his home, and yet she had little success to show for her plans.

It was inconceivable that all her investigations had been wholly unproductive in discovering anything about the real identity of Miss Bella Waters. The dowager had reentered society, entertaining and being entertained by her friends, in order to once more be apprised of the *on-dits* making the rounds. The *ton* was a small society where little passed unnoticed. Nowhere had she been able to find an iota of gossip that might give her an indication of who Bella was.

She had spent two frustrating days following a false trail that ended in a benighted cottage in Dorset. She had heard that Lord Esterhazy's youngest had run off. It had taken her untold visits and an annoying amount of money to pry the information out of the Esterhazy family and their servants, only to discover that the little slut had run off with her dancing master. The two were living in unbridled lust in a corner of Dorset far removed from her ancestral home.

By and large the dowager did not really care who Bella was, as long as Tristram married her. Her only interest in discovering her identity was in case there was some impediment to the marriage itself. Although she could not believe such a possibility, one must consider insanity, disfiguring diseases, or even misplaced husbands. She had enough consequence to weather any storm of scandal; she was not convinced that at her time of life she had the energy. But for all her inquiries, she had drawn a blank.

There seemed to be no woman of good standing missing or otherwise unaccounted for that she could discover. The dowager had even entertained the notion of actually confronting the little governess with her awareness of her assumed name, but was afraid that Bella might feel it her duty to leave London.

Thunder rumbled overhead, and the dowager shifted to a more comfortable position in her chair. She rested her head against the satin upholstery, feeling snug within the warm room. A fire had been lit, and the flames flickered in the sudden downdrafts, sending shadows leaping along the walls. She frowned at the lightning outside the rainwashed windows for a moment, and then returned to her thoughts.

As if her inability to identify the governess was not enough to irritate her, Tristram had made little push to get to know Bella. After he had brought her to London, he had absented himself from the town house as if its members had some putrid fever which might be contagious.

The dowager found this particularly annoying, since she had even been magnanimous in approving the plan for Bella to act as governess to the boy. And what good had that done? Granted the girl had visited with her every day, the rest of the time she was not much in evidence where Tristram might have the opportunity to run into her. To the best of her knowledge, Bella had rarely seen Tristram, with the sole exception of the fishing expedition at Leanderthorpe's.

It was the outside of enough! How could Tristram be induced to marry a woman he never saw? And marry he must. The boy could not inherit.

For a moment, the dowager's chin trembled with the memory of the boy's face pressed to the windows every time she entered the town house. Although, since his birth, she had refused to speak to him or acknowledge his presence, she was aware of him constantly. He watched her when she visited Dragon's Keep, and he watched her when she stayed at the town house.

He had only approached her once, many years ago. He had gotten away from that ninnyhammer of a nanny and come upon her in the great room of the Keep. She had not wanted to know what he looked like, but her own curiosity had gotten the better of her good sense. She was sorry now that she had given in to such weakness, because since then she had been unable to banish him entirely from her memory. It was so much easier to dismiss someone she had never met. The picture of the boy's sad gray eyes and tumbled dark curls, so like his mother's, tended to rise up like a specter to haunt her.

The dowager straightened her shoulders, pushing away the feeling of discomfort with her own actions that the thought of the boy had brought to mind. She was acting for the best interests of Tristram, despite the fact her grandson was too stubborn to understand the point. Their family went back centuries, and she would not have the title stained by the *bar sinistre.*

For all that he doted on the boy, Tristram had not fathered the child. Damn Johanna for her sluttish ways! The boy was the get of Johanna and that loose screw Henry Addison. Although she had never liked Tristram's wife, she could not understand how the woman had been so lacking in class that she had chosen to run off with such an unprepossessing twit. Good Lord! The man was a mere baronet, barely recognized in society. Addison had overblown manners and graces and an appalling sense of fashion that aped the more eccentric dandies. Aside from that, he had little personal beauty. Yet Johanna had taken the man to her bed. One might have excused such a lapse of character, but the outrageous woman had compounded her sins by running off with him.

At least Tristram had had the good sense to bring Johanna back to Dragon's Keep before he returned to challenge the scoundrel. His death had passed with little notice, since the duel had been held in secret and it was put about that he had died in a hunting accident. There had been some rumors, but no outright scandal as to Johanna's behavior. In the eyes of the world, the boy was Tristram's legitimate heir.

Over the last nine years, the dowager had wished that she had not known the true circumstances. It was the merest mischance that she had overheard the damning confession.

The dowager had come to the Keep, knowing that Johanna's time was near. She had never gotten on with the woman, but had been determined to make peace for the sake of the new heir. She had arrived unannounced and climbed the stairs in haste upon hearing that the babe had been born, but Johanna was not expected to survive. She had entered through Tristram's room, afraid of disturbing the dying woman.

She had stood transfixed in the doorway at the scene before her eyes. Johanna lay in bed, propped up on her elbows, her once beautiful face twisted by the anger that spewed from her snarling lips. Her brown hair hung lank and disordered like an old harridan's. The slowly weakening woman had spat out hateful and hurtful things as Tristram stood silently beside the bed. His face was closed, neither accepting nor rejecting her words. He showed absolutely no emotion until Johanna mentioned the child.

The dowager had reeled at the invective in the harshly whispered denial of Tristram's parentage. The dying Johanna had cursed him for killing her son's true father and gloated that the child would be a constant reminder of his ancestry. She let loose a stream of mocking laughter, fell back against the pillows, and gasped out her last breath.

The dowager had done what she could to support her grandson. Tristram had alternated between furious outbursts and a silence far too eloquent of the hurt he had sustained. He had refused to see the baby. He had told the entire story to his grandmother and sworn he would not acknowledge the child. Although appalled at the approaching scandal, the dowager had been just as adamant as her grandson that a bastard would never inherit the title.

Somehow they had gotten through the tradition-bound funeral ceremonies. Tristram had walked through it all as if in a trance, his face white and forbidding. Most put his behavior down to grief at the loss of his beautiful wife, not suspecting the real tragedy behind his mask of pain. Even Lady Wyndham had been reticent to intrude on his anguish. If only she had forced him to deny the child's paternity before it was too late.

A loud clap of thunder rattled the windows of the town house and sent the flames in the fireplace shooting upwards. The dowager shuddered and pulled the cashmere shawl more closely around her shoulders. She used to enjoy rainstorms, reveling in the raw display of nature's power. For the last nine years, she had hated them.

Two weeks after Johanna's death, a savage storm had hit the Keep. She had slept through most of it, awakening occasionally to the flashes of lightning outside her window. There had been one particularly loud crash, and she had gone to the window, looking down at the garden. A large beech tree had been struck. It had split in two, both halves lying flat among the flowerbeds. She had watched the foreshortened figures of servants working to cut and drag the tree away, but eventually had returned to her bed. It was only later that she learned this very event had precipitated their present tragedy.

Tristram had also seen the servants working on the fallen tree. Concerned for their safety amid the lightning, he had left his room to tell them to leave it until the storm had passed. He had heard the cries of the baby and had become concerned when no one responded to the sobbing child. The wet nurse, who had left the baby to join in the excitement over the split tree, returned to find Tristram holding the sleeping child. Two days later, the boy had been christened, acknowledged as the heir.

The dowager could recall her own horror at such a turn of events. She had argued and pleaded, but to no avail. Tristram had refused to listen to her, forbidding her to ever mention the matter again. He had said that as far as the world was concerned, the child was his and as such he would accept the boy.

But the dowager knew the child was a bastard. And knowing the truth, she could not permit the boy to inherit.

If Tristram had remarried, she knew she would have had an easier time of convincing him to set aside the boy in favor of his legitimate heirs. Her grandson had proved impervious to her attempts to manipulate him into another marriage. Through all her ploys, he had remained adamant that he would not remarry.

Miss Waters's arrival had given the dowager the first glimmer of a possibility that his stubborn refusal might weaken in the face of a lovely young woman. So it was with particular dismay that she viewed the present lack of communication between her grandson and the governess. Now that Bella's wardrobe had arrived, it was time to make some changes in the current situation. She had given it much thought and was fully prepared to concede a great deal if in the long run she achieved her goal of Tristram's remarriage.

The light show had faded outside the windows and the thunder was a distance growl when Tristram finally opened the door of the salon. The dowager was dozing lightly, but the tinkling sound of the decanter against the rim of the snifter brought her eyes open with a snap.

"Pour me something to warm my bones," she said. "This weather tonight has made me aware of my ancient state."

"I trust, madam, you have not called me here to discuss your will again." Tristram crossed the room with the two glasses, handed her one, and pulled a small burled table closer to her hand. "Every time you are less than pleased with my peccadilloes, you remind me that you have the option to bequeath your estate to cousin Eden. Although for the life of me I cannot imagine why you would prefer such a pompous man to your delightfully wayward grandson."

"Eden Danforth is a man of high principles," the dowager said with a slight twitch of her lips and twinkling eyes.

"Admit it, madam. The man is a pedant." He threw himself in the chair across from her, stretching out his long legs toward the fire. "I was appalled when he asked me to sponsor him at White's, for I hated the thought that everyone would think I actually speak to him."

"I suspect it was Glynis's idea for him to join White's. He should never have married the daughter of a cit. A pushy woman with aspirations well above her station in life. I can't imagine why he ever offered for her."

"Can't you?" he asked. "The way I heard it he was run up on tick. As next in line, he had borrowed the limit on his expectations. He was most distraught when I returned from the army with only minor injuries."

"Tristram! What a dreadful thing to say."

"I'm sorry, madam," he said. "I feel rather bloody-minded tonight."

The dowager noticed the lines of strain around her grandson's mouth. He looked decidedly haggard, and she wondered what had caused him to be so out of temper. He raised the snifter and his face seemed to relax as he breathed in the heady fumes. She smiled across at him, proud as always at how handsome he was. There was the look of her late husband in his finely chiseled features.

"Now, madam, what is this urgent matter we must discuss as your note indicated?"

"It is about the girl."

"Bella?" he asked in surprise. "Has Miss Waters proved unsatisfactory? I can't imagine how. Colin fair sings her praises."

"In actual fact, I find Bella most satisfactory," the dowager stated. "It is rather worrisome that I have been unable to ascertain anything about her real identity."

"Ah ha!" Tristram chuckled at the look of annoyance on his grandmother's face. "Do you mean that the woman who was able to winkle the information of Bishop Whitaker's preference for choirboys has been unable to ferret out the history of one small runaway?"

"Don't be cheeky, you scalawag!" she snapped. There was a momentary pause as she sipped her own drink. She placed the glass on the table with a sharp click of exasperation. "All right. I will admit that I have discovered nothing to any purpose. Despite the fact that this very failure reflects badly on my sources of information, it is decidedly worrisome."

"How so?"

"Think on it, Tristram. If a girl of good family suddenly disappeared, someone in society would be aware of it. A search would be in progress, and that kind of thing is always noticed. The mere fact that if any inquiries are being made, they are being kept extremely discreet indicates a sore lack of feeling for the girl."

"Perhaps her family wishes to avoid ruining her reputation."

His expression was bored as he flicked a speck of dust from his sleeve.

"Fustian!" She rapped the floor with her cane. "If they cared for the girl, they wouldn't care a fig for her reputation. They would wish for her safety first. She has been here an entire week and no one appears to be the slightest bit concerned for her welfare."

The dowager stared across at her grandson, satisfied at the expression of disquiet on his face. He pursed his mouth, and his eyes took on a faraway look.

"I'll admit it does seem unnatural," he conceded, lifting an eyebrow as he nodded in her direction. "What do you suggest? I assume you have a plan since you have obviously given this problem a great deal of thought."

"I have grown extremely fond of Bella. I suggested that I would be willing to sponsor her in society, but she shied away from such an idea as if I had suggested she join the ranks of the muslin trade."

"Actually, I once thought she aspired to such a position," he said. His lips twitched in remembrance as he raised his glass.

The dowager noticed that his face had lost the harried look he had worn when he'd entered the room. Her heart lightened as she again entertained hopes for her eventual success in her grandson's remarriage.

"I have invited Prudence Danforth to visit for several weeks." She was surprised at Tristram's reaction to this statement. He jerked upright in his chair and his eyes shuttered, giving his face an expression of guarded attention. She waved her hand to dispel his apprehension. "Never fear. You will only have to endure her parents for one evening. I did not invite them to stay on. Although I know Glynis would relish a lengthy visit to London, Eden prefers the quiet of their country house. The invitation was for their daughter."

Tristram relaxed in his chair, but there was still tension in his body. "Do you suppose Prudence is much like her mother?" he asked, his eyes narrowed in wariness.

"Bless you, lad." Now it was the dowager's turn to chuckle. "The poor chick is a definite throwback to some sweet, unassuming ancestor. Her mother has high hopes that the girl will make an impressive match, but there is little hope of such an occurrence. Prudence is painfully shy, unusually tall and has the grace of an unfledged bird."

"Sounds a treat," he snorted. "I hate to seem ungrateful for an opportunity to acquaint myself with such a social charmer, but to what purpose, if I may be so bold."

"It was my thought that you might take the girl about." She held up her hand at Tristram's groan. "No need to carry on until you have heard the entire plan. She could hardly go about unattended, so we would enlist Bella's help in keeping her company."

"Ah, madam. I suspect somewhere in your bloodlines there is a close, not to say lascivious, relationship with one or more of the Borgias. I thought at your age your capacity for intrigue should be sorely diminished."

"Surely, my dear, you do me a sad injustice to be so suspicious of my intentions," she said in high dudgeon.

Tristram grinned across at his grandmother, quite delighted with her machinations. He was fully aware that they were machinations, but at the moment he had not ascertained their purpose. He had caught a crafty look in her expression which indicated she was not making him privy to the real design of her plan. However, knowing her as well as he did, he could guess.

His grandmother had plagued him for the last nine years to remarry, and he suspected this was one more ploy to lure him into the clutches of some woman. He should be angry, since it was this very pressure that had precipitated their last major argument. However, it was such a relief to have her once more feisty and manipulative, he could put up with this latest start.

Was Prudence Danforth the newest candidate for his approval? The girl was only a distant relative so she would be considered eligible. Actually, in his grandmother's view, any woman above the age of sixteen who did not have a squint or teeth splayed outward like the rays of the sun was considered a meritorious find in the marriage market. Could she be hoping that Prudence would engage his attention? On the surface it would seem unlikely, since she had given the girl such a damning recommendation, but it was never wise to look only at the obvious when dealing with the dowager countess.

Tristram had too much on his mind at present to delve into

the motives of his grandmother. He suspected she would do as she pleased, so he might as well go along with her for fear she would go to further lengths that he might find less pleasing.

"What do you have in mind, madam?" Tristram asked.

"Society is light at present, so there is not as much entertaining, and Bella has made it quite plain that she will not be sponsored by me. It is my thought that when Prudence arrives we ask Bella to accompany her as she goes about town. Shopping, some sight-seeing, and perhaps the theater. Nothing to which Bella could object. It is my hope that if the mysterious Miss Waters is seen in public, surely someone will recognize her."

"And my part in this drama, madam?" His eyebrows raised and his eyes opened wide in mocking anticipation.

"Well, my boy, as a favor to me, I thought you might be the one to take Prudence and Miss Waters about. In your presence they are sure to be noticed. Hopefully that is not too much to ask?"

Tristram could have snorted at the look of ingenuous inquiry on his grandmother's face. He realized that what she asked would be simple enough to agree to and was surprised at the aura of tension that surrounded the old woman. Her request was apparently important enough that she was unsure of his agreement. Her eagerness put her in a vulnerable position, and Tristram decided to use this unusual turn of events to his advantage.

He took his time framing an answer and, to heighten the tension, refilled his snifter slowly as if deep in thought. Finally he returned to his chair, his face carefully controlled, ready to begin negotiations.

"Well, madam, your plan sounds reasonable as far as it goes, but I do think we shall have to improve upon it. Bella is not a flighty chit and will feel that her first responsibility is to her duties as Colin's governess. Therefore, it will be difficult for her to establish a relationship with Prudence unless Colin is invited to participate in some of the diversions."

It took several moments for the dowager to catch the import of Tristram's carefully chosen words. He could tell the moment she understood what he was bargaining for by the slight flare of her nostrils and a stiffening of her spine. He kept his expression bland as he continued.

"It would seem to me, Grandmama, that Colin might be included in the evening meal while Prudence is with us. Then it would seem quite natural to promote a friendship between the two young ladies. Without that friendship, I do not believe that it would be to any purpose for me to squire them about town."

"I see," the dowager said quietly.

"When are the Danforths due to arrive?"

"On Friday. They will be here midday. Eden and Glynis will leave the following morning." The clipped sentences issued from the dowager's tightly held mouth.

"That should work out splendidly then." He swirled the brandy in his glass, his gaze fixed on the rippling motion of the amber liquid. "After all it would only seem natural that Colin would join us for the evening meal with his visiting relatives. Suitably accompanied by his governess. No one could find anything to object to in such a situation, could they?"

Now it was Tristram's turn to raise artless eyes to his grandmother. For a moment he almost felt sorry for the old woman. For nine years she had refused to acknowledge Colin's existence. The pallor of her face indicated that she was aware of what was required in order to gain his cooperation. After a slight pause, she bowed her head in defeat.

"No one would object," she said.

No hint of victory showed on Tristram's face as he turned the conversation to other avenues. They talked pleasantly of social news, but he could see that the discussion had tired out the old woman. It was not long before she sought her bed and he sat alone in front of the fire. Despite the fact that he had won a considerable concession from his grandmother, he felt little desire to celebrate.

He felt curiously out of sorts. He had thought his life was going remarkably until Christmas and the beginning of his grandmother's "great decline". Since then it seemed everything contrived to unsettle him. And now there was the question that loomed large in his mind. Why was someone trying to kill him?

After the first shooting, he had sent Whitcombe back to the inn to retrieve his curricle and horses. He had given strict instructions to the wily Scot and had been most interested to talk to him on his return to London. As he had suspected, the wheel had not come off the curricle by accident. According to Whitcombe, there had been evidence of tampering to lend credence to the belief that someone wanted the carriage to overturn, hoping to injure or kill him.

In that case it did not take a great leap in imagination to see that the shot that felled him had not been the act of a bungled robbery attempt. It seemed more likely that when he was not injured in the carriage accident, someone had followed him and shot him, leaving him for dead.

Certain aspects of the attack that had bothered him would be explained if that were the case. It would certainly explain why he had not been robbed. For a while he had wondered why the assassin had not made certain that he was dead. Then he remembered that Bella, when she first saw him with blood covering his face and shirtfront, had thought he was dead. No doubt the attacker had drawn the same conclusion.

Perhaps he might be able to accept the fact that someone was interested enough in his early demise to take a single opportunity to kill him on the road to London. The shooting at the stream convinced him that the attacks were just the beginning. He did not for a moment think that the shooting at Leanderthorpe's was some poaching accident. The shooter had been standing on top of the embankment looking down on an open, grassy area. There was no way he could have missed seeing them. It had been a deliberate attack.

However, the second attack held a far more frightening conclusion. He had been the sole object of the first attempt, but he could not be so sure about the second. The bullet had cut between Colin and himself. Either could have been the target. The thought of anyone trying to injure or kill his son was enough to send a stab of fear through his very core. Until he could prove Colin was safe, he would have to take steps to insure the boy's protection.

It was hardly a surprise that someone wanted him dead. Over his lifetime he had made many enemies, but he could think of none who would so cowardly attack him. The gentlemen he had injured would be more likely to challenge him to a duel on the field of honor than connive in some hole-and-corner sort of scheme. These were not the impulsive acts of retaliation for some imagined injury or injustice.

Both attacks had the unmistakable stench of a hired assassin. A hired thug was indicative of premeditation, but to what purpose?

Colin was the only one who stood to gain substantially by his death. But if Colin's life was in danger too, that would put another light onto the situation. After his and Colin's death, the person who had the most to gain was Tristram's cousin, Eden Danforth. He conjured a picture of the man in his mind.

Short, dumpy, and pedantic was a perfect description of Eden. The man was a nonentity. He would more surely try to talk Tristram to death, which on occasion he had nearly succeeded in doing, but Tristram could not imagine his fastidious cousin resorting to any form of violence, no matter how far removed. According to the rumor mill, Glynis had brought Eden great wealth which had been added to recently by the death of her father. Money might have motivated him to desperate measures, but as far as Tristram could see, his cousin was exceedingly plump in the pockets. Would he commit murder for the title? At first glance it made little sense, but there was no point in taking chances. On Friday he would have a chance to reassess Eden's designs on the family title, but he could see little need to worry in that quarter.

Of course, there was a slight chance that the two incidents were unrelated. He knew little about the mysterious Miss Waters. He supposed he must at least consider the possibility that she had been the target of the attack. Granted, the bullet had not come close to her, but the shooting might have been done by a particularly inept marksman. He had always suspected something havey-cavey about her running away. She was obviously afraid of something, so he could not dismiss the fact that she might be in danger.

He did not know why such a thought should sit so poorly with him. He supposed it was because she was such a vulnerable little thing. At that he snorted, remembering the far from helpless wood sprite who had single-handedly saved his life.

For the moment he would have to take what precautions he could to protect himself and Colin and even the enigmatic Miss Waters. In the morning he would instigate some investigations of his own.

Satisfied with his course of action, he relaxed in his chair, smiling slightly at the thought of the interesting dinner party scheduled for Friday. Reminded of his grandmother's agreement to seat Colin at the dinner table, he could feel his mouth stretch in a wide grin of triumph, although it was tinged slightly by the realization that the boy's presence alone would not work a miracle. The old woman was nothing if not stubborn. She might still refuse to acknowledge Colin's existence. Once he had been close to making just such a decision.

The rumble of thunder from the storm that had passed overhead was a reminder of the night he had seen Colin for the first time. He had been so bitter in those days. He had known his marriage was a mistake, and he had been hurt and miserable. It had culminated with Johanna running off with Henry Addison. When Tristram had brought her back to the Keep, he had made an honest attempt to start over with their relationship. The announcement of her pregnancy had given him hope that perhaps the child would cement the shattered edges of their marriage.

The night of Colin's birth, Johanna had known she was dying. He had cleared the room, sitting beside her and holding her hand. He had spoken softly and tried to give her what comfort he could. She had been impervious to comfort. She was hysterical with anger and fear, striking out at him physically and, when she weakened, hurling words intended to hurt him. He accepted her words, knowing that he had not dealt well with her and willing to take on the guilt if it would ease her mind. It was his refusal to fight back that had driven her wild until she uttered the final confession of the baby's paternity.

Tristram was devastated by Johanna's betrayal. After her death, he had refused to even look at the child. He acted out of hurt pride and anger. The baby was not his, and he could not bear to see the product of his wife's adulterous affair.

The night of the storm he had heard the child cry. He had stood alone in the upstairs hall and the sound surrounded him. It was such a pathetic cry, echoing frail and hollow through the Keep. He waited for the wet nurse to attend to the baby, but the wailing continued until he became concerned. He might not be the child's father but it was no intention of his that it would not receive proper care. He stormed along the hallway to the nursery to discover why the baby was not being attended to. The nursery was empty. He approached the crib, leaning down to stare at the screaming occupant.

The baby was on its back, wound up in the blankets and trying, with little success, to free one arm. In the flickering candlelight, Tristram could see the little red face screwed up in what surely looked to be a fit of temper. Instinctively Tristram knew the child was not in pain. Every movement and cry was indicative of fury. He chuckled in amusement and reached out to loosen the blankets.

Fists flailed in joyful freedom. The baby sucked in air, and the crying stopped as if the child had been smothered. Tristram leaned forward in sudden fear and was caught in the unsmiling stare of the baby. He did not cry, but shuddering gasps shook the tiny body. Slowly the mottled red color receded from his face, and with a final hiccup, the child lay motionless.

In the candlelight Tristram slowly unwrapped the baby, examining every feature. He was not even aware when he started to speak to the child. The tone of his voice and the gentleness of his hands seemed to mesmerize the baby, who remained quiet throughout the examination.

Tristram had never seen a newborn. He was fascinated by the perfection of the baby's body. He did not know what he had expected, but the development of the fingers, down to miniature fingernails, touched him as nothing else had ever done. This tiny scrap of humanity was complete, a real person with emotions and feelings. How had he ever thought he could dismiss him so easily?

In that instant he acknowledged the child in his heart. The christening was stictly a formal announcement that he had accepted Colin.

Tristram's grandmother was the only person who knew the boy was not his child. Steeped in family traditions, she could not accept the fact that a bastard would inherit the title. She had been furious with him when he informed her of his decision. In the time before the christening she had begged and pleaded with him to set the boy aside, but it was something he could not do. If not prior to his birth, he was now the child's father. At the end, when he proved intransigent, his grandmother had sworn she would never accept the child. And for nine years, she had kept her promise, never speaking to the child nor mentioning him by name. Perhaps once she was forced to notice Colin and realized what a fine lad he was she would give in and accept him as the heir.

Tristram stretched out his legs toward the warmth of the

fire. He must remember to find a special present for Miss Bella Waters. It had been a lucky day indeed when he had encountered her. He had hoped then that her presence might bring his grandmother out of her state of the sulks, but had no idea that she might also be instrumental in bringing about a rapprochement between the two people he loved best in the world.

He would be particularly nice to the girl in their expeditions around London. Besides, it would keep him from falling in with his grandmother's plans for him to develop a tender for Prudence Danforth. Luckily he was wise enough to understand how devious his grandmother could be.

Chapter Seven

Bella swished her gauzy green skirt, pleased with the flutter of the muslin across her matching green slippers. This was her first chance to show off her new wardrobe, and she was slightly nervous as to the effect. Sarah had suggested the soft green gown, and Bella had followed the little maid's lead since she had never possessed so many dresses and had no clear idea which would be proper for the evening meal. After brushing her hair until it gleamed, Sarah had tied the rippling curls behind her neck with a ribbon of darker green to match the ribbon that ran beneath her breasts and fluttered down the back of her dress.

Lady Wyndham had been more than generous with the clothing and other accessories that now filled the wardrobe in her room. When the packages had arrived from the dressmakers, Bella had taken each item out of its wrappings with a cry of approval. She could not believe the number of things and wondered if she should accept such beneficence. When she met the dowager for tea, she had expressed her heartfelt gratitude and her feeling of distress. The old woman waved both sentiments away with the comment that it pleased her to buy pretty things, and any suggestion of hesitancy on Bella's part would send her into a fit of the vapors.

"Cheero, Bella. You look top of the trees," Colin said, striding along the hall toward her. She curtsied to him and he grinned, adding cheekily, "It's a marked improvement over your browns and blacks."

"Never say, good sir," she replied. "Those dresses were meant to add to my consequence."

"Your waist, most like. I was beginning to wonder if you'd gone to fat."

"Horrid child," Bella cried, but spoiled the effect by giggling. "I will admit that I feel considerably lighter. But, enough of me. Let me gaze upon your splendor."

Now that Colin was under scrutiny, a flush rose to tint his ears with crimson. He squirmed as she circled him, admiring his elegant evening attire. He was dressed in a dark brown, superfine coat and trousers to match, with a lighter brown waistcoat of brocade. His neckcloth was simply tied and sported a stickpin of onyx. It was evident that he had taken great pains to prepare himself for the evening, even to the extent of slicking his unruly dark brown curls into some semblance of order. Catching the hesitant look in his eyes, Bella cut short her perusal.

"You have the look of a Corinthian," she announced gravely. "I think your father will be extremely proud of you."

"Perhaps," he said, his expression glum. "I will admit that I am terrified of making some dreadful mistake. My hands are shaking, and I shouldn't doubt that I will knock over a glass at the very least."

"Just remember to move slowly. Besides, even if you should knock something over, it will not be anything of note. People are sometimes clumsy, and it would never do for a host to remark it."

Bella tried to keep her tone casual, seeing the nervousness behind the boy's complaints. After what Colin had told her about his relationship, or lack of one, with the dowager, she had been surprised when he informed her that they were to appear at the evening meal to welcome the Danforths.

"My mouth feels cottony," Colin said, his face taking on an expression of frightened resignation. "I feel as if my tongue is beginning to swell and I will trip over my words."

Bella patted the boy's shoulder consolingly as she turned him toward the main staircase. "It is always like that when one gets dressed up for company. I feel just the same, except that I imagine that I shall trip on my skirts and roll down the stairs right into the middle of the salon."

"That would be a rare treat!"

Colin chuckled, and by the mischievous light in his eyes, she could tell he was enjoying the mental picture. She kept up a light banter as they descended the stairs so that by the time they arrived at the doors of the main salon, the boy was smiling and much more at ease. She was very proud as he crossed the carpet to the dowager, but the old woman did not speak, only nodded. The boy did not seem overset by her behavior and turned to greet his father and the other guests. Bella spoke to the dowager for several minutes before she in turn was introduced to the company as Colin's governess.

Bella had expected some family resemblance between Tristram and Eden Danforth although she knew that the relationship was a distant one. There was little similarity between the two men. Tristram was elegantly dressed in black, his white linen highlighting the white hair at his temples. He was exceedingly handsome, albeit austere, but Bella spotted the twinkle in his eyes when he caught her looking back and forth between himself and his cousin. Eden Danforth was at least a head shorter than Tristram but weighed easily two stone more. His hair was an uncompromising black but balding. He continually ran his hand over the top of his head, as if to assure himself that the remaining hairs had not departed since he looked in the mirror last. He was probably ten years older than Tristram, and his fuller face had the blandness of a baby who had not yet learned to smile.

After her curtsy to the men, Bella left Colin in their care and turned her attention to the two Danforth ladies. Glynis was slightly taller than her husband and dressed as if she were attending a grand ball. Her gown was a soft apricot with wide, full ruffles at the low neckline and at the hem. Her blond hair was piled artfully atop her head, except for two curls which spiraled against her cheek to her shoulder. Every time she moved her head, which was often, the curls bobbed up and down as they straightened and recoiled in a fascinating action that held the eye. Her fingers were covered with rings, and there was a multitude of jewels at her neck that seemed to glitter at her every motion.

"Waters?" Glynis said. "Would you be related to Simon Waters who has a grand estate in Devon?"

"No, ma'am," Bella said apologetically. "I have no family in Devon."

"Pity. Well I shall assume you come of good stock, since the dowager has approved you."

"Mother!" Prudence Danforth said, her face reddening in her embarrassment. "It makes little difference what Miss Waters's background is."

"There you are wrong, my dear," Glynis said. "As I have learned to my despair, background matters a great deal. I have been trying to advise you this age that titles always make a difference in society. If you would only listen to me and make a push to encourage young Lord Sheldon, you would be assured of taking your rightful place among the *ton.*"

"I am sure that Miss Waters is not interested in such matters," Prudence said in agony. "Are you enjoying London?"

"It is quite a treat, Miss Danforth. I suspect there's much that you will find of interest during your visit here. Lady Wyndham has asked me to accompany you about town, so perhaps you might consider calling me Bella, since I do believe we are of an age."

"I would like that, if you in turn will call me Prue. Sometimes I find Prudence just a bit intimidating." The young woman shot a nervous look at her mother, but the older woman was now engaged in speaking to the dowager.

No one would call Prudence Danforth beautiful. Tall and gawky, she had the awkward grace of a colt, but unlike a young thoroughbred, one expected that she would not grow at ease with her body. Her hair was a pale blond, drawn into a tight braid at the back of her neck, and the pallor of her skin was accentuated by the hectic spots of pink that rode her cheeks. Her finest features were her clear, steady blue eyes, but Bella had little chance to study them for the girl mostly kept them lowered in her shyness. Although the girl fair towered over Bella, after only a few minutes they seemed to take to each other. After assuring herself that Colin was doing well, she and Prudence moved to a quieter corner of the room where they might talk more easily.

Tristram let Eden's words roll over him, grateful for the moment that the man preferred an uninterrupted monologue to the give-and-take of conversation. His cousin was propounding the theories of specialized feed for his horses, and since the subject of horses was always of interest to Colin, the boy could do the honors of paying attention. Tristram's eyes followed the progress of the two young women crossing to the window seat.

Despite the fact that his grandmother's description of Prudence had been right on the mark, it had not gone far enough. Granted the girl was no incomparable beauty, but it only took a moment of conversation to realize that she possessed a good mind and a sweet nature. He suspected that he would quite enjoy squiring her around London. He was sure her observations would be noteworthy rather than the simpered, bored comments of her sister debutantes. She might not be beautiful, but she would be easy company.

It was not Prudence that held his attention, but Bella. He had been hard-pressed not to gawk at the little beauty who had appeared in the doorway with Colin. He had known that she was well looking beneath her baggy, dun-colored dresses, but he had never imagined that she was quite so exquisite.

Without the oversized dresses, she appeared even more petite than he had guessed. He felt enormous when she stood beside him, tipping back her head to look up at him with her ingenuous eyes. Just looking at her arms beneath the puffed sleeves made him aware of the fragile bones beneath the surface. His night in the woods under her care seemed more a dream than a reality. Even now as he watched her across the room it amazed him that she could have saved his life. Her intelligence had obviously supplied invention where her childlike strength had been insufficient.

The soft green color of her gown brought out the creamy tones of her skin. He had been appalled when he almost reached out to touch her cheek in order to test the softness that he knew he would find. There was a glow that emanated from Bella. It was in the inquisitive sparkle of her brown eyes, in the soft sheen of her skin, and in the laughter caught on the edges of her pink lips.

The more he looked at Bella, the more he realized that the difference was not just in her clothing. When he had awakened in the woods to find her ministering to him, despite her competence, there had been a wariness and fear about the girl. She had not been afraid of him; she had made that amply clear by her behavior. There had been something else that he had put down to fear of her precarious situation. Granted she had reason to feel safe now that she was under his protection, but there was still a difference. Perhaps she was growing up and finding the world less frightening. He had thought of her as a child, but it was clear this evening that she was most definitely a woman.

Dillingsworth's announcement of dinner kept him from dwelling further on the puzzle of Miss Waters. Recollecting his duties, he set down his drink and crossed to help his grandmother out of her chair and lead her into the dining room. Eden and Glynis followed, and Bella and Prue, still chattering, were escorted by Colin.

Bella was delighted to be in the formal dining room, for it had impressed her on the occasions when she had peeked in through the doors. At the head of the table was a huge, square-headed fireplace opening flanked by carved mermaids holding up the immense mantel. Above the mantel was an enormous oil painting of a fox hunt and, continuing the theme, the red damask wall coverings held hunting prints, each one aglow with color and rich detail. Along one wall there were wide French windows draped in thick red velvet. The ceiling was plaster, ornately adorned with rosettes and fleurs-de-lis around the great crystal chandelier suspended above the walnut table. The marquetry floor was inlaid with panels of the Wyndham coat of arms.

Afterwards she could not remember what she had eaten for the strangeness of the atmosphere in the dining room. The meal had begun well enough, but eventually Bella was aware that there was a decided tension in the room.

Lady Wyndham kept the conversation general, touching lightly on the activities in London which were Glynis's main absorption. She included both Prudence and Bella by asking an occasional question, but never addressed a single comment to Colin. In fact, she seemed oblivious to the boy's presence. There was a tightness to her mouth and a stiffness to her carriage which made Bella wonder why the old woman had included the boy. According to Colin, he had never before dined with the dowager, and it seemed to Bella that the woman was not best pleased that he was here now.

For his part Colin never initiated any conversation and answered diffidently when a question was directed to him. It seemed to Bella that Tristram attempted to draw out his son, but it was as if Colin were afraid to intrude on the world of adults. At one point during the meal, Bella observed the boy staring at the dowager countess with a look that could only be interpreted as a deep longing.

The Danforths seemed unaware of anything unusual in the atmosphere. Glynis questioned both Tristram and Lady Wyndham about the people she knew in society, her eyes glittering at the slightest hint of scandal. Eden kept up a running dialogue on subjects as comprehensive as the theory of crop rotation and as specific as the origin of the Argand lamps which replaced candles in the theaters. It amused Bella that Glynis interrupted her husband's soliloquies with great regularity, but Eden was able to resume the subject without missing a beat.

Over it all presided the elegant figure of Tristram. Although he appeared totally at ease, Bella was aware of his sharp-edged concentration. His lazily hooded eyes flicked around the table, pinpointing one of the occupants and remaining fixed while his expression remained blandly interested in the topic under discussion. It was as if he were weighing the merits of each person in the room.

Only once did she catch him staring at her. She had looked up from her plate and seen the strangest expression on his face. His blue eyes had held a predatory gleam, as if she were a small rabbit and he an eagle. She had seen the same glitter of emotion in Derwent's eyes, and for a moment she could feel her body invaded by fear. Then Tristram blinked, and Bella realized she had been mistaken. His glance held nothing but a tender concern. She smiled as Eden droned on about the necessity for proper drainage ditches. Tristram raised an eyebrow, cocking his head to the side in such a comical way that Bella only saved herself from disgrace by hastily raising her napkin to cover her gulp of laughter.

After dinner, Colin was excused while the others retired to the salon. Bella was very pleased by the boy's performance. She noted with pleasure Tristram's proud, fatherly eye that followed Colin as he made his good nights. More intriguing still was the realization that Lady Wyndham also watched the boy beneath half-shuttered lids, although true to her character she still did not speak, merely acknowledged him with a sharp nod of her head.

Later Bella took Prue along to the room next to her own which the girl would occupy during her London visit. She assured the shy young lady that they would have great fun wandering around the city. Away from her parents, Prue seemed much more relaxed, and Bella knew that they would get along quite well. The girl was inquisitive and friendly, qualities guaranteed to increase their enjoyment of any activity.

All in all, Bella was well pleased with the evening. Snuggling beneath the covers, her delight enfolded her in a cocoon of happiness as her body drifted into sleep.

"Miss Waters."

The softly whispered words floated through Bella's mind as she fought her way up from the depths of her dream. It was dark in the room except for the checkerboard of moonlight that lay across the carpet between the windows and her bed. She lay quietly, wondering if she had really heard someone call her.

"Miss Waters." The name was accompanied by a light scratching sound in the direction of the doorway.

She sat up, rubbing the sleep from her eyes, and called softly in her turn. "Who is it?"

"Wyndham."

The paneled door opened more, and by the dim light in the hall, she could see Tristram's dark shape slip into the room. She threw back the covers and slid off the bed, hurrying across the floor on bare feet. They collided midroom in a shaft of moonlight. His arms went around her to steady her as she automatically braced her hands on his chest.

"What is amiss?" she asked in sudden apprehension. "Colin? Lady Wyndham?"

"Never fear," he whispered. "All is well in that quarter. It is the Lady Violet. Your noble little mare is about to bring forth her progeny. I asked Whitcombe to send word when her time had come so that you might be present."

"Oh, thank you!" She threw her arms around his waist, hugging him in her excitement.

All too aware of the dishabille of the girl, Tristram knew he should push her away but found his arms closing around her, holding her tightly to his chest. He could feel the beating of her heart as if she were part of his own body. Her face, aglow in the soft light of the moon, was turned up to his. The light and shadow sculptured the contours of her features, endowing her with a breathtaking beauty. He was reminded sharply of the danger of the situation as his body responded to her closeness.

"Get dressed, you flighty chit," he whispered, his voice harsh to cover his discomfort.

"I won't be a minute."

Without thought to the proprieties, she dashed to her wardrobe, throwing one of her old dresses on over her night rail, then fumbled around until she found her half boots and a light cloak. Through it all Tristram watched her, too fascinated by her nonchalance to remember to turn his back. True to her words, she returned to his side and, taking his hand, followed him out into the silent upper hallway.

Like two schoolboys sneaking out after hours, they stole down the stairs. Bella's eyes grew accustomed to the darkness, but she remained close to Tristram who was more familiar with the layout of the house. They wound their way through the kitchens and out the back door, stopping to be sure it was unlatched for their return. Then he pulled her into a run, weaving through the gardens and out to the mews. There were lights in the stable to guide them, and they arrived breathless and in time for the blessed event.

Unlike many she had heard her father talk about, the Wyndham stables were immaculate, run under the eagle eye of a dour Scotsman. Whitcombe held the title of coachman, but in actual fact he was the head groom. His duties in London encompassed the running of the stables and the care of all Tristram's cattle. He demanded a high quality in his workers, and the stable usually hummed with activity.

It was an old wooden building, freshly painted every spring. The corridors between the stalls were spotless, tack hung up properly and other accessories stored in special bins and barrels to keep the rats away. Cats prowled the premises, ready to pounce on anything that moved. The stalls were oak, aged to a fine patina, and the brass plates on each door were polished to a golden sheen.

After Violet had been brought to London, Tristram had

shown Bella the arrangements that Whitcombe had instigated to prepare for the birth. Two stalls had been joined so that the little mare would have plenty of room and in case of trouble others could be present without feeling as though confined in a box. A low fence with a wide gate was substituted for the normal doors and the corridor walls. This would enable Whitcombe and others to observe Violet and have easy access to the enclosure in case of emergency. Two grooms were designated to care for the mare, day and night. Violet could not be safer or more comfortable.

Arriving at the stable, Bella forgot everything in her concern for the chestnut mare. Violet had long been her friend, and she crooned softly to the horse, hoping her presence would ease the mother-to-be's travail. She stroked Violet's face and neck, and fought back a lump in her throat as the mare's soft brown eyes lifted to her own.

"She's been having a tough time of it, lass, but dinna' worry," Whitcombe said as he patted her shoulder consolingly. "It'll soon be o'er, and she'll no' be the worse for her efforts."

Bella was oblivious to all but the mare. She had seen a plentitude of birthings over her years on the estate, but this was the first time she was so personally involved. Fear for Violet and the new foal rivaled excitement at the miracle she was beholding. She held tightly to Tristram's hand as she waited with Whitcombe and the circle of grooms, some of whom had risen from their beds for the event.

As the foal emerged, Bella held her breath, watching in amazement as Violet broached the sack and freed the deathly still newborn. A nudge from his mother accompanied the first disjointed kicks of the colt's long legs. She licked him off while his eyes tried to focus on the new world he had entered. Tears slipped unnoticed down Bella's cheeks as the ungainly colt stumbled to his feet. Like a tipsy reveler, he rocked back and forth on his trembling legs, his head wobbling as he fought to keep his balance.

Low cheers and congratulations echoed around the stall as the onlookers joined in the celebration of the new life. Bella found herself once more in Tristram's arms, crying out her joy to the detriment of his ivory waistcoat. He didn't seem to mind and, after bestowing a wide smile of approval on her, he blotted her tears with his handkerchief.

"You will have to think of a particularly good name for the new member of your family," he said.

"He will be called Fortune," Bella said without hesitation. "It was surely Violet's good fortune the day we met. And mine," she finished so softly that Tristram had to lean down to catch her words.

Now that the excitement of the birth was over, the grooms dispersed to return to their duties or to their beds. Whitcombe remained behind, but moved away so that Tristram and Bella were alone with the two animals. Tristram unlatched the low gate and let Bella enter the stall. He was unsurprised that she immediately went to Violet, stroking the tired mare and whispering loving words into her ear. It was only after she had lavished praise on the mother that she turned to the new foal.

She knelt in the fresh straw, talking softly to the frightened foal who had backed into the corner of the stall. She waited patiently and the tone of her voice was so coaxing that finally the little fellow took a tentative step forward. The ungainly legs wobbled and shook, but he staggered across the straw until her hand touched his velvet muzzle.

"Hello, Fortune," she crooned. "I'm Bella and very pleased to make your acquaintance. What a little beauty you are. You have the look of your dam, but your legs are much like your sire's."

Tristram watched without moving. It was such a magical moment that he could feel emotion welling up within his chest. He blinked, unable to take his eyes off the disheveled girl and the miniature chestnut. Time seemed suspended as he listened to Bella's soft voice. His senses expanded, and he knew he would remember this night as if it were etched on his very soul.

Bella raised her eyes and seemed to include Tristram in her joy. "Thank you, Lord Wyndham," she said formally.

"It is my pleasure, Miss Waters," he responded, a grin of pure enjoyment lightening the features of his face. "I know you would like to stay, but I think we must return to the house. Grandmama would have my head on a platter if she knew I had permitted you to witness such an unladylike event."

"Fustian! Motherhood can hardly be termed unladylike."

She snorted in amusement, but after a last caress for Violet and Fortune, she rose to her feet. She wiped her hands and brushed the straw from her skirt as she exited the stall. Then, after thanking Whitcombe profusely, she followed Tristram outside.

The sky was beginning to lighten with the imminence of dawn. The air was fresh, untainted by the daytime odors of London. They walked through the gardens, their steps slow. It was not tiredness but the sense that the magic in the stable still surrounded them. In the growing light, the flowers were tinged with color. Just a hint, but it was there. In the very center of the garden, they stopped.

Bella turned to Tristram. She reached up, placing her hands on his chest. Her palms were flat and for a moment she stroked the material, then she grasped the edges of his jacket and pulled his head down. She kissed his lips, feather light, her thank you a silent whisper floating on the morning air. And then she was gone.

Tristram watched the dark shape of the girl until she reached the kitchen door. The latch closed behind her with a barely audible click. Still he did not move. He mentally followed her progress through the darkened house, and it was only when he was assured she had reached her room that he became aware once more of his surroundings.

He walked slowly across the flagstones, taking care to bolt the door after he entered the house. He took the main staircase to the first floor, but turned toward the library where he had been reading when the news of Violet arrived. He prodded the fire to life, all his movements deliberate as if he were afraid to break the rhythm of his actions. Once the flames licked around the edges of the new log, he returned to his leather chair and the brandy set ready at hand. He picked up the snifter and took a healthy draft without even tasting it. The sharp bite of the liquor took his breath away and broke the spell woven by the elfin Bella in the garden.

He had never known anyone quite like the multifaceted Miss Waters. She was never the same, one minute to the next. She had the quixotic enthusiasm of a child. Impulsive, compassionate, and innocent. Yet for all that, she engendered all the natural graces and charms of a beautiful woman. What was she?

He was ashamed to admit that when he held her in her bedroom, he was conscious of a rising tide of sensuality. He had been wholly aware of the feel of the barely clothed girl and the press of her body against his had forced him to a stern control of his senses. Just the thought of Bella in her nightgown caused a tightening in his groin.

The girl herself seemed totally unaware of him as a sexual threat. One part of his mind was irritated that this should be so. It had apparently never entered her mind that when he came to her room he might be there for some lascivious purpose. She might have at least had the grace to be slightly frightened by his presence. Instead, she had raced across the floor barefoot with only a thin wisp of material covering her. She had let him hold her and stared up at him with a face filled with trust.

Even in the garden she had kissed him with the innocence of a child. Her soft lips would have recoiled had he taken her salute for anything other than gratitude. She had kissed him in the moonlight with no awareness that he might consider taking advantage of her nearness and desirability. Devil take it! She treated him with the offhand casualness reserved for an ancient, emasculated uncle.

The more rational part of his mind was grateful that she behaved toward him as if he were a eunuch. He did not approve of the bedding of servants or others living under his protection. There were women he could go to if his sexual nature needed a release. He did not prey on children. He did not know Bella's age, but he assumed she was closer to Colin's age than his, so it was only right that he should think of her in a fatherly way.

Tristram nodded his head as if he had made a great discovery. He stood in the position of a temporary guardian for Bella and must remember his role. She knew no one in London and depended on him to protect her from all harm. Naturally he could never take advantage of such a situation. As her guardian, he would see that she was clothed, fed, and housed. He would give advice where he could, but he would have to guard against crossing the line between concern for her welfare and another more dangerous emotion he did not care to delve into at present.

Satisfied he had come to the proper decision, he banked the fire and retired to his bedroom. Once in bed, he closed his eyes, reliving the scene in the stable, pleased that all had gone well with Violet's confinement. However it was the vision of tumbled golden brown curls that occupied his mind as he drifted into sleep.

Chapter Eight

"If we were at Dragon's Keep we wouldn't have to plod along at such a slow pace," Colin complained as Bella cautioned him to rein his horse in to a slower trot.

"You must keep in mind, my lad," she explained in her best governess tone, "we are riding to be seen, not for exercise."

"It's jolly awful. Well-groomed trails. And crowded, too."

"Bella is right," Prue interjected. "When you are a beau on the strut you will look back on your words and understand. Just note that dandy in the blue riding habit. He would not dare trot, let alone gallop. It would ruin the set of his coat."

Colin snickered as he came abreast of the brilliant blue fellow. At a sharp cough of disapproval from Bella, he composed his face and managed to control his laughter until they were well past.

"Perhaps the walking stick in place of his crop was a bit much," Bella said, sending her companions off into whoops.

"No, it was the hat," Prue said, wiping her eyes with her handkerchief. "I have never seen a wider brim."

"Wait until I tell Father. I think I will suggest he get Weston to make him up a coat just like it. He would look a treat strolling through town in such a rig. Then we three could walk behind him and bask in his success as a fribble of fashion."

"Wretch!" Bella said, laughing as she cuffed him on the arm. "He's been very good to us so we must necessarily treat him with great courtesy. After all, he has spent much time taking us to all the most interesting places."

"I still wish he'd agree to take me to Sadler's Wells. I read in the *Times* that they are planning to show the launching of a ship on real water. It should be ever so wonderful and I promised to be quite good all week."

"I must agree with your father, Colin," Bella said. "The launch will not be put on until the end of the performance of the pantomime. You are still too young to be about so late."

"Rat's eyes," Colin muttered. "I suppose you agree, too, Prue."

"Yes, I'm afraid so, but for quite another reason. The crowd at the theaters is not fit for young gentlemen. It's a rough and ready group, and I can understand why your father does not wish to introduce you into such a society. The men get quite rowdy, and there is much fruit-throwing. You already have enough bad habits, I am sure."

"Give over, cuz," he said, sticking his tongue out but his curiosity got the better of him. "Do they really throw fruit?"

"Mostly oranges, or peelings at the least."

"Smashing!" he crowed, and both Bella and Prue laughed.

"Now see what you've done, Prue. He'll never give us a moment's rest until he sees that for himself. Come along, do. We best head back or we shall be quite late for tea. Knowing Colin, he will expire if he does not have his cakes and tarts."

"Fine one you are to talk," he said, rising to the bait. "Yesterday you took the very last sticky bun."

The threesome traded insults as they started toward the exit to the park. Each accusation was followed by a further exaggeration until they were hard-pressed to hold onto their laughter. It was only when Bella reined in her horse that they fell silent.

"Tansy must have picked up a stone," she said as she dismounted. She tossed her reins to Colin as she leaned over to lift her mare's front leg. After a quick inspection, she placed the hoof gently back on the ground. "Walk her forward a bit, Colin."

She watched the mare and saw that she was still favoring her right foot. Once more she leaned down to check. Finding nothing, she felt up along the leg, then patted the little mare on the neck.

"I can't see anything. It may be only a stone bruise, but I mislike riding her if she's an injury."

"You can take my horse and I'll lead her," Colin offered.

"Just imagine Lady Wyndham's expression when the governess arrives at the town house riding astride for all the world to see." Bella chuckled at the thought. "It will be far simpler if you two go on ahead and take Tansy. Whitcombe will know what to do for her."

"Never say, you'll walk," Prue said, looking quite shocked.

"I like walking."

"I meant without a groom. Unaccompanied."

"Ah, thank you, my friend, but those strictures are for well brought up young ladies, not governesses." Bella smiled up at her two companions. "I would actually enjoy the exercise. It's such a lovely day."

"I will walk with you then," Prue announced primly.

Bella gave her friend a speaking look as she indicated Colin with her head. "I would be better served if you would accompany Tansy. She sometimes is skittish in traffic. The sound of the iron-shod wheels on the carts makes her nervous."

Prue sighed and still looked disapproving, but she nodded her head in agreement. "I will go with Colin."

After promising she would speak to no one, Bella waved them off. It was pleasant to be in the park by herself, and in truth it was a lovely day.

She sat down on a bench beside the footpath. Across from her sat two nannies, gossiping while their charges slept in carriages beneath the shade of a nearby tree. Comforted by the presence of the two women, Bella felt safe sitting alone. In actual fact she was delighted to have the afternoon to herself. She could not say she found her duties onerous, but she did not have a great deal of time by herself. Each day she spent time with Colin and Prue, visited with Lady Wyndham, checked on Violet and Fortune, and was otherwise surrounded by servants.

The past week had sped by so quickly. Bella had been delighted when she was asked to accompany Prue. They had become good friends almost overnight. They both loved books and had endless discussions of all they had read. Lady Wyndham had a subscription to the library and they accompanied her, searching out books while the dowager gossiped with her friends. Bella was delighted that Prue liked Colin, so he usually joined them when they went abroad. Prue had been especially helpful on their afternoon rides, pointing out to the disgruntled boy the more eccentric fashions of the Macaroni set.

Prue was much relieved to be visiting London. It was apparent from what she said that her mother was forever pushing her into society when the girl much preferred a quieter life. She was painfully shy, and Bella's heart went out to her when she described her embarrassment at being the center of attention at her come-out ball. She had little desire to go to the occasional balls or parties, much to Bella's relief.

If that had been Prue's choice of entertainment, Bella would not have gone along. She could not permit Lady Wyndham to introduce her into society when she was living under an assumed name. Should she ever be unmasked, it would cause the dowager some embarrassment, and the woman had been ineffably kind. Bella had little fear that she would be recognized. She had seen no one in society since she was very young, and she had changed all out of shape since then.

She had expressed her concerns about society functions to Lady Wyndham who immediately agreed that the outings she had planned were merely to show Prue the more interesting and entertaining parts of London. And so far, that had been true.

For the most part the sight-seeing had been accomplished through Tristram's good will. He had been the one who had taken them about, and each day had been wonderfully exciting. They had been to museums, art galleries and even some private collections. Colin had been most impressed when they all went to lunch at a coaching inn in Holburn. The place had been a beehive of activity, and the boy could barely contain his enthusiasm when one of the mail coachmen let him handle his official steel-encased watch.

When left to themselves, Prue, Colin and Bella had made smaller forays to the parks close to the town house, but it was much more enjoyable when Tristram accompanied them. Bella had seen a return of the companionable relationship she had known in the woods and on their ride to London. She did tend to bristle when he treated her with the same attitude he bent on Colin. Tristram seemed to think she had somehow lost all her competence to fend for herself and could not get about town without his help.

It was interesting to see how others treated the earl. It was when they were abroad that Bella realized that the man whose friendship she enjoyed was both feared and adored by half the population in London. His bearing and arrogant assumption of authority demanded respect from the gentlemen to whom he spoke. And the ladies?

A low chuckle bubbled inside Bella as she rose to her feet to return to the town house. She exited the park, her mind still busy with her thoughts.

Ah, the ladies. Everywhere they went, the female population eyed Tristram. Young and old, rich and poor. They watched him boldly or beneath half-lowered lids, but they definitely observed him, taking his measure, their faces reflecting myriad emotions. For the most part it amused Bella, but it also reminded her that, despite his current refusal to marry, he might eventually meet someone he could love. She tried not to dwell on this thought. She would enjoy his company as long as she could.

"Bella?"

She spun around at the sound of the familiar voice and to her shocked amazement found her cousin Woodie standing beside a hackney pulled up at the curb. She was so surprised that she could do no more than gape at him.

"I was sure it was you," he said, crossing to her quickly and taking her arm. "I've been looking everywhere for you."

Bella tried to pull away but Woodie's fingers bit into her arm. "Unhand me, you idiot, or I shall scream."

"I wouldn't, if I were you. Surely you wouldn't want to cause a scene," he hissed. "Please let me explain."

"All right, but be quick about it," she snapped out, even though her heart was pounding and her knees felt as if she might collapse.

Before she could take in the purpose of Woodie's accosting her, he had dragged her to the hackney and bundled her inside. When the carriage took off, Bella opened her mouth to scream—until her cousin clutched her shoulder in a painful grip. Obviously overset by her behavior, Woodie rushed into speech.

"Please don't scream, Bella. My father is not in London, and you have little to fear from me. I just want to talk to you. Surely you will hear me out?"

Bella's mouth snapped shut. It was not that she was afraid but that she was so surprised. She had never seen Woodie act with quite so much boldness. In the seven years they had known each other, he had always followed her lead, rarely acting on his own. Knowing that her uncle was not in London, did much to alleviate her concern over Woodie's kidnapping. She could easily get away from him if she tried, but for the moment she was curious to hear what he had to say.

"Where are we going?" she asked.

Woodie released his grip on her shoulder and moved slightly away from her as if to indicate his good will. "To the Big Green Inn on the edge of town. I have a room there."

"I cannot go to your room." Bella turned a shocked face to him and was pleased to note his immediate discomfiture.

"Then I will secure a private parlor. Would that be acceptable?"

She cocked her head on the side as if considering his suggestion. Finally she nodded her head in agreement. "I am not best pleased, Woodie, but it will have to suffice."

"Thank you, Bella. I appreciate your cooperation."

Bella hid the smile that threatened to stretch her mouth. Her timorous cousin did not sound like a vicious kidnapper of young women. He sounded much like the Woodie she remembered. She held herself primly upright as the hackney rattled through the streets and was much relieved when the ill-sprung carriage arrived at the inn.

The Big Green Inn was not particularly impressive. The hostlers were a surly lot, and the innkeeper far too obsequious to be considered good-natured. He did however usher them into a private parlor and shouted up a servant to provide them with refreshments. After using the necessary and freshening herself up, Bella made herself comfortable in one of the overstuffed chairs and waited for Woodie to open his budget.

"I'm sorry to have accosted you in such a ramshackle way, Bella," he apologized. "I happened to see you by chance several days ago and have hung about the park hoping you would return."

"It was very clever of you really. I had not thought you quite so enterprising."

Woodie seemed taken aback by her compliment. He looked at her sharply with suspicion but at her grin, he relaxed in his chair and sipped his tea. From his wry grimace, Bella suspected that he would have preferred something stronger and raised her own mug to hide a smile of amusement. They drank in silence, and finally she realized that he would need some encouragement to continue.

"What did you wish to talk to me about, Woodie? Why are you in London?"

"I have been searching for you," he said. "I have been very concerned, but Father did not wish to noise it about. We looked everywhere near Mallory. When we did not pick up as much as a trace, I decided you might have set out for London and came here. I did not really think to find you in such a crowd of people. It was only by the merest chance that I happened to spot you."

"Mischance, more like," Bella snorted. "And now that you have found me, what do you plan to do?"

"I hope to convince you to marry me."

"Whatever for?"

"Beg pardon?"

"Why do you want to marry me?" she snapped in exasperation.

For a moment Woodie goggled at her. His mouth opened, but no words issued forth. His forehead furrowed in puzzlement as he tried to frame an answer to her question. Finally he shook his head as if to clear it and blurted out, "Father wants me to."

"I know that, Woodie. I overheard you and Derwent talking in the library. I know that your father lied to me about my inheritance and wants to keep the money for himself."

"Oh," came the astonished reply.

"And well you might say that, Woodruff Granger. You ought to be ashamed to face me after knowing how poorly he has used me." She almost giggled when the disconcerted young man hung his head. "I always liked you, and I am hurt that you would fall so easily into his plans."

"I'm sorry, Bella."

He looked up with such soulful eyes that Bella realized he really meant his words. He was sincerely ashamed of his actions.

"Do you want to marry me?"

He hedged. "I do like you—"

"But do you really want to marry me? Do you really want to live at Mallory under your father's thumb for the rest of your life?"

"No!"

At his adamant reply, Bella could not conceal her laughter. Woodie looked so affronted by her levity that she laughed all the harder. Finally she was able to master her amusement and wiped her eyes and smiled mischievously across at her cousin.

"Does that 'no' indicate the intensity of your dislike for the very thought of our marriage?" she asked.

His face was flushed as if he were about to fall into an apoplectic fit. "I apologize for making it seem so, but to speak plainly, I do not particularly wish to marry you," he admitted.

"Good. I also do not wish particularly to marry you," she said, earning a sheepish grin from him. "I would make you a very poor wife, I assure you. In fact, I would contrive to make you extremely unhappy."

"But Father is insisting."

"Have you told him yet that you have found me?"

"No. I did not exactly know where you were. I just saw you once leaving the park, but I was too far away and lost you after several blocks. But I will have to tell him something eventually."

"You never were a very good liar, Woodie," she said. Her tone of voice was accusatory, and once more her cousin looked crestfallen. "I do not wish to live for the next two years afraid that Uncle Derwent will snatch me off the streets of London and force me into a marriage that I do not want. I wish I knew what to do for the best."

"For starters, you might introduce me to your gentleman friend."

The drawled voice from the doorway quite literally left Bella breathless. In disbelief she raised her eyes to Tristram's elegant figure, leaning negligently against the frame. She blinked her eyes, but the man was not a vision. Apparently Woodie did not think so either, because he leaped to his feet and glared at the intruder.

"And just what business is it of yours?" he asked, thrusting his chin forward belligerently.

"I am the earl of Wyndham," Tristram said, striding forward after closing the door. "And you, sir?"

"Woodruff Granger, milord."

It was apparent that Woodie was awed by the presence of the nobleman, and any hope that Bella had of keeping her identity secret was dashed at the sound of her cousin's respectful tone. She was too overcome by the realization that she would have to leave the Wyndhams' town house now that her masquerade was over to do anything more than fight back tears of frustration.

"And the young lady is your cousin?"

"Yes, this is Lady Arabella Mallory. She inherited the baronetcy on the death of her father Sir Robert Mallory."

"I say," Tristram said, clucking his tongue in dismay.

"Give over," Bella snapped, rising to her feet in exasperation. "You knew all along that Waters was not my real name."

"You know this man?" Woodie asked, spinning around to look at Bella with surprise.

"He is, or perhaps I should say was, my employer."

"Bella! Whatever have you done?" Woodie cried.

"Stubble it, you looby." Bella glared at Tristram who was trying hard to keep the amusement from showing on his face. Unfortunately she could see the delighted sparkle of suppressed laughter in his blue eyes. "I have not accepted a slip of the shoulder as you so obviously think. Give me some credit for good sense. I was governess to the earl's son. And don't you dare apologize for insulting me. I have had quite enough of that for today."

"Well, now that we have all been introduced properly, I suggest we continue this discussion on the morrow. Perhaps you would care to call on me at ten," Tristram said to Woodie. "Would that be too early?"

"T—ten? That would be c—convenient." He stammered his answer, too bewildered by the proceedings to do otherwise.

"Excellent. Now that that is settled, we need not tarry. Come along, Bella."

Stunned by the high-handed behavior of the man, Bella could do little but gape at him. Tristram crossed the room and took her arm, leading her toward the door. One look at the hard glitter of his eyes convinced her it would be futile to attempt to resist. Woodie was far too confused to offer any assistance, and by the time she gathered her wits she was already ensconced in Tristram's landau. She settled for a glare of disapproval for her companion. Drawing her dignity around her, she braced herself for the thundering scold for which she was destined.

They arrived at the town house in icy silence. Tristram carefully assisted her to the walk, and then led her up the stairs to the front door. Although he did not drag her past Dillingsworth, he kept his hand firmly around her arm until they entered the library. Inside he released her and the door closed with an ominous click. Heart jarring within her rib cage, Bella crossed the room and sat down on one of the chairs across from his enormous carved desk. Tristram stalked to the windows behind the desk and stared out over the garden, controlling the anger that rode him.

It was just by the sheerest luck that he had seen Bella's abduction. He had been returning to the town house in his landau when he came upon Prue and Colin leading the limping mare. They quickly explained the situation and, after securing information as to where they had left the governess, Tristram took off. He arrived at the park in time to see Bella being accosted by a young man. Even at a distance it was apparent that they knew each other, but even so he was taken aback when the man hurried Bella into a waiting hackney. Face grim, he had followed in their wake.

He held himself in check when they arrived at the Big Green Inn. It surprised him at how difficult it was to let Bella enter the inn with the young man. He could feel anger billowing up in his chest, threatening to choke him. How dare the man lay hands on a young woman who was under his protection! He would like nothing better than to beat the young puppy into a bloody heap.

As for Bella, she was not immune to his feeling of ill-usage. How could she consider going to a posting inn with such a ramshackle fellow who had the unmitigated gall to kidnap her off the London streets! No matter that she appeared to recognize the fellow. The least she could have done was scream. Was that how she planned to conduct herself in a city renowned for its shady characters and wily sharpsters? He would be damned if he let her leave the house again without a full escort.

It was only after he entered the inn and listened to part of their conversation that he was able to face them with even a semblance of equanimity. Now as he stared out the library windows he tried to tamp down the anger that had returned and gain control over his emotions.

He closed his eyes, pinching the skin at the bridge of his nose. He had heard enough of the conversation to realize that Bella was running away from a wicked and conniving uncle so his first order of business must be to assure her of her safety. Thus deciding, he relaxed slightly and turned to face the room.

One look at the crumpled figure in the chair dispelled all feelings of calm. Bella looked like a lovely, lost child, shoulders hunched as if preparing to take a blow. Suddenly she raised her head and the brown eyes glared at him as she pulled herself upright in the chair. She resembled an angry puppy, her soft brown eyes sparking with annoyance. His lips twitched with amusement at her returning spirit.

"Well, Lady Mallory?"

"I prefer Miss Waters."

"I am afraid, my dear, that now that the cat is out of the bag, that little fiction will have to be jettisoned." Tristram came around the desk, sitting down on the edge facing her. "After all the energy she has been expending in trying to discover your identity, I am sure Grandmama will insist on calling you by your correct title."

"It will not matter," Bella said. She could not keep the note of sadness from her tone. "I shall be leaving here, of course."

"Absolutely not!" Tristram shouted, surprising himself at his own vehemence.

"Surely you realize, I cannot remain," Bella argued.

"I don't see why not. Perhaps we will have to change your status from that of governess to guest, but I see no reason to change else. Both Prue and Lady Wyndham enjoy your company, and Colin would no doubt fall into fits of despair if I permitted you to sneak off," he concluded.

This drew a smile from Bella, and she relaxed more naturally against the back of the chair. "Well there is that to consider. I should not wish to abandon the boy."

"Although I heard a great deal of your conversation with your charming cousin, I would appreciate it if you told me a little of your background and what precipitated the flight from your home."

After some initial hesitation, Bella briefly sketched the events that had led up to her escape with Violet in the dead of night. Tristram watched her face, catching nuances beneath her crisply spoken commentary which revealed far more than she knew. There was no self-pity in her tone, just a bald recital of the facts, but he was quick to note the fear that fluttered across her expressive face every time she mentioned her uncle. Derwent Granger had much for which to answer.

"So you can see," Bella concluded, "that it will be impossible for me to remain here. Now that Woodie knows, Derwent will eventually force the information out of him. I must leave here for the simple reason that I am no longer safe. Derwent is my legal guardian."

"Devil take it, Bella! Do you actually think I will permit you to fall into the hands of such a rogue after all you have told me?" Once more Tristram could feel anger building within his body. "You ran away before because you had little choice in the matter. You had no one to turn to for advice or protection. However, you are now a member of my household. Would anyone dare to challenge Wyndham?"

Bella could not restrain a smile of amusement. Perhaps a life of privilege led him to believe that he was above the normal touch. For a moment hope rose in her breast, but it was short-lived and she shook her head in returning sadness.

"Uncle Derwent is my legal guardian," she repeated.

Tristram stared at the set face of the girl in the chair. He knew enough about her by now to know that she would never admit to fear, but he could tell by the whiteness of her face that she was in fact afraid. He had the overwhelming desire to sweep her into his arms and tell her that he would protect her from all harm. In a sort of fatherly way, of course, just as he used to do when Colin was injured and needed consoling. His fingers gripped the edge of the desk to keep from reaching for the girl.

"Be assured, Bella," he said, his deep voice resolute. "I have absolutely no intention of permitting Derwent Granger to decide your fate. I have the solution, if you will hear me out. I will marry you."

"What!"

Bella's squeal of surprise was an echo of Tristram's feelings. He had made no conscious decision to offer for her; the words had flown from his mouth without thought. However, now that he considered the situation, he could see that it was easily the best solution to the problem.

"You will marry me, and then you will be fully protected from your uncle and any plans he may have constructed to marry you to his hapless son. I have enough friends and influence to force him to approve the marriage. I assume from what you have said that he would not be overjoyed by too close an investigation into his stewardship of your estate. For that reason alone, I believe he would agree to your marriage."

Tristram had been staring at a spot above Bella's left shoulder, but now he dropped his eyes and took in the stunned expression on her face. He paused for a moment, waiting to see if she would make any comment. She merely looked at him in confusion and he hurried into speech.

"As you know, I have been adamantly opposed to remarrying. I will not offer you false coin. I do not want a wife. I am done with all the emotion that commitment entails. I would like a mother for Colin. I think he would approve of my choice. What I am offering you is a marriage of protection. With my name, you will be safe for the rest of your life."

Bella was truly staggered by Tristram's proposition. She realized the generosity of his offer and was pleased that he should make such a sacrifice. On the other hand, she was saddened, knowing he had no feeling for her, other than a certain fondness which made the offer even more surprising. She had assumed that he had not remarried because he had not found someone he could love. It was apparent that he truly did not wish to marry.

She stood up, conscious that such a gracious offer deserved her heartfelt gratitude. She stared into his brilliant blue eyes and knew an instant of sharp disappointment that she must reject his proposal. Even for the security he offered, she could not accept.

"While I am conscious of the honor you have done me, Tristram, I cannot agree to such desperate measures," she said, her voice soft but firm.

"What!"

Now it was Tristram's turn to be stunned. He knew his own desirability as an eligible party, no matter what conditions were attached to the offer. It had never occurred to him that any female would refuse him, and he felt curiously hurt by Bella's rejection. He had never met such a contrary wench!

"I can understand perfectly that you have no wish to marry," Bella continued, trying to explain her position. "I have no intention of marrying, either. I will never put my person or my inheritance under the control of any man again. I am fully capable of taking care of myself."

Her calm, reasonable tone did nothing but exacerbate the already tight check Tristram had maintained on his emotions. She stood before him, a veritable babe, and suggested that she was up to handling her own protection. It beat all to flinders, he thought, grinding his teeth in rising anger. She had less strength than his own son, and yet she stood prepared to withstand the abusive control of a wicked uncle, not to mention every fortune hunter in the whole benighted English countryside.

"What idiocy is this?" he shouted, grasping her shoulders and pulling her forward until she was standing directly in front of him. He glared at her, somehow pleased at the flash of uneasiness he read on her face. "Have you any idea what would happen to you should people discover that you were an heiress without family protection?"

"I will not broadcast my news, milord," she snapped. "I will take another position as governess under the name Miss Waters."

"Oh ho! And that I am assured will protect you from the fortune hunters, but not, I think, from the realities of life. There is a certain segment of society that preys on little governesses like you. And they need not even have the startling looks that you possess." His hands tightened on her shoulders, and he shook her in his frustration. "Older sons, fathers, even the servants in a household would make short work of your defenses. At the very least they would handle your person with greedy hands. At the worst they would bed you in the most brutal form of violation you could possibly conceive."

Bella pulled against his painful grip, wanting to cover her ears at his hurtful words. She shrank physically and mentally from the venom in his voice, but in his rising fury he was oblivious to her discomfort.

"How will you protect yourself from this?"

Tristram pulled her savagely against his chest and took possession of her mouth. Although Bella had never been kissed by anyone other than her father, it was just as she had always imagined it would be. Tristram's lips moved on hers in a brutal kiss, meant to dominate and humiliate her. Fear raced through Bella, and she fought against the pressure, striking out blindly in her terror. She felt Tristram shudder, and suddenly he released her. She shrank away from him, covering her bruised mouth with the back of her hand.

The sight of Bella's stricken expression drove a shaft of pain into Tristram's body. He could read fear and disgust in her face and felt heartily ashamed of his loss of control. He could not believe that he had been driven to such measures just to frighten her.

"Please forgive me, Bella," he said, his voice hoarse with emotion. "I do not know what came over me. You must believe me when I say that this will never happen again."

The sparkle of unshed tears and the tremble of Bella's chin was his undoing. He groaned at what damage he had wreaked in his anger.

"Come here, Bella," he said.

His voice was soft but the tone was commanding. For a moment she did not move and he prepared to repeat his words. But the girl had pluck. A shudder traversed her body, but she straightened her spine and stepped forward until she stood before him with lowered eyes.

"Look at me, Bella."

Slowly she raised her eyes. Her body vibrated with a tremor of fear, but Tristram was amazed to note the trust that still glimmered in her eyes.

"Have you ever been kissed by a gentleman?" he asked.

For answer, she shook her head, flags of color shimmering on her cheeks.

"I have done you a sad injustice that your first kiss should be given in anger. It should not be so. When you find a man you can love, he will not use you thus. When you find a man you can love, he will kiss you gently and softly, and you will be neither afraid nor ashamed."

Thus saying, once more he lowered his head and kissed her. This time his lips were gentle. They pressed her own with a cool firmness. His arms held her securely, nesting her against his hard chest in a comforting embrace. Slowly her fear ebbed away and other emotions rose in its place.

There was a sweetness to Tristram's kiss that sent a wave of dizziness through her body. She had no desire to push him away. Instead her fists relaxed, flattening out against the firmness of his chest. Her eyes closed and she lost herself in the tide of pleasure that filled her. She felt an instant of disappointment when he released her.

Silence held them both in its grip, each aware of the other's every movement. Reluctantly Bella stepped away, breaking the rising tension.

"Thank you, Tristram," she said softly.

Without another word, she left the room. She walked up the staircase, methodically placing each foot in front of the other. Her actions were automatic and, without knowing how she got there, she arrived at the door of her room. She managed to close the door behind her before the tears slid silently down her cheeks.

Bella was not aware of any reason for tears, but a deep emotion had taken possession of her. Perhaps she cried for the gift Tristram had given her. For surely he had done that. He had shown her that she had no reason to fear passion, it could be tender, as well as hurtful. Yet she did not think that was why she cried. Somewhere within her heart she was hurting, knowing she had lost something very precious at the same time that she had found it.

Chapter Nine

"Well, my dear, I must agree with Tristram in this instance," Lady Wyndham said. "I see absolutely no reason for you to leave. Surely you do not wish to live in the shadow of fear. It would be much too wearing on your constitution. You will live here as our guest, a visitor just like Prudence. I must insist you use your proper name. We might even put it about that you are some sort of relative. Far removed, naturally, so you need not be aware of any family history. After all, Bella, here we can offer you our protection. No one would dare offend Wyndham," she concluded archly.

"I do not like to impose," Bella said, still not completely comfortable with her situation.

"Fustian!" Lady Wyndham snapped. "I quite enjoy having young people about. We all get on well, and I see no reason to change the status quo."

"Even your cousin approved of the idea, Bella," Prue said. "He did, didn't he, Tristram?"

"The young cub fair leaped at the idea." Tristram grinned across at Bella, his eyes alight. "I cannot imagine why he should be so set against the marriage. You must have plagued him when you were a child."

"I did not!" Her face pinked at some of her memories. "All right, I will admit that I did insist we play according to my rules. But that was when I was very young. In the last years we have got on quite well. We spent most of our time on horseback, prowling around the estate. If truth be told, I believe Woodie would prefer the estate to the excitements of London. I think he stayed away from Mallory because Uncle Derwent was there."

"Is he so dependent on his father?" Tristram asked.

"I don't really think so." Bella squinched her forehead, trying to remember all that she had heard. "There was some talk about the fact he had his own money. I think it came from his mother's family. He is not really my cousin. Aunt Emma is only his stepmother. I think he is afraid to cross his father."

"Well, for the moment I have assured him that he need not fear a forced marriage. He is pleased that you are safe. In actual fact the nodcock is terrified of your displeasure. For all your bullying, he is quite fond of you."

Bella made a moue of annoyance at Tristram's words, but spoiled the effect as she felt a bubble of amusement well up inside. She could not hold back a giggle and smiled when she saw an echo of amusement in his bright blue eyes. She loved it when he found something to be humorous. His face lit up and lost the severe expression he usually wore. His mouth was made for smiling. His finely chiseled lips . . . Bella dropped her eyes to her lap, feeling a rush of heat rising to her cheeks as she remembered the feel of Tristram's lips on hers. She was grateful when Lady Wyndham stamped her walking stick for attention.

"As far as I am concerned, the problem is resolved," she said. "You do agree, Bella?"

"I will accept your kind hospitality for the moment, Lady Wyndham," she temporized.

"Excellent!"

Bella was mystified by the look of triumph on the woman's face. She had assumed that the dowager would be rather overset to discover her masquerade, but she seemed to be overjoyed instead. Her eyes had sparkled during the recital of Bella's history, and she had a gloating look to her that Bella might have understood if she had known Lady Wyndham better.

In any event, Bella was pleased that she could relax for the moment. Woodie had been interviewed earlier and even he was accepted by the household as a fit companion. In fact, they were waiting for him now to take Prue and Bella for a drive in the park. Thus reminded of his imminent arrival, Bella hurried off to her room for a hat and her parasol.

From then on, Woodie joined the afternoon forays about town. Bella was surprised when she realized she was seeing a whole different side of her cousin. Around her, he generally stammered and stumbled, but with Prue and Colin he was much more assured. Perhaps he was intimidated by her as Tristram had suggested. She tried to treat him more patiently and was rewarded for her efforts. He made a charming companion.

The thing that amused her most about their outings was that it was becoming ever more apparent that Woodie had formed an affection for Prue. Since Bella and Colin were always impatient to be moving on to the next event, Woodie and Prue were thrown more and more together. They suited each other. They talked endlessly of the country, and it turned out that Prue enjoyed the hunt, a subject Woodie adored discussing.

At first Bella thought Prue was just being kind to Woodie because by nature she was a dear and sweet person. Eventually it began to dawn on her that Prue enjoyed Woodie's company. He was rather shy himself so he appeared to understand the gawky girl's tendency to retire within herself. He did not require a great deal of conversation and was content to ask questions when a subject interested him. Since there was no pressure to charm or beguile him, Prue began to speak to him with the same ease she had discovered with others she liked. Soon it was evident that she was smitten with a true fondness for Woodie.

Once Bella assured herself that Prue returned her cousin's regard, she relaxed and gave them more time together. Although she did not know much about Eden and Glynis Danforth, she thought Prue's parents would have enough social influence to counter Uncle Derwent's hold on Woodie. If it was true that he had his own funds, she could see little chance that Derwent could cause any trouble. Besides, although Prue was painfully shy in company, she was fiercely loyal and not easily cowed.

At the end of two short weeks, it was apparent that Prue and Woodie were in love. The shy young woman seemed to glow with an inner light of approval that gave her usually pale complexion a rosy tint. She smiled more often and was so filled with well being that she appeared almost pretty to those who watched her. Although Tristram rolled his eyes in the presence of the two lovebirds, he did seem generally pleased by the outcome. Even Lady Wyndham had given her nod of approval to the match.

The only dark cloud on the courting couple's horizon was the imminent arrival of Eden and Glynis Danforth. Prue was particularly apprehensive because she was convinced that her mother would never agree to her marriage to Woodie. While it was true that he had a good income, he was an untitled gentleman. According to Prue, her mother had groomed her to be the wife of a nobleman and would settle for nothing less.

Bella applied to Tristram and he suggested a theater party. In such an entertaining setting, Prue's parents would be able to see how well-suited the couple was. Although Bella had refused to attend any society functions, she agreed to be included in the group going to the Green Mews Theatre. She had never been to a theater and was looking forward to the evening. She was especially excited because she had heard much about the celebrated actress Maggie Mason, who was scheduled to perform in the pantomime.

Sitting in the darkened theater, Bella thought the evening had gone exceptionally well. Lady Wyndham had hosted a family dinner at the town house for Prue's parents, with Woodie as the only invited guest. She was pleased that her cousin had presented such a charming picture. Woodie had learned much through being in Tristram's company; he appeared far more sophisticated now. It touched her heart when she looked at Prue. Her friend's face glowed with an inner contentment whenever she chanced to look in Woodie's direction.

They had arrived at the Green Mews Theatre after the performance of Hamlet, which had been the early bill. Tristram had felt that the pantomime which followed would be more in keeping with the lighter tone of the evening. Bella had been delighted by the glittering parade of those attending and would have been content if they had gotten no farther than the lobby. However she followed in the wake of Lady Wyndham and was suitably rewarded when she walked through the red velvet curtains into the private box.

The theater was laid out before her. She did not know where to look first and sat forward on the velvet covered gilt chair, her eyes dazzled by the sights and sounds. Above, there were enormous chandeliers and below was a sea of faces. The men milling around the pit held her in thrall for a while until she swung her gaze upward to admire the occupants of the private boxes. She was so bewitched by the scene that it was only from a distance that she heard Glynis Danforth's raised voice above the roar of the crowd.

"This actress Maggie Mason is called 'La Solitaire', I am told," Prue's mother said, her voice sharp with disapproval. "No doubt a blowsy slattern no better than she should be."

"You will be surprised," Lady Wyndham said, her voice noncommittal. "I have seen her several times and have quite enjoyed her performance. She was a protégée of Sarah Siddons, don't you know. Besides being an exceptional beauty, she is a first-rate actress."

Bella heard Glynis sniff her disbelief just as the theater darkened and the green curtain rose. Once the pantomime started, she was lost to all awareness of those around her. It was as if she had entered a magical world that took possession of her senses and her emotions. She was not watching the play; she was involved in it. It was as if she had known the heroine Theodosia in another life. Each time she was kidnapped or otherwise separated from the hero, Prince Tatum, Bella worried that they might never find true love.

At the back of the box, Tristram moved his chair so that he would have an unobstructed view of Bella. From the moment they had arrived at the theater he had been aware of the excitement bubbling inside the young woman. There had been such a look of wonder on her face as her eyes darted around that he had been fascinated. It was as if she were seeing something that the rest of them were missing. She seemed to be filled with a wellspring of joyous innocence, and for some reason he wanted to be a part of it.

In the light of the chandeliers, he noticed how lovely she looked. Her dress was a simple yellow muslin with puffed sleeves and a wide satin sash beneath her softly rounded bosom. It was unremarkable in style, yet set off her beauty, like the plain gold setting of a diamond. Her golden brown hair was dressed in a Psyche knot with soft tendrils at her cheek and her neck. She wore no jewelry, only a yellow ribbon tied at her throat. She needed no adornments; she was exquisite.

When the lights dimmed, he could still watch her, her face bathed in the soft glow from the stage. He could follow her every emotion by the changes written clearly on her expressive face. During the sword fight, her dainty hands were pressed to her bosom in an agony of suspense. She laughed and clapped at the antics of Clown. She held her breath in tension as the acrobat walked the wire suspended above the stage. Silent tears rolled unattended down her cheeks as La Solitaire sang of her lost love.

In some respects it was like watching a child. Bella had an innocence about her that Tristram had rarely encountered. Compared to her purity of spirit, he felt jaded and dirty, afraid that any contact with him might somehow tarnish her. Yet at the same time he was drawn to her, wanting to be within her orbit, warmed by her very presence.

At the intermission Bella sagged in her chair, and Tristram wondered how she would survive to the denouement of the play. He rose to his feet and leaned over her chair.

"Bella?"

Tristram's voice floated over her shoulder and she turned in her chair to face him. She blinked her eyes to bring him into focus and found he was smiling broadly down at her, just as if he understood how far away her mind had been.

"Would you care to walk about for a bit? It will help, I assure you," he said.

Bella took his hand, excusing herself to the others, and walked through the curtains at the back of the box. Out in the hall people were strolling about, and for several minutes her companion remained silent. Finally Bella was able to speak.

"Thank you for the most wonderful evening of my life," she said.

"There is more to come, my dear," he said, patting the small hand on his arm. He led her carefully down the stairs to the crowded lobby. "Have you never been to the theater?"

"Never. It is a whole new world. I feel as if I have been transported across the oceans to a land of enchantment." She noted the amusement in his eyes and felt a flush rise to her cheeks. "I fear you must think I am a green girl, but I am enjoying it ever so much."

At her words, Tristram's face took on an expression of gravity. "On the contrary, Bella, it is only in observing your enjoyment that I feel again the same joy of my first visit to the theater. It has given me additional pleasure to watch the performance through your eyes. I should be grateful to you for reminding me."

"Is she as beautiful as I think she is?" she asked.

"La Solitaire?" he asked. At her nod, he continued, "Yes. I think so. There is magic in her acting. I have seen her many times and I have the same feeling that you do. I am not sure what is the reality and what the illusion. But I believe she is very lovely."

"Glynis must be very disappointed. From her words earlier I had expected someone else entirely. Miss Mason appears to be very ladylike and truly elegant. Her powdered hair makes her very striking, but it is the fineness of her features that holds one's attention."

"Here, too, I would have to agree," he said.

They had reached a series of sheltered alcoves, and he led her into an empty one and indicated a marble bench. Bella sat down, grateful that she could still view the assemblage without feeling crushed by the press of the crowd. They spoke for a few minutes, discussing the various scenes of the pantomime. Finally, after assuring himself that Bella would not mind being alone, Tristram excused himself to speak to a friend.

She watched as he approached an elegant gentleman with wavy brown hair. The man was clearly delighted to see Tristram, for his mouth spread into a smile and his green eyes flashed with pleasure. Although his friend was handsome, Tristram was still the more striking of the two. She was totally content to be able to watch him without fear of being observed. She was so immersed in her inspection of Tristram that she jumped when a hand closed over her arm.

"I've found you at last, you ungrateful chit," a voice hissed close to her ear.

"Uncle Derwent!" she gasped, choking back a cry of fear.

"In the flesh." His black eyes glittered against his pale skin, and the unrelieved black of his clothing gave him a sinister air.

"What are you doing here?" she asked, through stiffened lips.

"Never thought I'd find you, did you?" He gave a chuckle that was far from amused. When she would rise, he pressed her back on the marble bench. "No need to make a scene, my girl. We will wait until the play begins again, and then you will leave quietly with me."

Although Bella wanted to stand up and run from her uncle, she did not think her legs would hold her. She felt the veriest coward, but there was something about the way he looked at her that made her cringe away from him. His eyes blazed as he surveyed her from head to toe.

"Who would have thought the little brown wren would have blossomed into a bird of exotic plumage," he said. "Little Arabella is most surely not a child anymore. Quite ripe for the marriage bed, I should think."

His words shamed her, and she had the urge to cover herself, but his iron grip prevented her from moving her arm. Although he blocked her escape, she could look beyond him to Tristram's figure deep in conversation with his friend and take courage from his nearness. A spurt of anger stiffened her spine, and she glared up at Derwent.

"I will not leave with you," she announced. She was pleased when her defiance surprised him, but her triumph was short-lived as his fingers tightened around her wrist.

"Do not mistake me, girl. I am your legal guardian and I can do anything with you I so choose," he snarled. When she slumped on the seat, he chuckled. "I thought there was something havey-cavey from the tone of Woodruff's letters. So I decided to pay a visit to London. And what should I find but my delightful little ward hobnobbing with the swells."

Bella tried to pull away from the pressure of the fingers biting into her wrist. "Please, Uncle Derwent. You are hurting me," she said.

"This is nothing compared to what I plan to do to you," he warned.

At these words, Bella's whole body began to tremble. She should have known that her uncle would find her. The thought of once more being under his control almost sent her into a swoon. Pride came to her rescue and, taking a deep breath, she pulled herself straighter on the marble bench. No matter the situation, she would not give in to her fear.

"How dare you lay hands on Lady Mallory."

Tristram's quiet voice shook with the intensity of his anger. There was a tightness to his jaw and a stiffness to his body that indicated how difficult he found it to control his fury. He moved forward until he was standing beside Bella. She started to rise, but his hand shot out and pressed her shoulder, holding her in place.

"Remove your hand this instant," Tristram said between clenched teeth.

Derwent's face flushed at the challenge to his authority. He was aware that others in the crowd had noticed the contretemps and was determined to keep the upper hand. "Who are you and what business is this of yours?" he snapped.

"I am the earl of Wyndham, and Lady Mallory is my affianced bride."

Tristram's words had not been loud, but the effect on the crowd was as if they had been shouted. There was a general gasp of surprise, and then a rumble of conversation burst from the onlookers as they passed this startling information from ear to ear. Derwent was shocked into silence, the color fading from his face in his stupefaction. Bella could feel her own face whiten, but when she looked up at Tristram he seemed unfazed at the consternation of everyone in the vicinity.

Derwent released Bella's wrist as if contact with her skin had singed him. He opened his mouth several times but no words came forth. In the silence Tristram stepped forward, speaking in a whisper. He spoke only a few words, but Derwent nodded his head several times. Then, with a last glare at Bella, the older man turned and pushed his way through the crowded lobby.

It had all happened so quickly that for a moment Bella wondered if she had dreamed the whole thing. One look at Tristram's carefully shuttered expression disabused her of such an idea. Without a word he extended his hand. She took it, rising to her feet as a crowd of well-wishers closed in around them. He accepted the greetings of his friends without halting his pace. She could feel the color burning in her cheeks and shrank against him as he led her back to his box. In the privacy of the anteroom, he pulled her around to face him.

"I am sorry for such a scene, my dear," he said. "I should not have left you alone. My only excuse is that I had not seen Drew Farrington for several months. I apologize for any embarrassment my absence may have caused you."

"My embarrassment? What about you? Everyone will be

saying that you plan to marry me," Bella said, her voice shaking in her agitation.

"I do plan to marry you." His words were quiet but firm.

"But you don't want to marry."

"I have changed my mind."

Bella closed her eyes, shutting out the grave expression on his face. She was appalled that her actions had precipitated such a situation. She knew he did not want to marry her, but had been forced to such a statement in a misguided attempt to save her from her uncle. Tears threatened, but she forced them back, not wanting to create more of a scene than she already had.

"I shall tell the others that I offered for you several days ago but you were unsure of your answer until this evening." Tristram's words snapped open Bella's eyes, and she stared up at him in shock. He gave her a slight smile and patted her perfunctorily on her shoulder. "I realize that this is all very awkward for you, but do you think you can carry off such a stretching of the truth?"

"No," she announced bluntly. "I do not want to marry, either. I see no reason to carry on with such a fiction when it will never come to pass. I am sure once we explain the situation to Lady Wyndham, she will understand why you said what you did."

"What a contrary child you are," Tristram said. He glared at her, and it was apparent he found little to favor. "Like it or not, I intend to marry you. I have given my word to your uncle, and a Wyndham never goes back on his word."

"What a coil!" Bella was drained by the events of the evening and felt less than able to fight the determination she saw written on his face. "Everything was going along so wonderfully until Derwent found me," she cried.

"I am sorry that your uncle's arrival should have ruined the evening for you," Tristram said. "I think we will be forced to leave. The news will have traveled the length and breadth of the theater by the time the pantomime is over. I would not wish Grandmama to hear of my good fortune from one of her cronies. If you will wait here, I will explain to the others the need to return to the town house."

After sending a lackey to call up his carriages, Tristram parted the curtains and entered the box. The action of the play had already resumed and Bella could hear muted voices from the stage. She waited in an agony of whirling emotion until the others left the box and then, with Tristram's arm firmly supporting her, she was whisked from the theater. Lady Wyndham and Prue's parents, evincing great curiosity as to the aborted theatrical visit, were assisted without explanation into the first carriage. Riding with Tristram and Bella, Woodie and Prue were not less curious, but were so involved with their own relationship that they were oblivious to the sudden change in plans.

Tristram led a shaken Bella into the salon. He seated her carefully on the silver-striped sofa, placed his hand on her shoulder for support, and then turned to the mystified occupants of the room.

"I am sorry if our abrupt departure from the theater has caused you any discomfort," he said, his words clipped but unhurried. "But, you see, an event has occurred which I felt could only be handled under my own roof. Lady Arabella Mallory has agreed to become my bride."

For a moment, the words seemed to echo in the hollow silence of the room before anyone reacted to the news. Then, of course, there was a babble of unintelligible voices until finally Lady Wyndham rapped her stick for attention.

"It's about time," she said, a look of triumph on her face. She crossed to face the couple. "May I be the first to wish you happy?"

Bella wanted to rise, but she knew her trembling legs would not support her. Lady Wyndham sat down beside her and embraced her warmly while the others gathered around to extend their good wishes. Prue and Woodie emerged from their own dream world long enough to congratulate the couple. Bella suspected that their enthusiasm for the match stemmed from the fact that they hoped it would soon be their turn to announce such exciting news.

The elder Danforths were more restrained in their comments. It was only on their arrival that they had learned that Bella was no longer a governess but a young woman entitled to be called Lady Mallory. They had been given an expurgated version of Bella's history, and they were having trouble adjusting to such a series of changes in the young woman's status.

Through it all, Bella was aware of Tristram's elegant figure at her side. He responded when spoken to, but did not enthuse on the situation as one might expect of a happily engaged young man. He called for champagne to toast the betrothal and accepted the good wishes of his family with a grimness of visage that might have presaged a visit to the hangman. It was apparent to Bella, if to no one else in the room, that he was in a towering temper, held in check by the responsibility to show at least a token appreciation of his good fortune.

After the excitement had lessened and the talk became more general, Bella pleaded exhaustion from the events of the day. She accepted the dowager's warm embrace with a flush of discomfort, feeling herself the veriest of traitors. She knew Lady Wyndham would be much overset when she learned that in actual fact there would be no wedding. Tristram accompanied her to the hallway to bid her good night. She stood on the first step, facing him. When he took her hand, she felt a jolt, like some sort of shock to her nerves, run through her body at his touch.

"We will leave for Dragon's Keep tomorrow," he said. "My announcement this evening will create a flurry of sensation. Gossiping biddies, anxious for a look at the woman who succeeded in leg shackling me, will descend on us in droves. Will you mind leaving?"

"No," she answered softly, all too aware of her hand in his. He was staring down at it, as if surprised to find it in his own larger palm. "I am anxious to quit London."

At this he looked into her face and her breath caught at the intensity in his blue eyes. For a moment she could not speak. It was as if he were searching the far reaches of her soul. Her heart pounded, and she wanted to reach out to touch his face, so close to her own.

Her gaze dropped to his mouth, and for a moment she remembered the two kisses in the library. The first had been frightening in its power, but it was the second one she remembered most clearly. It had been tender and sweet, offering her security and love. She swayed toward him, wanting him to take her in his arms so she might once again feel his protection. Instead she rocked back on her heels, annoyed with herself for such weakness. A flush rose to her cheeks, and she licked her dry lips before she could speak.

"Might I ask a favor?" she asked.

"Of course, my dear."

"I realize that there is bound to be gossip after tonight, but I would rather not announce anything further until we have had an opportunity to talk."

"Why?" he asked, eyes narrowed in suspicion.

"Because I have not decided if I will marry you," she blurted out.

Tristram's grip tightened on Bella's fingers, but he did not speak immediately. He stared down at her flushed cheeks, a curious expression of exasperation and anger on his face. Finally his mouth twitched with amusement, and he nodded his head.

"I will put it about that I have asked for your hand, but you are so overcome at the honor that you have not been able to formulate an answer," he drawled. "Would that be acceptable?"

"Y—yes," she stammered. "And Colin?"

"I will have a chat with the cub," he growled. "Anything else before you seek your bed?"

"No. And thank you, Tristram. For everything."

"As always, I am your humble servant."

He raised her hand and tenderly kissed it, but Bella's throat was so choked with tears she could do no more than nod her head at the gesture before she fled up the stairs to her room.

Inside, she staggered to the window seat, collapsing on the satin cushion. She leaned her forehead against the glass, reveling in the coolness against her overheated skin. Her body cried for the soothing release of tears, but she knew in her heart that nothing would relieve the pain she was experiencing.

No matter what Tristram said, she could not marry him. It was not fear of scandal, fear of marriage, nor even fear of Derwent that held her back. Tristram did not want to marry her; therefore, she could not agree. She would not hold him to words said in the mistaken belief he could save her from her uncle. She could not accept such a sacrifice for the simple reason that she had discovered to her joy and sorrow that she was in love with Tristram.

She was not sure when she had first fallen in love with him. It might have been during their night in the woods when she had first stared into his clear blue eyes. It might have been when he was joking with her about a picture at the art gallery.

It might have been any one of a million inconsequential things. All she knew was that suddenly she was in love with him, and it seemed as if she always had been.

For so long she had sworn she would never put her trust in a man. She had seen the kind of tyranny Derwent played out on Aunt Emma and promised herself that she would never place herself in such a position. Marriage for her had always meant a loss of control. The thought that someone would have control of her person and her actions terrified her. Under Derwent's domination she had felt powerless. Now she realized that her uncle had been abusing his power and that she need only look for a man who would never try to force her to his will. Her uncle was not a fair representative of men. He was an aberration, not the norm.

In her dealings with Tristram she understood that although he might not approve of things she said or did, he would not try to enforce his will on her. She trusted him implicitly. Perhaps that was part of loving someone, but she did not think so. Tristram was a man to be trusted.

It would be so easy just to agree to the marriage. She truly loved him and would happily consent to spend her life with him. But Tristram did not love her.

She knew he was fond of her and that they had become good friends, but he did not view her in any loverlike capacity. He treated her with the doting affection he reserved for small children and untrained puppies. Without love, their marriage would be a disaster.

Her eyes burned with unshed tears, and she raised her hands to rub them. Her fingers pushed up across her forehead and dug into her hair to help release the tension in her body. She was glad they were leaving London.

Once in the country, she could decide what to do for the best. Perhaps it was time to discuss the situation with Lady Wyndham. It might make the breaking of their engagement easier if the woman understood the entire problem. Perhaps it would be a nine-day wonder, but Bella could only act according to her beliefs.

She undressed slowly, unwilling to think beyond their trip to the country. She knew that the breaking of her engagement to Tristram would force her to leave his household, but she could not face such a decision at this time. Climbing into bed, she burrowed beneath the comforter, already feeling the desolation of her future.

Tristram paced the floor of the library. His teeth were clamped shut in anger as he attempted to walk off his excess emotion. Tomorrow he would meet with Derwent Granger, and the thought of having to be civil to the man infuriated him. He gripped his fingers tightly behind his back, wanting nothing more than to choke the life out of the bastard.

He had always known there was something not quite right about Bella's running away. When she had told him the story, she had not explained enough about her relationship with her uncle. The moment he had seen the look in Granger's eye, he had understood her desperation to get away.

Over the years he had met men of Granger's stamp. They were men who thrived on the domination of the weak. They were cruel men who were aroused by pain, the pain of others, naturally, never their own. They preyed on women, physically unable to defend themselves, and they gloated in the ability to break their spirit through the use of brute force. Derwent Granger was such a one.

Tristram could still remember the rush of emotion when he placed his hand on Bella's shoulder and felt her body trembling in fear. He had been conscious of the delicate bones beneath her translucent skin and the very fragility of the young woman. Fury such as he had never known flooded his body, and if it hadn't been for the presence of a lobby full of people, he would have killed the man where he stood.

He had managed to control his immediate blast of anger, but when Granger released Bella's arm, the livid marks on her wrist brought a return of his killing rage. Even now as he stalked across the library, he could feel the pulse of blood in his temples. Granger did not deserve to live. Tristram would have no difficulty erasing the man from the earth, but he suspected Bella would not approve of such drastic measures.

He had already sent a note to his man of business to initiate a full-scale investigation into the man's background. Tristram had enough friends and influence to protect Bella's inheritance, and he would make Granger accountable for every penny. Knowing the kind of man Bella's uncle was, Tristram knew that stripping him of money would hurt him on a very elemental level. Money meant power to men of Granger's ilk, and the loss of Bella's fortune would be painful. Although it hardly satisfied his personal need to destroy the man, Tristram would at least have the satisfaction of thwarting the greedy bastard.

He could also be satisfied that Bella was protected from her uncle. Even as her guardian, Granger did not have the ability to stop their marriage. Tristram would explain in very precise terms that if the man did anything to cause Bella the slightest discomfort, he would have him brought up on charges. Fear of retribution, both the law's and Tristram's, would keep Granger in line.

Once he had settled with Granger, he would move the family and, of course, Bella to Dragon's Keep. His absence from town would soon put period to the wealth of gossip that would greet the news of his engagement. Eventually another delectable piece of news would be discovered, and the *ton* would lose interest in his marital affairs.

Besides, he would feel that the family was more secure surrounded by his own people. Although there had been no further attempts on his life, he was not convinced that they were free from danger. He had been unable to uncover anything of note, but wanted to be able to protect his family as best he could. It would be difficult for a stranger to cause trouble on Wyndham land, where every new face would be quickly noted and the intruder questioned.

Satisfied with the arrangements, Tristram could feel the tension leaving his body. It was not a wholly satisfactory conclusion, but at least it was an acceptable one. He crossed the room and settled in the comfortable leather chair behind his desk. He stretched his arms, easing the tight muscles of his back, and laced his fingers on top of his head.

Although at first he had been surprised that he had bound the girl to him by his quickly spoken words, now it seemed quite logical. He was a practical man, no longer ruled by the impulsive passions of his youth.

He would have to talk to Bella about their marriage. She must understand that their marriage would be a platonic one, based on friendship rather than passion. He knew she did not wish to marry him, and he was sorry that he had been impelled to insist. He understood that part of her refusal to accept his offer was because she was afraid. She need not fear him. He would never force his attentions on such a young woman. He would treat her with the same paternal affection he had always felt for her.

He shifted uncomfortably when he recalled the delicate beauty of the girl during the pantomime. He suspected she would bring the same excited joy to the marriage bed that she had brought to the theater. He reminded himself that the marriage would be in name only. After all, Bella thought of him and treated him like a favorite uncle, and that must be the role he would assume. He enjoyed her company, and she would make an excellent mother for Colin. That must be the first consideration. He did not need or want a wife. He was done with that sort of commitment.

For all the logic of his arguments, he could not help but picture her with hair floating free, wildly tumbled against her creamy skin. He groaned, furious with himself for such prurient imaginings and forced his mind to concentrate on his interview with Granger.

Chapter Ten

"So you see, madam," Bella concluded, "I cannot marry Tristram."

"Goose feathers!" the dowager demurred. Her mouth remained pursed as it had throughout Bella's recital, a clear sign of her displeasure. "Tristram must marry."

"Perhaps. But not necessarily to me. As I have explained, he only stated that we were engaged to save me from my uncle. It is totally unnecessary to go to such extremes. I was helpless under Derwent's original guardianship, partially through my own ignorance and partially because I lacked anyone of sense to counsel me. Tristram has put me in touch with a solicitor who can protect my inheritance. And thanks to your good offices, I now have friends to advise me. There is no need for Tristram to marry me."

The dowager seemed oblivious to Bella's words. Her eyes were focused on the garden outside the windows of the great chamber of Dragon's Keep. Her face was set in grim determination, hands clenched atop her cane and she seemed intent on an internal dialogue of her own that left little room for other arguments. After several moments of silence, she blinked her eyes and turned her attention back to the room.

She smiled warmly at Bella and reached out to pat the fingers tightly gripping the material of her skirt. There was a frail translucence to the blue-veined hand in contrast to the lightly tanned tautness of her skin, but Bella was comforted by the strength of the older woman's concern and relaxed under the soothing touch.

"Believe me, my child, I understand your anxiety," the dowager said. Her face had lost its frosty quality and was filled with tenderness. "I have heard all of your arguments, but at my age one learns to listen more carefully to what is not said. And that has revealed much to me."

"Oh," Bella said, a flush of guilty color rising to stain her cheeks.

"Let us have no missish airs. I am too old for such evasions. Do you wish to marry Tristram?"

"Yes. No." Bella tried to find the words to explain her answers, but nothing came to mind.

"Perhaps it might help if I rephrased the question," the dowager said, her tone holding a hint of amusement. "Do you have some affection for my grandson?"

"Well naturally I am fond of Tristram. I have enjoyed his company, and he has been extremely kind to me. He is very handsome, and most women would be delighted that he had asked them to marry him." Bella could feel herself babbling and was almost grateful when the dowager's sharp voice interrupted her rambling discourse.

"Cut line, my girl," she snapped. "You are in love with Tristram."

Bella opened her mouth to deny the statement but no words came out. She stared at the dowager, appalled that the woman should have so easily guessed her secret. "D—does he know?" she finally managed to stammer out.

"He hasn't a clue."

Sagging against the back of the sofa, Bella blinked rapidly in relief. "I am glad."

"Men, my dear," Lady Wyndham continued, "are rarely perceptive when it comes to matters of the heart. Most of them do not believe that love exists until one morning they wake up and find they have turned into a blithering idiot at the thought of a certain pair of eyes. Tristram, like most men, sees the world according to his own lights. He wishes to see you as a child, so he has not even considered the fact that you might hold him in some affection."

"I am grateful for that at least," Bella said. "I would not wish to embarrass him with an emotion he could not return."

"Are you so convinced of that?"

"He treats me in the same way that he deals with Colin."

"Yes, I am aware of that, and have found it most amusing." The dowager snorted at the subterfuges of men. They seemed to think they needed to protect themselves from the very females who would do them the most good. "Most marriages are made for reasons far removed from considerations of the flesh or other more laudatory sensibilities. In this more casual age, one hears a great deal about love, but in most cases it is only another word for sexual interest. Love is slow in coming, in most cases. It is based on many things. Friendship, trust, and humor, all play a part. It is rare for love to blossom within the short courtship period. It takes time to grow, and in most cases this happens after the marriage takes place."

"Do you think this might be the situation in our case?"

"I do."

Bella repeated the dowager's words in her mind. Was it possible that Tristram might eventually see her as a woman, a woman he could love? She realized that a part of her wanted to believe in the truth of Lady Wyndham's arguments. Yet, she was aware that Tristram liked her, and that was a very strong basis for love. She was already willing to place herself in his custody, trusting that he would cherish her, not abuse her. Could she risk marrying him with the hope that one day he would learn to love her?

Suddenly she was reminded of his words and blurted out, "But he does not want to marry me."

"My grandson does not want to *marry,*" the dowager said. "That is an entirely different situation. I suspect he has not even considered the reason that he placed himself in such an awkward position if he were truly adamant in his refusal to remarry."

"He must have loved his first wife very much."

"Although I am strongly tempted to state my opinion on such a matter, it is not my place. Only Tristram can explain his feelings for Johanna and his refusal to remarry. Before you do anything foolish about breaking your engagement, I would suggest that you ask him about those two matters. As a favor to me, will you do that?"

After a brief hesitation, Bella agreed. "I will ask him. Until

I know the answers I will not be able to make up my own mind."

After embracing her warmly, the dowager sent her on her way, suggesting she try the library or the stables. Bella was afraid she would lose her courage if she waited, so she walked briskly along to the main staircase.

She had loved Dragon's Keep from the moment she set foot on Wyndham land and got her first view of the place. It was old and seemed filled with a sense of history. Each room held a collection of antique furniture or an architectural detail that fascinated her, and she found herself constantly asking Lady Wyndham or Tristram for the story behind each piece. Most of all, she loved the main hall. As she had done since her arrival at the Keep, she stopped at the top of the stairs, looking over the railing in delight.

The walls and the floor of the main hall were stone. The ceiling soared above her, supported by massive chestnut beams. Across from her was a minstrel gallery that overlooked the central hearth. Hanging from the gallery were glorious Flemish tapestries of hunting scenes in rich reds and greens and blacks that lent a warmth to the stonework. Animal heads and weapons lined the walls, interspersed with black embroidered pennants edged with a heavy border of red.

From her vantage point at the top of the stairs she could almost picture the scene below as it had been long ago. There would be an enormous fire in the hearth and the smoke would rise, mingling with the odor of food and the scents of the people seated around a huge refectory table. She could imagine the riot of colorful clothing and the roar of conversation, a feast for the eye and the ear. Dogs would snuffle through the rushes on the stone floor and servants would bustle about with great trays of food.

Bella smiled as she returned to the more mundane life of present day. Walking down the stairs, she took her time so that she could examine the balustrade composed of carved walnut panels depicting battle scenes. Her fingers caressed the peaks and valleys of the carving in the last panel. She was so entranced with the intricacy of the work that she let out a squeal of surprise when she looked up to find Tristram standing beside her.

"I'm sorry that I startled you. I wondered what you were looking at so intently," he said.

"The carvings," she answered. She had been so surprised to see him that she was quite breathless as she looked up into his handsome face.

"And do you approve?" he asked, curious to hear her impressions.

"Oh, yes." She sighed. "It would be wonderful indeed to be able to create such beauty."

"I fear that I have neither the talent nor the patience for such work. In my salad days I thought I might take up painting, but it was only the artistic yearnings of an unfledged youth. My miserable attempts made even my staunchest admirers double over in laughter."

Tristram chuckled at the memory, and Bella joined in as he took her arm and led her toward the main doors. Outside, the weather was warm but not uncomfortably so. They walked down the shallow steps that led to the carriage sweep and veered across to the extensive parkland that surrounded the Keep. Bella could see down the gently sloping hill to the wrought-iron gates at the end of the long drive. Beyond the gates was a vast expanse of rolling green.

"I like this view with the woods behind the Keep and the flowers and grass to give it color," Tristram said.

"You must still have the soul of an artist," Bella said, smiling up at him before she looked back at the building. "It is really quite breathtaking. There is such a solidity to the structure that one's first thought is permanence."

Dragon's Keep had an imposing facade. The walls were vast slabs of pale-colored limestone and hard, coarse ragstone. There were many windows and towerlike, jutting bays ran up four stories. There was nothing soft about the building. Everywhere were harsh angles and steep projections. Yet there was a cold beauty to Dragon's Keep that spoke of security and endurance.

"You do not find it drab or ugly?" he asked.

"Oh, never that. It is really quite beautiful. One would not have expected anything else in such a setting. This is no place for a frothy manor house."

Tristram sighed. "I am glad to hear that. I have always loved the place, but there was a time when I began to wonder if in actual fact it were no more than a great pile of stones."

"Why is it called Dragon's Keep?"

"It is ancient history. Are you sure you are up to such a lengthy tale?" At her smiling nod, he laughed. "What a curious child you are. I feel a bit like Scheherazade since you have arrived, spinning tales when you ask about a piece of my heritage. Shall we walk to the garden as I tell you? That way when I have quite exhausted you with my words, you will find solace among the flowers."

"Your stories never bore me, good sir," she said, taking his proffered arm and walking happily beside him.

"My ancestors came over with the Conqueror. William built many fortresses around London in which to garrison soldiers and to awe and dominate the populace. He knew he must control the cities in order to hold England. So he had countless fortresses built around the country. They were called keeps. Many of them were constructed of wood, surrounded by water in a moat, and had a single entrance. They were not beautiful. Their purpose was to impress the citizens with the power of the Norman conquerors and dominate the cities. One of them was built here."

"Is there anything left of the original structure?"

"Only a few artifacts in the library. Legend has it that my ancestor torched it in a fit of temper. The roar he made as the building burned could be heard for miles around. Flames licked the skies and the natives trembled in their beds, convinced that a dragon was on a rampage. When the new building was raised it was called Heart's Content, but the locals, remembering the night of the fire, always referred to it as Dragon's Keep."

"What a charming story," Bella said as she sat down on the stone bench in the garden. "It is a wondrous place. I am very impressed with your management. The tenants fair trip over their tongues to sing your praises. I will admit that aside from the main house, I am most taken with the stables. Whitcombe was near bursting with pride as he showed me around."

"Whitcombe thinks London is a heathenish place," Tristram said, sounding inordinately proud of the man. "He is always so grateful to be back in the country that he is most garrulous for several days. It wears off eventually and he returns to his taciturn manners."

"For all his fierceness, he is truly a dear man. He sent for me when Violet and Fortune arrived. He wanted to be certain that I approved of their lodgings. The colt is thriving under his care." Bella's face was grave as she turned to Tristram. "I realize you have made most of the arrangements, and I appreciate your kindness with all my heart."

"I am delighted that you approve," he said, bowing elegantly to cover his pleasure. "Colin gives me daily reports on the little fellow. The lad seems to think Fortune is destined to be a fine racer."

"I fear the staid pace of London horseback riding has done much to dampen Colin's enthusiasm for the city. He is delighted to be home."

"The boy is a constant source of surprise to me. I had always thought he was far too quiet. I worried that he spent too much time with his books, but in London he was forever tearing about. Since our return, he has been on horseback, riding neck or nothing, and chattering without restraint about his adventures."

"Perhaps it is just that you are spending more time with him," Bella suggested.

"Perhaps," he agreed. "It is more than that, though. He was always so serious before. Now he seems much happier and more at ease with himself and others. Of course, he has gained a little town bronze and beyond that it may just be that he is growing up."

"As far as I am concerned, he is a total delight. It amuses me to observe him when he is among adults. His eyes flash around and he appears to be memorizing everything. The next day he will have a few choice comments on the proceedings, which usually leave me either howling with laughter or amazed at his perception."

At Bella's words, Tristram's face pinked with pleasure. He placed a well-shined boot on the bench and leaned his arms on his knee. As he beamed down at her, she knew that the warmth entering her body had nothing to do with the sunshine in the garden.

"You will make a very fine mother to Colin," he said.

She was reminded of the questions she had promised the

dowager to ask, but based on the suspicion that the happy mood would be dissipated, she hesitated. Tristram noted the sudden gravity of her expression and raised an eyebrow in question.

"I am eager to hear what thoughts have brought such a frown to your face," he teased. "I was looking for you earlier because I thought it was time for a discussion of our plans. Have you any immediate concerns?"

"My immediate concern is that we should not marry," she said. "The original necessity to protect me is gone. You told me Derwent was far too concerned about the opening of an inquiry into the handling of my funds to offer any further threat."

"That is true."

"Then I do not see any reason that we need continue such a fiction."

Tristram fairly glared at the stubborn chit. He could feel the muscles along his jawline tighten in rising anger. He had already decided that his remarriage would be best for all parties and his own peace of mind. Grandmama would cease thrusting young ladies in his path, and Colin would have a mother. It seemed perfectly simple to him and he wondered at the contrary nature of this young woman that she should continue to object to such a plan.

"Any woman of sensibility would swoon at the opportunity to lead me to parson's mousetrap," he stated.

"I am not a woman of sensibility then. I am far too practical for such conceit."

"Then you should continue the practicalities," he snapped. He cleared his throat, annoyed that he had lost his temper. He supposed he was handling this badly, but he could not understand how one small, brown-eyed chit could so fluster him. "As my wife you will be protected both physically and financially. Although your inheritance represents an adequate amount, my assets are such that I have no need for such income. Socially you would be the envy of most. You will have position and security, a son and a husband. You have everything to gain by accepting my offer."

Except the one thing she wanted, his love. Bella sighed at his words, wondering if Lady Wyndham could possibly be correct in her assumption that eventually Tristram would love her. On the face of his dry recital, she had serious doubts. He hardly looked besotted, merely annoyed.

"Yes, I can see that," she said, a flutter of nervousness shaking her as she considered how to broach the real questions in her mind. "I have had a long talk with your grandmother, and she has suggested I apply to you for some answers. I would not pry into personal matters, but it is necessary in order for me to form a final opinion."

"I see." Tristram took his foot off the bench and scuffed the dirt on the path with the toe of his boot before he sat down beside her. "I am amazed that Grandmama did not choose to enlighten you. I know that is not fair. She is an extremely honorable woman, but it would have been interesting hearing her pungent comments on the situation. Please ask me what you wish to know. If we are to be married, there is no possibility that I would consider withholding any information."

"I knew that you were opposed to remarrying and assumed that your refusal was based on the fact that your first wife was so exceptional that you had found no one to replace her in your affection."

Bella jumped at Tristram's sharp bark of laughter. She was startled that he would find her remarks humorous until she noticed that the tone had little in common with amusement. It was almost savage in its bite.

"Devil take it!" he swore as he jerked to his feet. "You don't suppose that all these years people looked on me as a grieving widower. What a blow to my ego!"

He paced in front of her as she stared at him in rising consternation. She dug her fingers into the material of her skirt and waited, knowing that whatever she had said had resulted in his anger. Finally he stopped and stared down at her in returning amusement.

"Now that I think on it, it seems to me that only you in your innocence and universal good will, could ever entertain such a thought." He smiled warmly to take the sting of sarcasm from his words. "The majority of the *ton* were privy to the details of Johanna's life and our disastrous marriage. She made little attempt to keep it secret."

Returning to the bench, he sat down and pried one of her hands from the wrinkled material of her skirt and chafed it between his own warm palms. Quietly he told her the story of his meeting with Johanna and their subsequent marriage. He stroked her hand, his actions automatic as his mind returned to the events that led up to Johanna's death. At the end, he sat quietly, his eyes intent on her face.

"I am dreadfully sorry, Tristram," she said, and there was little doubt of the sincerity of her words. There were tears sheening the warm brown eyes and a tremble in her voice. "It must have been hellish for both of you."

"How typical of you to see both sides," he said, squeezing her hand with approval. "Grandmama could only blame Johanna, but it is never that simple."

"No," she agreed. She was silent for a moment as she thought back over all he had told her. A frown tugged at her forehead, and she looked into his face with puzzlement. "I can understand after such a devastating experience that you would be hesitant to remarry. But you must have been aware that there were other marriages and that, while they might not have been perfect, they were at least good ones. You are not so stupid that you would condemn the behavior of all women based on Johanna's actions."

Now it was Tristram's turn to hesitate. He realized that he must be honest with Bella, but was concerned for her reaction. He thought he knew her well enough to guess what her feelings would be, but he was loath to put them to the test. Finally he plunged ahead.

"It is because of Colin that I refused to marry. I did not think a wife would think it fair that Colin inherit instead of her own sons. You see, Bella, I am not Colin's father."

"Impossible," she blurted out.

"Colin was fathered by Henry Addison, the man Johanna ran off with. She did not tell me until she was dying. She said herself that it was her revenge for my killing Addison." He hung his head, staring down at the ground between his feet. "I have had some guilt over killing the boy's real father, but I must admit I would do it again. After Johanna died I was convinced I would not acknowledge the child, but there was a certain charm to Colin even at that age that quite won my heart. I have raised him as my own and have always felt he was the child of my heart, if not my loins."

"Have you told him?"

"No. No one knows except Grandmama."

"So that's the reason," Bella said in dawning understanding. "She has refused to accept him even though you have. That is why she never mentions his name or speaks to him. I would not have thought it of her."

"You must know Grandmama to understand her position. She was raised to believe the honor of our family name was all important. She disliked Johanna and blamed her entirely for the breakup of our marriage. Her actions are not quite as cruel as you would first imagine. The reason she has refused to acknowledge Colin is for her own protection. If she pretends the boy does not exist, she cannot become emotionally involved. If she ever speaks to the child, she will realize the tragedy of shutting him out of her life."

Bella's face reflected the sorrow she felt at such a dreadful situation. "Why has she suddenly consented to have him join the evening meal and enter into some of the family entertainments?"

Tristram chuckled, and this time his voice was filled with warm amusement. "We made a bargain. Colin would join the family dinners, and I would squire Prudence Danforth around London."

"You stooped to blackmail?" Bella was shocked by his actions, but on second thought found it rather amusing. "Poor Lady Wyndham. She must have been furious to be so manipulated."

"Quite!" He grinned at the memory and once again squeezed her hand. "To give her justice, I can understand what a quandary she has been in. You see, according to her lights, Eden Danforth should still be my heir. She cannot like the man, and so she has insisted that I remarry and produce an heir who would supersede Eden. But that I cannot do. I have no guilt where Eden is concerned. He is plump in the pocket, thanks to his marriage to Glynis. Most of what Colin would inherit are my personal assets, not part of the entail. Perhaps the title might be a subject of legal discussion, but that is of little interest to me. In all but the act of creation, I am Colin's father. As my son, he has the right to inherit."

"But what does all that have to do with your remarrying?" Bella asked, unable to see the logic of Tristram's thinking.

"How can I marry a woman and expect her to accept the

fact that Colin will inherit over any legitimate sons she may have?"

Bella tried to assimilate his words, but her brain felt as if too much information had been received. Her mind was loggy, slow to hear the real message in Tristram's question. Finally she understood and with knowledge came anger.

"You would condemn all women as greedy and selfish?" she asked. Her voice was low, but there was an intensity of emotion simmering beneath the surface. "If you chose a woman of character there would never be a question of who should inherit. She would love Colin as you do and never consider anything but his welfare."

"It is easy for you to say since you already love him," Tristram said in defense of his actions. "But it is a risk I am not prepared to take."

The anger at his blindness dissipated at his words. Bella bowed her head, knowing that there was no possible way to convince him that in the matter of heredity only the character of the person was important. He knew that, but it was fear for the possible injury to Colin that held him back from acceptance of the idea. She wanted to reach out to comfort him, explaining that she understood, but when she looked up she was alone.

She sat on the bench, her eyes blind to the beauty of the flowers that surrounded her. Slowly she went over the things that Tristram had told her and tried to sift out all but the pertinent facts. The more she studied the information, the more certain she was that there was a key piece that was missing from the puzzle.

She did not believe that Colin was illegitimate. The boy looked nothing like Tristram either in build or physical characteristics, but strangely enough she could see a very definite resemblance to Lady Wyndham. Colin's eyes were gray, but they were very like in color to the silvery blue of the dowager's eyes. To Bella's unprejudiced eye, there was a great similarity between the old woman and the young boy that could only come from the same heredity.

If this was true, then why had Johanna lied? Bella thought back to Tristram's description of her death. She had been wild with anger and had struck out at him in her fury. She had wanted revenge. Tristram had assumed that her revenge had been in telling him that Colin was not his child. But what if Colin was his child? Would any mother risk hurting her own baby just for the sake of revenge?

The answer to that lay in the character of Johanna. The woman Tristram had described was self-centered, shallow, and vindictive. It was entirely possible that in her desire to hurt Tristram, Johanna had struck at his most vulnerable quality, his pride. She would have known how much he would hate the thought that the child was not his own. If she had known she was dying, the lie would live on after her, a festering wound, reopening every time he looked at the boy.

If this was true, it proved how little Johanna had understood her husband. Tristram would never have blamed an innocent child for an action he had no part in. There was no doubt that his wife's declaration had hurt him deeply, but the loving qualities he possessed had brought victory out of an act of revenge.

Bella nodded her head as if she had come to a decision. In a way, she had. First she must prove that Colin was Tristram's son. She was not sure just how she would accomplish such a trick, but she could begin by interviewing everyone who had been at Dragon's Keep nine years ago. As Tristram's affianced bride, it would not seem peculiar that she would wish to know everything about the family. By now all the servants realized that she was curious about the estate and were well used to her constantly asking them questions.

In a way the second part of her mission was the more difficult. She must try to make the dowager accept the boy before she discovered that he was the true heir. If ever Colin discovered what had happened, her acceptance of him would go far to lessen his hurt at her refusal to have anything to do with him earlier. Besides, knowing the honorable nature of Lady Wyndham, once she realized how wrong she had been, she would be devastated.

Bella stood up and shook out her skirts. There was much to do before she could make her own decision. She did have some hope that once Tristram understood Colin was no longer at risk, he would consider regularizing their marriage. And then he might learn to love her.

•

Chapter Eleven

"Actually, I was planning to kidnap you if you refused my invitation to tea," the woman in the pony cart stated as she smiled up at Bella.

"In that case, I will accept with great speed," she said, turning her horse back along the way she had come. "I would hate to put you to any trouble."

"That's the ticket," Millicent Heathrow-Finchley said.

She jiggled the reins and, with an annoyed shake of its head, the pony began to plod along the country lane. The pace was slow enough that the two women were able to continue the conversation they had begun when they chanced to meet.

"Tristram told me that you were determined to call," Bella said. "He is very fond of you and has told me much about when he and your husband were in school."

"Dull tales, indeed, compared to their early days in London. You must remember to ask Tristram about the time they placed the night watch in the bell tower." Millicent chuckled as she beamed up at her companion. "They hung him with the aid of a harness borrowed from an irate carter."

Bella laughed, well pleased with her new acquaintance. She had felt in need of some exercise and had been riding along the lane when she chanced upon the woman in the pony cart. Blond hair fluttering behind her like a pennant, she had been clipping along at a brisk pace toward the Keep. Introductions followed, and Millicent invited her back for tea.

They kept up an easy conversation until they arrived at the manor house. Bella dismounted and handed her reins to a waiting servant, then turned to her hostess. It was only when Millicent stepped to the ground that it became apparent that she was extremely pregnant. Noting her start of surprise, the older woman slipped her hand through Bella's arm and led her up the stairs.

"My condition is the reason that I have been condemned to drive that humiliating contraption," she sniffed. "I am better used to horseback and cannot like the sedate speed."

"It seems you were making excellent time when I happened upon you," Bella said, removing her gloves as she entered the foyer of the house.

"Daisy has learned I am not content to stroll about."

Thus saying, she led Bella on a brisk tour of the house. It was old and rambling, filled with a great deal of ornately carved wood along with plenty of comfortable furniture. Millicent's husband Neddy was hunting-mad, and dogs of every breed roamed the house, chased by the Heathrow-Finchley brood, five rambunctious girls no older than seven. Millicent was unfazed by the activity around her and, despite her top-heavy appearance, moved with rolling grace through the rooms at a pace that left her guest breathless. When tea was served in the salon, Millicent banished the children to the nursery so that they might visit undisturbed.

"Will you have another scone, Bella?" Millicent asked. "My cook has a wonderful hand for pastry."

"She certainly does." She patted her mouth with a lace-edged napkin. "I'm afraid if I eat another one, I'll have to walk behind my horse all the way back to the Keep."

"I'm delighted that you were free this afternoon," Millicent said as she eyed the pastries with eagerness. "I don't feel so guilty about eating when I have a guest. Cherry tarts are my favorites."

"You sound just like Colin," Bella said, sipping her tea.

"He is such a dear. He brought presents for the girls from London. They have always adored him and clustered about while he told them what a jolly time he'd had on his visit. They will give us no peace now until we take them to the city." She sighed in despair, but brightened as her fingers closed on a pastry. "We have just come back from London ourselves.

Neddy knew I was feeling particularly cumbersome, so he took me to town to shop. I am so tired of looking like a ship in full sail, and I had a lovely time. A veritable orgy of buying. Once this latest addition to the household appears, I shall return for final fittings."

"I wish you a healthy baby and an easy confinement," Bella said, raising her cup in a toast.

"Thank you, my dear," she said, lifting her own cup in salute. She sipped, then smiled across at her guest. "Tristram called here also. He wanted to tell us all about you before we began to hear the latest gossip. I understand that he has offered for you, and I can tell you, I have never been more pleased to hear that he is finally thinking to remarry. He is a very fine man and would make an excellent husband."

"I am sure he would." Bella hedged. "But despite the rumors, nothing is decided yet."

She shifted in her chair, uncomfortable with a discussion of the marriage since she was not totally convinced the happy event would ever take place. Hoping to turn the conversation, she asked, "How old are the children?"

"Carolyn is six, Jennifer five, Letitia four, and the twins Bethanne and Amy are three." Millicent smiled at her guest, her face flushing in pride. "They are quite a handful. I'll admit that perhaps I am not such a good mother to permit them to run wild through the house. But I confess I enjoy the activity."

"By the smiles on their faces I can tell you are a very good mother indeed. And I quite enjoyed viewing their collection."

Millicent laughed. "You were a good sport. It is their greatest treat when we have guests. I thought only boys delighted in creepy, crawly things, but the girls are hoydens to be sure. They invariably have captured some loathsome creature and can't wait to parade it through the house to the accompaniment of shrieks from the maids. You were lucky today that it was only a mouse."

"I hope they weren't disappointed that I did not scream."

"They might have been, if you hadn't suggested a new trap for the foxes. Although I am sure their father would be disturbed to know they were moving the foxes about the estate like the pawns on a chess board. More tea?"

"Yes, please," Bella said, accepting a refill. "This is excellent."

"I'm delighted you approve. I have it specially blended by an importer in Salisbury. I prefer just a hint of lemon, especially on depressing days when I am in need of something to pick up my spirits."

"I would think your children would take care of that."

Millicent beamed, pleased that her guest had enjoyed the children's presence. Not all her guests were so delighted. "I fair dote on the girls, to the detriment of their manners. You see, Neddy and I had been married for four years without being blessed with children. I was absolutely thrilled when I discovered I was increasing."

"That is not always the case," Bella said, chuckling. "To hear the tenants' wives talk, it is a condition to be mourned."

"I'll admit I am disgustingly unfashionable. The tenants' wives are not the only ones to bemoan such an event. I've had many friends over the years who have heralded the discovery that they were to bear a child with the same dread they would feel if they had contracted the plague. And look at the miraculous result. An adorable child to carry on your life. I think of that most often when I look at what a fine young man Colin is becoming. I see so much of Johanna in him that I do not feel that she is really gone. If she had known how things would turn out, she would never have been so resentful over her pregnancy."

At Bella's startled expression, Millicent flushed and raised a hand to her mouth. She dropped her eyes in embarrassment, not knowing what to say.

Since Bella had decided that Tristram was Colin's real father, she had been eager to learn more about the events that led up to his birth. She had spoken to the servants who had been at the Keep when Colin's mother resided there, but they offered little enlightenment on the situation. From what Tristram had told her, she knew Millicent had come out at the same time that Johanna made her bow to society. Perhaps she might remember enough of Johanna's life to give Bella a clue as to whom she might apply to for information.

In the short time that they had been together, Bella had taken to the woman. She sensed in Millicent an honesty and a common-sense approach to life that she admired. She suspected that Millicent would have keen insights on Johanna's character and Bella would have liked nothing better than to explain the situation. But it was not her place to reveal such a confidence. It was Tristram's secret, and only he could speak about it.

"Please, Millicent, you have not committed a *faux pas,*" Bella said, placing her teacup back on the table. She leaned forward in her chair in her eagerness to ease the embarrassment of her new friend. "I was only surprised when you mentioned Johanna's name. Everyone refrains from speaking of Colin's mother, perhaps in fear that somehow I will take offense. I have been eager to know much about her, but everyone seems curiously reticent to discuss her."

"As Tristram's fiancée, I thought you might be affronted when I mentioned her," Millicent said. "I am forever speaking when perhaps it would be wiser to be quiet. Please forgive me if I have offended you."

"Not at all. Sometimes it is easier to deal with things when one knows what has gone before. Was she a particular friend?"

"In a way. We came out the same year and after she was married she was glad of a friend in the neighborhood. We visited back and forth most every day. I was convenient, and Johanna felt I was not beneath her notice. You see, my father is Viscount Dunwoody, heir to the earl of Chetham. Johanna was very impressed with titles. Despite the fact that she could never understand why I had conceived a passion for poor untitled Neddy, she did accept me as a friend." Millicent flushed with color, shifting uncomfortably on the sofa. "I would not like my words to appear unkind. It was just Johanna's way. I understood that and was pleased to have the company since oft times there is a paucity of adult conversation, especially during hunting season when Neddy is away so much."

"I'm sure that Johanna had need of companionship. I gather she sorely missed London," Bella said.

"Indeed she did. It was apparent that all was not well with the marriage. I hoped that I might offer advice if she should need it, but unfortunately she never asked." Millicent sighed. "She hated the isolation of the Keep. She was very beautiful and needed other glittering beings around her. It was almost like a sickness with her. She loved the excitement of London and felt she was dying in the country."

"Unless you have a love for country life, I am sure it must

seem deadly dull after the wealth of entertainment to be found in the city," Bella replied.

"I suppose so. I find it very hard to understand because I much prefer the quiet of the country. I tried to cheer her up on days when she despaired ever seeing the city again. She was quite miserable that last year. She had spent the summer at the Keep and was longing for her return to London when she discovered she was with child. She came to me in near-hysterics and I tried to convince her that her life was not over. Tristram was not so archaic that he would immure her at the Keep for nine months. Despite my words, she was inconsolable, and I felt so terribly sorry for her."

Millicent paused, her eyes unfocused as if she were trying to picture that time so long ago. Bella sat patiently and sipped her tea in silence. Finally her hostess continued, but the words were slow in coming, as if she were reliving the events once more.

"I knew it was not good for the child for Johanna to be so sunk in despair. I tried to talk to Tristram, but it was apparent he did not wish to discuss Johanna. And, of course, he was right. I had no business prying into their affairs. Neddy and I have had our differences over the years, and I would have taken it poorly if some outsider had attempted to interfere."

"I can find no fault in your good intentions," Bella said. "You were acting as one would hope a friend would act."

"Over the years I have regretted the fact that I never did speak to Tristram. In a way, what I did instead, had far more dreadful consequences. Tristram has never mentioned it, so perhaps he did not blame me, and I have always felt that one cannot stop the course of history." At Bella's puzzled expression, Millicent chuckled. "That is typical of a man. Tristram told me that he had told you everything concerning that last year, but apparently he did not fill in all the details. Men never seem to understand that it is the details that most interest women. You see, my dear, it was I who introduced Johanna to Henry Addison."

"Oh." Bella felt at a loss for words, but thankfully Millicent seemed to understand immediately the reason for her surprise.

"I knew of Johanna's elopement because it was I who went to Tristram with the information. I doubt if anyone else ever knew, but Johanna had come to me to say good-bye. I think she did it, knowing that I would be forced to go to Tristram. Even knowing that, I could do nothing else."

"In any case it could not have been easy for you," Bella said, seeing the pain of remembrance on her hostess's face. "I am not sure I would have had the courage to face Tristram."

"Thank you for such kind words, but from what Tristram has told me about you I would think you would have done just as I did." A smile of approval crossed Millicent's serious face before she continued with her story. "When Johanna was in such despair over her pregnancy, I felt terribly sorry for her. She was furious with Tristram, of all things. She said she would never forgive him, although I cannot believe that he was wholly to blame for the blessed event. At any rate, I decided to have a party in order to pick up her spirits. And it was there she met Henry Addison."

For a moment Bella thought she had not heard correctly. She replayed the words in her mind, and then leaned forward in her eagerness.

"Until your party, Johanna had never met Henry Addison?" she asked.

Millicent looked startled at the question, but she answered without hesitation. "No. He was a friend of my brother. He had not been in London when Johanna came out, and then of course at the end of the season Tristram married her and they left for the continent."

"Perhaps she had known him earlier?" Bella persisted.

"No, I am quite sure of that. I can remember Johanna accusing me of hiding such a paragon of virtue from her sight. It surprised me so because I always thought Henry was a buffleheaded fop. And so he was. But Johanna thought his air of sophisticated fashion was quite the thing. I have always felt guilty that my inviting him to the party eventually caused great injury to a friend I valued. But, coward that I am, I have never had the backbone to apologize."

Bella was stunned at the discovery of the one piece of information that would prove to Tristram that he was Colin's father. If only Millicent had spoken before, Tristram himself would have known the truth. Once he heard the story, he would believe it, for he would know that Millicent would have no reason to lie. Bella wanted to fly across and hug her hostess, but she realized the poor woman would never understand such treatment.

"Believe me, Millicent, you have no need to apologize," Bella said, smiling happily. "Tristram knows you have always been a good friend. And soon I believe he will be telling you so himself."

Her hostess seemed most confused by her words, but Bella was not at liberty to say anything more until she had spoken with Tristram. She realized that her hasty departure would appear rather strange, but she could no longer remain quietly drinking tea while there was so much to think about. After making polite apologies to a bemused Millicent for her need to return to the Keep, Bella left.

She rode along the lane, oblivious to the beauty of the afternoon. She couldn't wait to tell Tristram. It would not change anything in his attitude once he knew that he was Colin's father. He could not love the boy any more than he did now, but the realization that Colin was actually his son would be especially wonderful because of that love.

The greatest change for Colin would be in Lady Wyndham's attitude toward him. He would now receive the love and approval she had withheld. Bella felt sorry for that. She did not know if the boy would be bitter, but he would have the right. It was too bad that the dowager could not have grown to love the boy for himself before she discovered his birthright.

It was out of all of their hands now. Bella had no right to withhold the information from Tristram. It was much too important to risk waiting with the hope that Lady Wyndham would suddenly accept the boy. Both she and Tristram had done what they could to keep Colin within the dowager's sight, but the woman had remained stubbornly silent, never addressing a word to the boy. For the dowager, Colin did not exist. And now the time was gone when she might make amends for such behavior. Once Tristram knew the truth, he would quite naturally tell Lady Wyndham.

Bella rode around to the stable and then cut through the garden to the kitchen entrance of the Keep. She was conscious of a need to freshen her appearance before she talked to Tristram. She reasoned that he would find it easier to believe her story if she did not look like a harum-scarum girl with her hair windblown and her face covered with dust. However, in her heart, she knew it was vanity. Tristram continued to treat her like a child, and she wanted him to begin to see her as a composed young woman. There would only be hope for a full relationship if he began to realize that she was closer to his age than Colin's.

She threw open the doors of her wardrobe and eyed each of the gowns. Choosing one, she laid it on the bed while she washed and brushed her hair. She tied the tumble of curls behind her head with a yellow ribbon, and then stepped into the dress. She struggled with the buttons but was satisfied as she turned in front of the cheval glass.

The gown was a buttery yellow silk with a high, wide band of ivory lace at her throat and across the top of the bodice. The soft sleeves floated down her arms to the lace at her wrists. The material was drawn in beneath her breasts with a yellow ribbon, and then fell softly to the floor and the yellow slippers peeping from beneath the edge of her hem. It was a woman's dress. Perhaps she still looked young, but the simplicity of the gown made one aware of her softly matured figure. Bella nodded at the mirror, satisfied by her reflection.

Her slippers were only a whisper on the carpet runners as she traversed the corridors in search of Tristram. He was not in the great chamber, nor the conservatory, nor even in his estate office. She asked the footman in the entrance hall if Tristram had gone out, but the man assured her that the earl had just returned from a tour of the tenant farms. She was already upstairs on the way to the family quarters when she remembered she had not tried the library.

The library was at the back of the Keep, a beautiful room, fully two-stories high, which looked out over the stables and the kitchen gardens. Tristram had showed her the room proudly, and Bella had fallen in love with it. On the lower level, the wooden floors were covered by deep-piled forest green carpets. There were comfortable leather chairs, several mahogany writing desks, and long tables which displayed brilliantly illustrated manuscripts. There were long French windows, uncurtained but draped in heavy green velvet to match the carpet.

The walls were bookshelves, filled with leather-backed volumes and art objects to delight the eye and intrigue the mind. The room did not have the musty smell of stagnant learning. Perhaps the loft that ran around three sides of the room lent an airy quality to the atmosphere. The loft was also filled with books and overstuffed chairs where one could sit and read. It was reached from below by a black iron circular staircase or could be entered on the second level by a door off the upstairs hallway. Already upstairs, Bella quickly crossed the hall and opened the door of the loft.

She was met by the sound of voices below and hesitated, unwilling to interrupt. She caught a glimpse of the dowager seated facing Tristram before she actually heard the significance of the older woman's words.

"There is no question about it, Tristram," Lady Wyndham repeated. "You must marry Bella. You have compromised the girl."

Bella's knees trembled and she leaned against the doorframe for support. She did not mean to eavesdrop; she did not have the strength to leave.

"Devil take it, Grandmama!" Tristram exclaimed. "You know full well, Bella was as safe with me in the woods as if she were my own daughter."

"The simple fact is, young man, that Bella is not your daughter. She is a maiden of good family, a titled gentlewoman who inherited the baronetcy on the death of her father. The knowledge of her presence overnight with you in the woods, no matter the reason or your incapacity, will quite ruin her reputation."

"As far as I am aware, madam," Tristram drawled, "there are only three people who know of the circumstances. Bella, myself, and you."

There was a long silence and, above in the loft, Bella closed her eyes wishing she would hear nothing further.

"Do not attempt to force my hand," Lady Wyndham said, her voice hard and cold with decision. "It would only take a small slip of the tongue, among friends mind you, to put period to such a situation."

"Damnation! You would injure Bella in such a way just to serve your own purposes? I thought you loved the girl."

"I do love her," the dowager defended. "I love you both, and I think you well-suited. It is only your stubbornness that would force me to such tactics. I have never made a secret of the fact that I wanted you to remarry, Tristram, and to achieve that goal I would risk much more than Bella's reputation."

"I cannot believe that our family name should be so important to you, madam, that you would risk your soul." Tristram's voice was bitter, his words sharply clipped.

"I can live with my conscience as I have for the last nine years."

Once more there was silence below, and Bella could picture the two opponents staring belligerently across at each other, each bound by pride, stubbornness and love. Tristram's words broke the silence.

"You win, madam." Despite the quietness of his tone, it was apparent that he was truly angry. "I will marry the girl, though I cannot like it. But I swear to you that I will give you no triumph from your victory. I will be civil to Bella as befits her role as my wife, but I will never take her as my bride. I will not shame her with a passion and love I can never give her. She will be a wife in name only. You may have forced the marriage, Grandmama, but I will not support such a wretched fiction with anything other than the merest formality."

Bella opened her eyes in time to see Tristram angrily storm from the library, his face set in determination. Slow tears rose and rolled over the edge of her lids, sliding unchecked down her cheeks. She was so involved with her own pain that she was oblivious to the rustle of motion as the dowager rose and left the room. Bella did not know how long she remained in the loft, but when she turned to go to her room she felt as though ages had passed. She moved like an old woman, placing her feet carefully on the hall runners as if she were afraid she might trip. She opened the door of her room and closed it carefully behind her, then crossed the floor and crawled up onto the bed. Drawing her knees up, she curled into a ball, fighting the shuddering sobs that coursed through her body.

She knew Tristram well enough to know that he would consider himself honor-bound to agree to the marriage. He would not accept her refusal and would attempt to force her to accept the inevitable. She was weak where Tristram was concerned. She was all too aware of a portion of her mind that would accept a marriage to him on any terms, just for the opportunity to remain close to the man she loved. She had too much pride to shame herself by such weakness.

Tristram eventually would hate her for agreeing to the marriage. He would begin to wonder if she had been aware of the dowager's machinations and approved of the trickery. Any fondness he had for her would wither under such suspicion. In other circumstances, she might have the option to remain and fight for the man she loved. But in this case, she had no choice but to leave.

This time she would make better plans than she had when she'd left Mallory. She would not go to London. She had seen enough of the city to realize that there were too many dangers for a woman alone. She had enjoyed seeing the sights and entertainments, but she was afraid of the dark, ugly streets and the evil that hung over many of the poorer sections to ever feel anything but fear. From Salisbury she would go to the north of England. Far from London and Tristram, she would seek a small town where she might find honest employment. She would arm herself with a recommendation as to her good character from Lady Arabella Mallory, and under an assumed name would try to get a position as a lady's maid. Surely there was a woman somewhere who would have need of such services.

Bella tried not to think about Colin, but his cheerful, boyish face rose before her mind. She loved the boy and would miss him. She could not leave without giving him at least some explanation. He was mature enough to have some understanding of the situation and, besides, she would not want him to think she had deserted him without a thought. She could explain about her inheritance and promise to get in touch with him again in two years.

When Sarah arrived to dress her for the evening meal, Bella pleaded a headache as her excuse for going to bed. She was embarrassed at the maid's solicitude, and was relieved when she was tucked snugly beneath the covers and Sarah was tiptoeing from the room.

Alone, she stared up at the bed canopy as tears overflowed her eyes and mingled with her unbound hair. She cried without sound, the silence far more indicative of the depth of her pain than uncontrolled hysterics would be. She cried for the sham marriage that she could never accept. She cried for the ultimatum of the dowager that forced her to leave the Keep. But most of all, she cried for a love that would never be.

Chapter Twelve

"Hurry, Bella," Colin shouted from the bottom of the stairway. "Father is ready to leave, and Lady Wyndham is already in the carriage."

"I'm coming," she said.

She moved slowly down the steps, one hand holding to the balustrade. Despite the fact she had gone to bed early, she had only dozed during the night; in between were long periods of wakefulness. When she woke, she was tired but determined. Colin's note about the outing to Prue's estate had forced her to hurry through breakfast and then change to traveling clothes.

"Father is not in a very good mood, so you better not dawdle," he said, looking apprehensively over his shoulder. "Lady Wyndham's behaving very touchy, so I wager they've had another falling out. What a dreadful time for it. If Father's on his high ropes, he might not be in the mood to purchase a hunter, and then I'll really be in the basket. How can I convince him I'm ready for the hunting season, if I don't have a proper horse?"

"I'm sure your father would not drag us all off to Prue's if he wasn't planning to consider the horse," she said placatingly.

She followed the boy as he waved her toward the door, and soon she was ensconced in the carriage beside the icily erect Lady Wyndham. Tristram sat next to Colin on the seat with their backs to the horses.

Except for her original nod of greeting, Lady Wyndham glared out the window, her stiffness a fair indication that she desired no conversation with the other occupants of the carriage. Even Colin was aware of the tension and pressed himself into the corner, trying to control his natural exuberance. Occasionally Bella glanced at Tristram whose face was set in a brown study. The muscles along his jawline rippled with his effort to control his temper, and there was a stiffness to his movements which indicated he was having difficulty restraining his restlessness. The general air of gloom inside the carriage was so palpable that it augured ill for the success of the day.

The fictional headache of the night before became a reality as the party rattled along the road to the Danforth estate. She was annoyed at herself for what she considered her weakness in taking to her bed the night before. She had been so involved in her own pain that she had quite forgotten the momentous news that she needed to impart to Tristram. It did not matter what she had heard; she should have been brave enough to face him with the clear evidence of Colin's legitimacy.

She realized that she had been living on hope. She had believed that Tristram wanted to marry her, if for no other reason than he was fond of her, and that eventually he would learn to love her, but the overheard conversation had indicated how far off the mark she had been. He had said he could never give her passion or love. Without hope of either of these, the marriage was doomed from the very start.

Bella leaned her head against the side of the carriage, watching Tristram from beneath her lids. She feasted her eyes on his clean-cut face, memorizing the features as if to store up the memory for the days ahead when she would no longer see him. After she had spoken to him about Colin, she would have to leave. She was much too weak to withstand the pressure of Tristram and his grandmother, who was bent on an early marriage. Her vision blurred and she bit her lip to keep from crying out her pain.

Her sadness lifted slightly on their arrival at the Danforths' when she discovered Woodie was also in attendance. She sighed, watching adoration shine on her cousin's face as he spoke to the shyly flushed Prue. It would seem that his suit was beginning to be accepted by Eden and Glynis, and Bella could only be thrilled for the young couple's success. Even the dowager unbent sufficiently to appear pleased at Prue's evident happiness.

When the gentlemen and Colin set off for the stables, the ladies adjourned to the drawing room for tea. Bella was thankful to be able to settle in a soft seat while Prue chattered away about Woodie's visit. It appeared that he had been there a week and was planning to remain for another. Face glowing with quiet joy, Prue confided that her father had consented to Woodie's making her an offer, and the announcement would be made at a special ball being given in about a month. Bella hugged her and wished her happy.

Eventually the men returned, and Colin could bearly contain his excitement when he revealed that the hunter had been purchased. Bella smiled, listening to the boy's enthusiastic description of the horse's attributes.

"He is a great, enormous brute, Bella," he said, his words whispered but vibrating with pleasure. "He's a chestnut, which you know is my special favorite. He was wizard on the jumps."

"Your father let you try him, I see." Bella glanced across at Tristram who merely nodded his head.

"They were only baby jumps," Colin said, his tone deprecating but resigned. "I'm sure once I have him at home, Father will let me work him on larger ones. He said he wanted a chance to try him out first to see how well-schooled he is."

"Very sensible."

"He is seven, which is not so very old," Colin continued as if she had not spoken. "His name is Rory for his reddish coat, but I don't think that is such a good name. Father said I might call him anything I like because he is now my very own horse."

"I suspect you have already thought of an excellent name for such a noble steed," Bella teased.

"Well I should hope so. I shall call him Todd, which is like the Scottish word for fox," Colin said. His face was grave but his silvery eyes sparkled with mischief. "It seems only fair to set a fox to trap a fox."

Once Colin had exhausted the subject of the new hunter, he spied the trays of food and launched into a quiet decimation of the fare. Bella watched him for a while, but then her eyes returned to Tristram. He was standing with his shoulders braced against the mantel, his eyelids lowered to shadow his eyes. There was tension in his figure, and at first she thought it was rekindled anger at his grandmother; but when the old woman asked him a question, he answered her civilly enough.

When he left the others in conversation and approached the corner where she sat with Prue and Colin, she was slightly apprehensive. Since he had entered the room, she had caught him staring at her, a brooding look on his face, but when he spoke, his words partially explained his dark mood.

"I cannot like the look of the sky to the west," he said. "I think we must start back earlier than planned. Grandmama should not be out in damp weather, and it appears we are in for a storm later this evening."

"Can we take Todd with us?" Colin asked.

Tristram hesitated, but after one look at the longing in Colin's face his expression lightened. He reached down to ruffle the boy's dark curls.

"I will tell you what, brat," he said. "While you finish gorging yourself on the sticky buns and cakes, I will ride on ahead with the horse. It will give me an opportunity to check his paces and see how much work Whitcombe will have to expend to bring him up to snuff. Will that be suitable?"

"Topping good, sir!" Colin crowed, and then more quietly he said, "Thank you for your kindness, Father. I will take very good care of Todd."

"I never doubted it," Tristram said, laying his large hand on the boy's shoulder. "You are a son to be proud of."

Bella found her eyes awash with tears as she listened to the tremor of feeling in Tristram's voice. She was filled with an urgency to blurt out her knowledge of their true relationship, but restrained herself. It was neither the proper time nor place. When they returned to the Keep, she would tell Tristram, and then she would be free to see to her own plans.

Beside her, Prue rose to her feet and placed a hand on Tristram's sleeve. "I also would like to give you my thanks. It was truly brilliant of you to mention to Mama that you would introduce Woodie to some of your friends in Parliament." She chuckled. "For all her admiration of inherited titles, she has always had an awareness of the power of political office. She now sees Woodie in a totally different light. She is convinced he will make the perfect prime minister."

Tristram's blue eyes twinkled as his mouth spread in a grin.

"She told me as much," he said. "Naturally she added that the prime minister was more powerful than the king."

"Oh la." Prue giggled. "Well at any rate, after your talk with Mama she indicated that she would support Woodie's suit, and for that I will be forever in your debt."

"I hope you will feel the same after ten years of married life," Tristram said, raising an eyebrow for emphasis. "Well, I am off to the stables. I will send the carriage around while you finish your tea."

"I'll come with you," Prue said. "There is something I wish to ask."

After they left, Bella persuaded Colin to finish the last of his tart, and then they rejoined the others who had been notified of the early departure. Prue returned shortly and immediately came to Bella's side.

"I have asked Tristram if he could spare you for a few days," she said. "I have not seen much of you since our return from London, and this is much too short a visit. Woodie is forever off in the woods with Father, and I would love to while away the hours in a comfortable coze. Say you will stay on. Tristram has promised to send your maid with your things on the morrow."

Bella hesitated before giving an answer. She did not relish a return trip in the carriage with Lady Wyndham, and the thought of being free from worry for several days was appealing. Colin did not need her, and Tristram would perhaps be relieved at her absence. She almost agreed until she remembered that she could not put off talking to Tristram. If only she hadn't been so missish the day before, she would be free to accept the invitation.

"I wish I might stay on, Prue," she said. "But there is something that I must attend to before I can continue our visit. I do not wish to disappoint you, but I must return with the others."

Prue, soft eyes taking in the gravity of her friend's expression, squeezed her hand in ready understanding. "You are welcome here anytime."

A footman entered to announce the arrival of the carriage. When Glynis discovered Tristram had gone on ahead, she was overset.

"I do not think it a good idea to set out in such weather without him. Why don't you all remain here until the storm has passed," she urged.

"Nonsense, Glynis," Lady Wyndham stated. "I always sleep better in my own bed. It cannot be much more than three hours to the Keep, and I doubt if the storm will break before then."

Outside, dark clouds scudded across the sky and the sun looked curiously leaden. The afternoon sunlight had a blue-gray cast. One look at the ominous weather was sufficient to speed them on their way. As the day continued to darken, the coachman kept the hurried pace, hoping to beat the storm. The coach rattled along the road, while inside, Bella and Lady Wyndham spoke only occasionally, saving their energy to brace themselves for the bone-jarring bumps that were inevitable as they traversed the ruts in the road. Only Colin was enjoying the journey, grinning in delight as he was bounced from side to side.

Bella thought ahead to her talk with Tristram, wondering how she could best approach the subject. She knew he was a fair-minded man and would not reject her words out of hand. But it was never good to tell a story secondhand, and she debated whether it would be better to ask him to go with her to the Heathrow-Finchleys. Once he heard the tale directly from Millicent, there would be no question of Colin's legitimacy.

The day continued to darken as the carriage rattled and bumped along the road. Bella knew they were getting close to Wyndham land when suddenly one of the wheels hit a particularly large rock. There was an ominous cracking sound that seemed to vibrate through the frame of the vehicle. The carriage shook, and Bella reached out to save Lady Wyndham from falling off the seat. The carriage careened from side to side while outside the coachman screamed at the horses. The seat tilted, and Bella was thrown against the window, her head slamming against the frame. The carriage lurched sickeningly to the side, but miraculously righted itself as it scraped against the bushes lining the road until finally it came to a grinding halt.

Pain pounded at her temple, and Bella shook her head to keep from fainting. She touched the spot and her fingers came away sticky. She knew it was blood, but thankfully there did not seem to be a great deal. Outside it was nearly dark. She could see no movement, but she could hear the piercing scream of a horse in agony. She blinked to focus her eyes in the semidarkness of the coach. She still held Lady Wyndham braced in her arms and was thankful to see the older woman's eyes open and only slightly glazed with shock.

"Are you all right, madam?" Bella croaked through dry lips.

"I shall have to speak to Tristram about the condition of the roads."

The dowager's voice which had begun rather shakily finished in an acerbic tone. Bella sighed in relief at the older woman's returning spirit, then she remembered Colin and called out in fear.

"Colin? Are you there?" There was a rustle near her feet, and she called again. "Colin?"

"I'm here, Bella." The boy's voice came from the floor of the carriage and held a tight, breathy quality. "Is Lady Wyndham all right?"

"Yes. It appears that we have all survived, although I cannot like the fact the coachman has not called out."

At Bella's words, the dowager pushed herself away, and even in the half-light Bella could see the older woman draw herself up. She looked around for her walking stick but, unable to locate it, she folded her hands neatly in her lap. "We must find out what has happened," she said.

"I'll go, madam," Bella said, reaching for the door handle.

Bella pushed the door open and stepped down into the road. The air was heavy with moisture, a clear indication that the storm was approaching. She stumbled around to the head of the carriage, where the horse was still screaming. One of the grays lay tangled in the traces, his two front legs doubled beneath his heaving body. It took only a glance to realize there was nothing they could do to save the poor animal. After a hasty survey of the area, she returned to the carriage.

A thin shaft of light filtered inside, penetrating the interior gloom. Lady Wyndham sat upright in the middle of the seat, her hat slightly askew but her manner unruffled. Colin was crumbled on the floor of the carriage, his left arm cradled in his lap. He was blinking his eyes rapidly to hold back tears, and it was apparent that he was in a great deal of pain. She found herself close to tears as he attempted a brave smile.

"How bad is it?" she inquired, with a nod at his arm.

Colin shot a quick glance at Lady Wyndham before he answered. "Must have wrenched it," he said. As she eased him out of the carriage, he gritted his teeth and leaned against the side, taking deep, shuddering gulps of air.

"There is no sign of the coachman, madam," she said to Lady Wyndham. The woman's mouth tightened, but she merely nodded her head for answer. "A wheel has come off, but the hedges kept us from overturning. One of the grays is down, and I'm sorry, ma'am, but there's little to be done for him."

The screaming of the horse seemed to surround them and Bella sensed rather than heard Lady Wyndham sigh. "There is a gun in the box beneath the forward seat."

Bella scrambled back inside and fumbled beneath the seat until she found the box. With shaking hands she carried it outside, laying it on the ground.

"Father keeps it ready loaded," Colin said. His arm dangled uselessly at his side, but he seemed more in possession of himself.

"We'll have to release the other horse first, Colin. Can you help me?" she asked, eyeing him in concern.

He nodded for answer and, wordless, they made their way to the front of the carriage. While Colin held the bridle of the horse, she unbuckled the harness. Once free, the gray trembled and shook, whipping up its head in near panic. The downed horse continued to scream, and it took both Colin and Bella to force the uninjured horse to the rear of the carriage where they tied it.

In the waning light of the day, Bella knelt in the road to open the lid of the wooden box and gingerly remove the gun. She had never handled a firearm, and the skin of her hand seemed to pull away from the contact. Rising to her feet, she held the pistol at her side, barrel pointed at the ground.

"I will do it, Bella," Colin said.

There was such a note of frightened authority in the boy's voice that Bella's heart went out to him. His face was creased with pain, but determined.

"Are you sure?" she asked, unwilling to give such a dreadful task to the boy.

"Yes," he answered shortly, taking the gun from her frozen fingers. "You will have to hold the other one steady. Be careful. He's already out of his head with fear."

Bella placed her hand on Colin's shoulder, all too aware of the fragile frame of the plucky child. She squeezed gently and then, too overcome to speak, she hurried to the rear of the carriage. The horse was stamping and shaking, and the sudden movement jostled Bella. Pain shot through her head from the bump she had received earlier and sent a wave of sickness fluttering across her stomach. She fought the nausea and buried her face into the horse's neck to block out the sight of the boy with the gun aimed at the screaming animal's head. When the shot came, the horse jumped beneath her hands, but even he seemed to relax in the blessed silence that followed.

Bella heard Colin retching and waited until the ugly sound subsided, then hurried to the front of the carriage. The gun lay on the ground beside the dead horse, but there was no sign of the boy. Looking around wildly, she found him doubled over on the far side of the road. Silently she handed him a handkerchief. He wiped his mouth and tried to hide his tears, but when she opened her arms he came to her without a word. She stroked his hair and patted him, careful of his injured arm. Finally he pushed away and she released him.

"Have you found any sign of the coachman?" she asked.

"Over there," he whispered, waving to a spot just beyond the lip of the road. When she moved, he grasped her arm with his good hand to hold her back. "He's dead, Bella."

"I see." She spoke briskly, hearing the bleakness in his voice. "Then we shall have to go for help. Have you any idea where we are?"

"We are on Wyndham land," he said. "We passed the markers well back. If you'll stay here with Lady Wyndham, I'll look around."

Bella moved along the side of the carriage to the open doorway. The dowager obviously had heard everything, and she leaned back against the seat, her eyes closed. Bella raised her face to the night sky, watching the clouds race past. The wind was picking up, and the moistness against her cheek indicated rain was imminent. It seemed an age before the boy returned.

"I know where we are," Colin said. The excitement in his voice said much for the amazing resilience of children. "We could be home in ten minutes if we cut through the woods, but I think it's too dark for such a plan. The road swings in a wide circle around the woods, so if we go that way, we are only about a mile from the Keep. Best of all, I know the perfect place to stay until Father can bring help."

"Thank heavens, Colin," Bella cried. "Is it far? It's already beginning to rain."

"No, it's just off the road. It's a small cabin, and I know it well. We will have to hurry if we hope to stay dry."

Lady Wyndham rose without a word, and Bella helped the woman to the ground. A trace of amusement cut through Bella's worry when the dowager shook out her skirts and straightened her hat before accepting her arm. She might be shaken by the events of the day, but obviously there were still proprieties to be observed. She had not recovered her cane and leaned heavily on Bella as they followed in Colin's wake. They walked slowly across the uneven ground, rounded some hedges until they came to the door of a thatch-roofed, one-room cabin.

"It is not very elegant, but I promise it is free of rodents," Colin said as he opened the door. He entered, calling back over his shoulder. "If you give me a moment, I will set a light."

They waited in the doorway and listened to the sounds of movement within the darkened room. Suddenly a lucifer flared and the flame was touched to a candlewick. The light flickered weakly in the current of air from the open doorway, but steadily brightened, lighting the inside of the little cabin.

One look at the contents of the room explained the boy's familiarity with the place. It was apparent that they had stumbled on Colin's hidey-hole. There was a tattered oriental runner on the beaten earth floor and a kettle hanging from an iron hook in the stone fireplace. There were toys and books and a worn, overstuffed chair, and on the straw mattress of the bed was a brightly colored quilt.

Bella led Lady Wyndham across the room. She eased the woman into the chair, watching in concern as she leaned her head against the back. Then, turning to Colin, she grinned. "It's very cozy in here."

"Thank you," he replied, returning her smile. "When the tenants left, Father said I might have it for my very own. It may not be what you are used to, but it will keep you dry while I go for help."

"No, Colin, I will go," Bella said. She had seen the pain in his face and the way he held his body and recognized the fact that he was in no condition for a ride through the storm.

"It is my duty to go."

"You sound very much like your father," she said in exasperation. "You must stay here to guard Lady Wyndham."

She gave him a speaking look, indicating the old woman with a wave of her hand. The boy lost his stubborn expression, nodding his head in agreement.

"All right, Bella," he said. "Do you know how to find the Keep?"

"No."

He chuckled at the honest answer. "If you climb on the horse and let him loose, he will take you right to the stables. You will have to hold him if there is lightning. He's already frightened and will spook at the slightest thing." Then as she started to the door, he said, "You will be careful, won't you, Bella?"

His shaky voice reminded her of his youth, and she gave him a grin and a jaunty salute. "I will be very careful," she replied solemnly as she opened the door on the rainy night.

She ducked her head, faced into the rain, and plodded across the muddy ground back to the carriage. The scene of the accident was lit with a faint light from the west. Bella averted her eyes from the body of the dead horse as she approached the restless gray. He tugged wildly at the tether and rolled his eyes at her sudden appearance, but she crooned softly as she reached up to stroke his neck. He trembled and shuddered at first, eventually quieting beneath her hands.

When she felt he had calmed sufficiently, she hiked up her sodden skirts and, using the back of the carriage as a mounting block, threw a leg across his back. A sudden clap of thunder panicked the horse, and he threw up his head. Bella was only partially mounted, bent over his back, when the horse's neck slammed into the side of her head. Blackness threatened as pain arched through her body. She threw her arms around his neck to keep from falling back on the ground.

She touched her head, feeling the ooze of blood as the cut reopened. She raised her face to the night sky, letting the rain wash her face. The cool dampness revived her. Her heart pounded, an echo to the pain in her temple, and she breathed deeply to clear her head.

Her fingers were wooden as she tried to unfasten the bridle from the back of the carriage. When she leaned over, she was caught by a wave of dizziness, but she bit her lip, knowing she must hurry before she lost consciousness. Finally the knot gave way, and she dug her hands into the horse's mane as he wheeled away from the carriage. Rain pelted her, soaking her clothing and pulling heavily at her body. She lay atop the gray, face buried in the side of his neck as he took off down the road in what she hoped was the right direction. Each jarring step drained her of energy, and she felt her grip loosen until she knew she had lost control of the horse. Her mind drifted, and she no longer noticed the chill that invaded her body and the pain that radiated from the bruise on her head.

Overhead thunder barked and the horizon was backlit with lightning. The gray was spooked by a particularly loud crash. Bella was nearly unconscious when she lost her grip and toppled to the ground, landing in a sprawled heap beside the road. She raised her head, watching the frightened horse tearing away into the night, but she could do no more than follow his movement with her eyes. Blackness closed in around her, and she gave up the fight, falling back on the grass in a faint.

Colin closed the door after Bella and remained with his hand on the wooden panel as if to take comfort from its firmness. He felt bereft, perhaps with the knowledge that the old woman in the chair did not want to be left alone with him. He wished he could have gone, but knew Bella was correct.

His left arm was broken. He had actually heard the bone break when he fell against the side of the carriage. The pain wasn't too bad if he didn't move it much. He didn't relish the time it would take for Bella to get to the Keep and send help. He hoped his father would hurry, but until he arrived it was his duty to take care of Lady Wyndham. He pushed away from the door and turned to face the room.

Lady Wyndham was sitting straighter in her chair, her face white and pinched, the only spot of color two dots of rouge high on her cheekbones. Her hands were folded on her lap. Colin found it strange to see her without her walking stick, for it had always seemed a part of her. As he watched her, she shuddered and he hurried forward.

"I will try to get a fire going, ma'am," he said. "It's getting chill in here, what with the rain and all."

Since he had taken over the cabin, he had made it a practice to always leave a fire ready laid. He never knew when he would be able to come to his special place, and sometimes when it was cold he needed the warmth of a fire when he arrived. Carefully, so as not to jar his arm, he used the candle to set a small area aglow. He fanned the blaze until he was sure it was well started, then, using the water jug standing near at hand, he filled the kettle and swung it over the fire.

He was aware that Lady Wyndham was watching his every move and tried to hide his nervousness. Crossing to the storage cupboard, he pulled out a chipped china teapot and some mugs. He had trouble opening the tea canister, but eventually succeeded by holding it between his knees to pry off the top. By the time he had finished his preparations, the fire was beginning to fill the room with heat. He moved to the fireplace, waiting for the steam to rise in the kettle.

"Come here."

Lady Wyndham's voice was sharp in the silence of the room. Colin was so unused to her speaking to him that for a moment he looked around to see who she was talking to. As his eyes met hers, she nodded briskly. Heart pounding in his throat, he approached her chair.

"Is it broken?" she asked, indicating the arm hanging limply at his side.

"Yes, ma'am," he said. "I heard it snap when I fell."

"Can you move it at all?"

"Not unless I want it to hurt." He grinned sheepishly and was amazed when she returned his smile. He couldn't remember ever seeing her smile. She didn't seem quite so fierce when she did.

"It shouldn't be hanging down. It's already quite swollen. We need something to support the weight." Her mouth pursed as she looked around the room and, for a moment, Colin felt ashamed that she was finding the cabin wanting in amenities. "We shall use my shawl."

Colin watched in fascination as she untied her shawl, laying it across her lap to fold it into a triangle. It was a flowered muslin, gossamer thin, and looked much too fragile to be useful. Her long-fingered hands smoothed the creases, and he was mesmerized by the motion.

"Come closer and I will tie up your arm."

Colin did as she asked, touched by her concern. She had

never paid him any attention, and he felt honored by her ministrations. She laid one end of the material over his shoulder, then, with great gentleness, she cupped his elbow and raised his arm. Slow as the movement was, pain shot through his arm. He sucked in his breath, but did not cry out as she folded the material around his arm and tied the ends behind his neck.

"You are a very brave boy, Colin," Lady Wyndham said.

"Thank you," he said.

He bowed his head, knowing his words were inadequate. He ought to say something more, but was much too moved to speak. It was the first time that Lady Wyndham had said his name, and he was ashamed at the sudden rise of tears and the lump in his throat. He had tried not to cry over his injuries, but now the old woman's kindness nearly unmanned him. He struggled for control and turned to the fireplace, noting with relief the ribbon of steam rising from the spout.

"I'll make us some tea until Father arrives."

His voice sounded shaky to his own ears, and he hoped the old woman wouldn't notice. He crossed the room and swung the kettle on its hook out away from the fire. When he turned, he was surprised to find Lady Wyndham beside him with the teapot. He tilted the kettle with his good hand, holding his breath as the dowager caught the water neatly in the teapot. Then he watched in amazement as she set about setting up a tea tray. She rummaged about among the tins and boxes until she discovered some shortbread he had purloined from the kitchens. He heard her chuckle of triumph, and he joined in, feeling happier than he could ever recall.

She carried the makeshift tray back to her chair, setting it on the small table. Colin stood beside the fire, afraid to move for fear he would wake from what was obviously an impossible dream. Lady Wyndham crossed to the cot, removed the quilt, and folded it to a bulky square. She placed it on the floor, close to the fireplace, but almost in front of her chair. Then, smoothing her skirts, she sat down, indicating the quilt at her feet with an imperious finger.

"Sit," she ordered.

Still speechless, Colin sat down on the quilt, his eyes raised to the old woman. Her face was expressionless but her silvery blue eyes twinkled as she bent over the tea tray. She poured the tea with the same formality she would in her own salon.

She handed him a mug, holding it carefully until he could grasp it with his good hand. She raised her own, took a sip and sighed.

"Well, drink up, Colin," she barked. "It'll put some color in your cheeks."

He raised his mug, grateful for the heat that rose to his face. He sniffed and then took a small sip, closing his eyes as the warmth filled his mouth and spread down his throat. Tea had never tasted so good. He took another sip, and then smiled over the rim of his mug at the old woman in the chair.

"How's the arm?"

"Much better, ma'am. Now that it's up, it doesn't throb quite so much." Colin grinned and took another gulp of tea. "It was ever such a clever idea to make the sling."

Lady Wyndham nodded graciously at the compliment. She reached for a piece of shortbread, bit into it, and made a face.

"I'm sorry it's a bit stale," Colin apologized.

"Quite all right, lad," she said. "I shall just have to make sure Cook supplies you with better provisions. I should hate to think anyone would think you a pinchpenny host. After all, one never knows when you will have company here."

She waved her hand around the room, and Colin giggled. Hearing his amusement, she raised an eyebrow and pursed her lips, and he was hard-pressed not to laugh louder.

"Do you come here often?" she asked.

"Sometimes I come every day. Other times maybe only once a week. I like to read here and just think about things." He let his eyes circle the room, enjoying all his treasures. "Mostly I come here when Father's away. I get lonesome, and when I'm here I don't feel quite so alone."

"I see," Lady Wyndham said.

There was a curious, choked quality to her voice, and Colin looked up at her but her head was bent over her mug. There was a tremor in her hand, and he wondered if she were warm enough. He looked at the fire, but it was snapping crisply, filling the room with warmth. When he looked back, Lady Wyndham was staring at him, her face expressionless.

"Do you play chess?" she asked. "I noticed the set in the corner and remember it was Tristram's when he was small."

"Father gave me the set and showed me the moves, but I

don't play very well," Colin admitted. "I'm afraid Father is able to beat me with the greatest of ease."

"I used to play myself. As I recall, I was quite good. I used to play with Tristram, but eventually he began to beat me and I refused to continue. It was pique, I suppose. I do not like to lose." She glared at him fiercely over the rim of her mug. "Perhaps I might play again. It is an enjoyable pastime. I'm rather rusty, don't you know, and I wonder if I would offer you much of a challenge."

Colin could feel his eyes widen as the meaning of her words penetrated his mind. He blinked up at her, unsure if he had heard correctly.

"Pardon?"

"Would you consider playing chess with me, Colin?" she asked.

"Oh, ma'am," he whispered. He was so overwhelmed that his chin began to tremble and he ducked his head before he could disgrace himself.

"I'm very sorry, Colin," she said. "I have been a stubborn old fool."

She reached out to touch the tumbled brown curls. Her fingers stroked the silky head of the boy, and he sighed as he leaned against her knee. Tears filled her eyes as she thought of the lost years and silently promised she would somehow make it up to the child.

Chapter Thirteen

Still dressed in buckskins from his ride back to the Keep, Tristram entered the library. His forehead was furrowed in concentration; his mind focused inward as he grappled with a sense of unease. He tried to pinpoint when the feeling had first come over him, but knew that it was during his visit to the Danforths' stable.

He had been examining Colin's new hunter when he caught sight of one of the grooms. There was an instant of recognition which perplexed him because he could not recall ever seeing the man before. The familiarity of the man puzzled him. It seemed important somehow and, as the day wore on, it continued to nag at his memory. He had used the new hunter as an excuse to leave ahead of the others, in hopes that the elusive memory would slide back into his mind once he was alone.

He crossed the room to stare out the windows. The storm was imminent, and the day had turned dark. The afternoon sunlight overlay the grounds, tinting everything a bitter red-orange. The first raindrops began to fall, marking the window and sliding down the pane in wavy, crisscross patterns.

His ride back had been uneventful. Todd appeared to have good stamina and reacted well to jumps. Tristram had put him through a fairly rigorous pace, but the animal had a strength of spirit that would make him an excellent hunter. The horse had responded quickly to Tristram's commands and, despite the fact he had used a light rein, the stallion had not been difficult to control. For a youngster, Colin had strong hands and should be able to handle the new addition to the stables. All in all, he was pleased with the purchase.

Turning away from the windows, Tristram scanned the bookshelves but was too restless to read. He looked around the room and was sharply reminded of his interview with his grandmother the day before. Anger returned in a burst, and he kicked a small stool in a fit of temper.

He had always known her for a meddler, but this time she had gone too far. The moment he indicated any reservations about his marriage with Bella, the stubborn old woman had tried to blackmail him with the fact that he had compromised the girl when he'd remained with her in the woods the night he had been shot.

If it wasn't so outrageous, it would have been laughable. He had hardly been in a condition to molest the girl. He had been physically incapable of mounting any form of seduction in the event that such an idea had even crossed his mind. He had never thought of Bella in sexual terms. Well, perhaps once or twice, but that was just a weakness of the flesh that he had immediately suppressed as unworthy of consideration. The thought of making love to Bella was quite out of the question. After all, he had already decided that his relationship with her was one of a favorite uncle for a young girl. He had been trying to explain that to his grandmother when she had made her outlandish accusation.

He was nonplussed that he had reacted so strongly to her charges, and in his anger had suggested that he would not honor his marriage with Bella. Since the night he had declared himself engaged in front of myriad witnesses, he had given the idea serious consideration. His refusal to marry had always been based on the fact that his new wife would not accept Colin's inheriting once she realized he was not Tristram's natural son. If he married Bella, that would never be in question.

From the moment she'd entered his household, she had taken Colin to her heart. He knew from her anger when he told her of the boy's heritage that she could honestly not understand how anyone would ever consider Colin not the rightful heir. For Bella, the matter of heredity had nothing to do with the true character of the boy. She loved Colin and would always defend his rights to his father's estate.

He had a sudden vision of Bella in the woods the night he was wounded. He had opened his eyes to discover the fairylike creature staring curiously into his face. He had thought she was a vision, some spirit of the woods who would disappear if he blinked his eyes. Even then he had been certain that her leaving would somehow make his life less full. And it had proved true. Bella had brought a sense of happiness to his entire family that had been missing before. For that alone he would marry her.

He was sorry that he could not offer her love or passion, but in all else he would try to be a good husband. She would be financially secure and safe from her conniving uncle. She would have social status and friends of her own age so that she would not miss that side of marriage that he was not free to give her. He hoped it would be sufficient.

Lowering himself into a chair, he leaned his head against the cool leather and contemplated the future. The storm broke overhead, raindrops drumming against the windowpanes. He closed his eyes and immediately Bella's piquant face appeared in his mind. Flashes of memory reminded him of the many moods of the delightful young woman. He relaxed, and a smile of pleasure pulled at the corners of his mouth.

Suddenly the face of the unknown groom superimposed itself over Bella's face. He tensed, but let the memory fill his mind until finally he remembered where he had seen the man.

It was thinking about Bella that had given him the clue. He had first seen the groom on the day he had met her. The wheel of his curricle had come off just outside a small village. He had walked back to the inn, a place called the Toot and Whistle. While the innkeeper was arranging to retrieve his horses and repair the carriage, he had gone into the public room for a draft of ale. The man he had seen in Danforth's stable had been sitting at a table near the hearth.

He could remember the expression on the man's face as he pushed through the door. It was part recognition, part surprise. Tristram had stopped, wondering if the man were an acquaintance, but he did not know him. Eager for the cold ale, he had dismissed the unknown man from his mind. It was after he left the Toot and Whistle on the rented horse that he had been shot.

Tristram pulled himself straighter in the chair. His eyes narrowed as thoughts raced through his head. Suddenly he latched onto the piece of the puzzle that had been missing and understood why he had been possessed of such a feeling of uneasiness. His nostrils flared as if he scented danger, and slowly his thoughts began to solidify into a series of questions.

Had the mysterious groom been involved in that first attempt on his life? Was he the one who had tampered with the wheel? Perhaps that would account for the look of surprise on the man's face when he entered the public room. And then, knowing that Tristram had survived the accident, had the groom followed him and fired the shot that felled him?

Tristram was stunned at the possibility. The more he thought about the incident, the more reasonable it appeared. And if the groom had been involved in the first incident, was he also the one who had fired on them beside the stream?

He jerked to his feet, pacing the room in an attempt to release some of his pent-up fury. The groom worked for Eden Danforth. Surely that meant that someone on the Danforth estate was involved with the plot. He ran his hands through his hair, appalled at the thought that one of his relatives was somehow implicated.

There was a knock on the door.

"Come," he called out impatiently.

One of the stable hands stood in the doorway. He was wet from his run across the yard, and slightly breathless. He shifted uncomfortably under Tristram's baleful glare, snatching off his cap before he spoke.

"Sorry to interrupt, milord. Whitcombe asks that you come to the stables. It's urgent, he says."

Tristram knew Whitcombe would never send for him except in an extreme emergency. He pushed past the groom and charged outside. His boots splashed through the puddles as he ran through the gardens. He outpaced the servant who followed in his wake, leaving the old man puffing and gasping for breath. The heavy rain lashed at Tristram's face which was coldly chiseled and grim in the occasional flashes of lightning. He was hatless, his black hair plastered to his forehead, but he was oblivious to the discomfort, intent only on reaching the stables.

"Ho, Whitcombe," he shouted as he spotted the bandy-legged Scotsman in the doorway.

"Your lordship." The head groom hurried forward, meeting Tristram in the middle of the yard. His wizened face, wrinkled from years outside, was stiff with worry as he drew his master through the cluster of activity in the doorway. "It's glad I am that you've come. I couldna' leave."

Whitcombe stopped in front of one of the stalls and opened the upper half of the oak door, clucking softly to the animal inside. One look was all it took to constrict Tristram's heart in a band of pain. The carriage gray, still lathered from its run through the rain, was being brushed down by one of the grooms.

"He come tearin' into the yard just a few minutes ago," Whitcombe said without prompting. "There was blood on his neck, but it wasna' his."

The sparsity of words tightened the band inside Tristram's chest. He did not need further explanation to know that the occupants of the carriage were in need of help. He forced down his wildly spinning emotions, knowing he would need a clear head. He clamped his teeth together and felt the muscles in his jaw bunch. Taking a deep breath to get control of himself, he nodded to the tensely waiting Whitcombe.

"The gray did nae break free. The buckles of the bridle were undone, nae torn away. Someone was on his back, the coachman most like. I've sent out two men. When they find the carriage, one of them will return. I told them to look sharp by the roadside for the coachman, and that we'd follow with another carriage." Whitcombe hesitated, then added, "I've also sent one of the boys for the doctor."

"Good man, Whitcombe," Tristram said. His face was hard as granite as he pulled on his gloves. "My horse?"

"Bein' tacked. Along with as many as we've men to mount."

Tristram was icy calm now that action was imminent. He sent some of the younger grooms with a list of supplies. By the time Diomedes was brought around from his stall, house servants had appeared with the requested supplies, which included a flask of brandy. Leaving the rest to be stowed in the carriage, he tucked the flask inside his coat and leaped to the saddle. Beside him Whitcombe mounted a bay hunter. The hastily prepared carriage was just coming in sight as they flashed out of the yard.

Tristram bent over Diomedes's neck, trying to hold back the

fear that had invaded his body from the moment he had heard the first news. The thought that the carriage had overturned was uppermost in his thoughts, and scenes of carnage appeared in his mind, adding to his dread. Lady Wyndham was of an age that such a shake-up could very well cause her death. And Colin's body was still too small to withstand much punishment. Was he hurt? Lying beside the carriage, his body bent in some grotesque shape?

He should never have left them at Eden's. He should have stayed beside them, especially after he felt his first uneasiness. Guilt tore at him with the realization that his failure to identify the mysterious groom might have put his own family at risk. Everyone at the Danforths' thought that Tristram would return in the carriage. Had the accident been the result of a further act of sabotage?

Questions whirled through his mind as he rode through the rainy night. He would have to hold back his urgent need for answers until he had dealt with the accident to his family. All he could do for the moment was beg a beneficent God to spare his son and his grandmother.

His sole consolation was that Bella was safe. Thank God she had stayed behind at the Danforths'. It shocked him that when he was first called to the stable, Bella had been uppermost in his mind. He had had a flash of terror that he could not explain, but as he ran through the rain to the stables he had been frightened that something had happened to the girl. He suspected now that his fear had been for Violet and Fortune. The mare was Bella's friend, a solace in the lonely years after her father died, and she already adored the new foal. He knew if anything happened to them, she would be inconsolable.

Rain pelted his face, rolling down his cheeks like a river of tears. He stared ahead into the darkness. Hearing a shout from up ahead, Tristram reined in his horse. Diomedes shied nervously as the groom appeared out of the mist. He held the prancing stallion with hands of iron and clenched his jaw in anticipation of the news.

"We've found them, milord," the man called when he came within hailing distance.

"Excellent, Hastings," Tristram bit out.

"They're right and tight in the old Windbourn cabin. The carriage lost a wheel, but didn't overturn." The words came more distinctly as the groom came abreast of Tristram and Whitcombe. "I'm sorry, milord, but the coachman is dead. And one of the grays."

Although sorry about the coachman, Tristram released his breath, relieved at the safety of his family, and turned to slap Whitcombe on the shoulder. The Scotsman grinned and moved back as the groom turned his horse to lead the way. The pace of the horses was slower, or perhaps it just seemed so to Tristram, now that his first urgent need for information had been satisfied. As they approached the scene, Whitcombe and the groom continued on while Tristram turned Diomedes toward the snug cabin nestled in the trees. He had never thought when he gave the place to Colin it would one day shelter his family. He dismounted, tied the reins to a nearby bush, and pushed open the door.

The tableau before the fireplace was so unexpected that he stopped in his tracks, too stunned to move. Lady Wyndham sat in a worn armchair, an expression of concern etched on her face. Colin was curled up on a quilt beside her chair, one arm wrapped in a floral shawl. He was sound asleep, his head pillowed on the old woman's knee while she smoothed the curls off his forehead. The teapot and mugs were a homey addition, and Tristram could feel the sharp sting of tears as he took in the intimate scene.

Lady Wyndham raised her eyes to his. He opened his mouth to speak, but she held up her hand in an imperious gesture. Nodding his head, he closed the door and tiptoed across the room, kneeling down to stare into the white face of his son.

"He'll need a doctor, Tristram. His arm is broken," Lady Wyndham whispered, her hand once more stroking the brown hair of the sleeping child.

"Dr. Danderfield has been sent for," Tristram answered hoarsely, watching in fascination as his grandmother caressed his son. "Are you well, madam?"

"Slightly stiff, but otherwise none the worse for our ordeal." She spoke quietly, never taking her eyes from Colin's face. She lifted her hand from the boy's hair and placed the back of it against his forehead and then his cheek. "He's flushed, but I don't think it's fever. The warmth of the tea relaxed him enough to fall into a natural sleep. However, you should wait to move him until the last minute."

"The coach is right behind us. We'll wrap him in blankets to cushion him for the return trip." Tristram reached inside his jacket and brought forth the flask, smiling as he spotted the light of interest in his grandmother's eyes. "Perhaps a drop to ward off any dire consequences of your adventure?"

"Quite appropriate, my boy," she said, reaching out with her free hand to the empty mug.

He poured her a healthy dollop. He would be relieved once she was returned to the Keep for, although she appeared to have taken no injury, there was a whiteness to her skin that worried him.

Lady Wyndham raised the mug, staring at Tristram over the rim. "To Colin," she said quietly. "A worthy heir."

Tristram bowed his head, too overcome by the emotions that filled him to do more. He had never thought to hear such words from the starchy, pride-bound dowager. His heart expanded as he reached out blindly to take her hand. With a gesture as formal as an obeisance to a queen, he lifted her hand and kissed it.

He rose to stir up the fire, grateful for the familiarity of the actions which kept him from dwelling on his emotions. Once the fire was blazing merrily, he turned back to the room. His grandmother's color was better, cheeks flushed by the alcohol, and she seemed more relaxed now that rescue was at hand. He leaned down to caress the cheek of his son.

"Colin shot the horse when there was no way to save it," Lady Wyndham said.

"Brave lad."

"Aye. He was in great pain, but he wouldn't let Bella do it."

"Bella?" Tristram's eyes widened in a sudden burst of fear.

Lady Wyndham continued to explain. "He brought us here and would have gone for help, but Bella could see the condition of his arm."

"Bella is here?" His mind felt wooden as he fought to understand the situation.

There was silence as Lady Wyndham caught the first hint of his anxiety. "Bella went for help on the carriage horse."

"The horse was riderless!" Tristram shouted as he charged for the door.

He heard his grandmother cry out as he streaked out into

the night. He grabbed Diomedes's reins and leaped to the saddle, turning the stallion's head as he kneed him back toward the road. The rain had stopped and a low mist rose in ghostly columns to soften the sharpness of objects picked out in the light of the moon. He found the carriage and reined in beside Whitcombe. In short sentences he explained about Bella, and they made plans to initiate a search.

The men were called away from their tasks, and they fanned out on either side of the road. Torches were lit and passed along the line as they walked back toward the Keep.

Tristram rode behind the line, his fingers cramped with the pressure of reining in himself and Diomedes. The pace seemed incredibly slow, and he ground his teeth to keep himself from tearing off blindly into the night. His face felt stiff, and his body was tight with tension. He refused to think, terrified to let the image of Bella, injured or worse, take over his mind. Inside his chest, pain roiled and twisted as, unbidden, her lovely face rose to haunt him.

The instant of agony when he discovered Bella was missing made him finally understand his feelings. What a fool he had been to ever think his fondness for her was fatherly affection. He had been struggling against his own emotions while he tried to rationalize his relationship with her. But the thought of danger had removed the scales from his eyes. He loved her; she was as much a part of him as his own body. She had taken possession of his heart and his soul.

Bella. Bella. Her name pounded in his head to the rhythm of the horse's hooves. Silently he prayed.

A shout drove him forward, and he leaped to the ground to kneel in the mud beside the crumpled figure. Bella lay on her side, knees drawn up and head cushioned on one outstretched arm. She did not move as the men gathered in a silent circle around her.

"Bring a torch!" Whitcombe cried.

Tristram's fingers shook as he brushed the rain-soaked hair away from her face. In the wavering light, her skin shone ghostly white, colorless except for the crescents of dark, spikey lashes that lay atop her cheeks. He pressed his fingers against the side of her neck beneath her jawline. His own heart was pounding so loudly in his ears that for a moment he felt nothing. Then, like a faint echo of his own life force, he felt Bella's pulse flutter beneath his fingers.

"She's alive," he whispered.

He felt, rather than heard the men's exclamations, shaken as he was by the miracle that had been granted him. He was vaguely aware that Whitcombe was organizing the men to return for Lady Wyndham and Colin, and to bring up the coach. For the moment he could focus only on Bella and his fear for the extent of her injuries.

"Hold the torch steady," he snapped.

He turned her onto her back, cushioning each movement as best he could. Expertly he examined her arms and legs, and was jubilant when he could find no apparent broken bones. He was frightened by her stillness and checked her pulse frequently, more to reassure himself than for any practical reason. Once more he brushed back her hair, and his heart jolted when his hand came away sticky with blood.

Gently he turned her head to the side until he found the cut. It was just at her hairline, the edges slightly puckered and red with blood. He pressed his handkerchief to the wound and felt her moan.

"It's all right, Bella. We'll soon have you home."

While he waited for the carriage, Tristram held her, speaking softly into her ear. He had no recollection later of what he said, but he was determined that she would know she was no longer alone. His voice would somehow penetrate the confusion of her mind and keep her from slipping away into eternal darkness.

When the others arrived, he tenderly wrapped her in blankets and cradled her in his arms as they returned to the Keep. Lady Wyndham sat on the opposite seat, Colin, well-cushioned by blankets, held close to her side. Though the coach was well-sprung, the boy sucked in his breath at each bump.

"Will Bella be all right, Father?" he asked, his voice trembling on the edge of tears.

"God willing," Tristram said. He raised his eyes from Bella's white face and stared gravely across at his son. "You have done well tonight, Colin."

"I had to shoot the gray."

"I know. It must have been very difficult. Remember, though, he was in agony and you saved him from more pain."

"Thank you, sir."

"You took excellent care of Lady Wyndham. A chivalrous act, indeed."

"More like she took care of me," Colin said.

In the light from the moon, Tristram saw the boy grin up at the dowager. Without a word, she bent her head and kissed the top of his curls then checked to be sure the sling supporting his arm was secure. Tristam smiled for the first time since he had discovered Bella missing, then returned his attention to her limp figure in his arms.

Bella's stillness terrified him. He had never felt so helpless in his life. He had no way of knowing how serious the head injury was, but he would feel some relief if she would at least open her eyes. His body ached with tension as he held her close in his arms, her head pillowed on his chest. Her breath touched his cheek, featherlight, like the kiss of a butterfly. She seemed much too fragile to be able to survive such a series of accidents as had befallen her this night.

For a moment fury welled up in him, threatening to choke him. Whitcombe had already apprised him of the fact that the carriage wheel had been tampered with. The thought that someone would endanger his family, let alone the woman he loved, tore at him, sending him into a near killing rage.

The Keep was a blaze of lights when they arrived. With iron control, Tristram forced down his anger and waited while Lady Wyndham and Colin were helped from the carriage before he stepped down with Bella in his arms. Her head was against his shoulder and her one arm curled trustingly around his neck. The similarity to his arrival in London, with her asleep in his arms, cut through him like a knife. He pressed her close to his heart and hastened up the stairs to the doorway.

The hall was filled with servants, and for a moment Tristram hesitated. His mind was obsessed with the need to help Bella, but he had other responsibilities, as well. Thankfully his grandmother was perceptive enough to understand his dilemma.

"The doctor is not here yet, Tristram," she said. "Take Bella upstairs. I shall take Colin along to his rooms and wait with him until the doctor arrives."

With a nod of his head, he took the stairs to the upper floors, moving quickly along the hallway, followed by a train of servants. Bella's maid Sarah ran ahead to open the door and, without ceremony, Tristram entered. He was gratified to see a steaming tub placed before the fireplace. Not only was Bella filthy, but her skin was cold to the touch. Hopefully the warmth of the bath would ward off the chance of an inflammation of the lungs. Gently he laid his precious bundle across the end of the bed as Sarah and the two female servants pressed closer.

Bella was cocooned in blankets, with only her head and one arm visible. In the soft light of the wall sconces, her face looked deathly pale, whiter than the handkerchief covering the cut on her head. Her lips were bloodless; the only color a livid bruise high on her cheekbone. Her golden brown hair was coated with mud, the matted curls a Medusalike headdress atop her head.

Reaching down, he carefully folded back the blankets. Her dress was water-soaked and streaked with mud. He tried to close his mind to everything and concentrate on the girl on the bed. He reached for the top buttons of her gown, his fingers wooden in his agitation.

"Lord Wyndham!" Bella's maid cried, her face a picture of horror.

"Be quiet or I will send you all out of the room," Tristram snapped, exasperated with such niceties. "I am not planning to ravish the girl, merely undress her."

Aware of the intake of breath from Sarah and the other two servants, Tristram smiled grimly. He quickly stripped off Bella's sodden stockings and outer clothing, but for the sake of propriety he left on her underthings. When he lifted her, his heart was touched once more by the fragility of her body and the awareness of the abuse it had undergone. He carried her across to the tub, kneeling down to slide her carefully into the water. Bella's maid folded a towel on the rim of the tub, and he placed her head against the improvised pillow.

For a moment no one moved; each intent on watching the lifeless face of the young woman in the water. Tristram held his breath as a flush of color moved up from the neckline of her shift, rising inexorably like the tide to coat her cheeks. Suddenly Bella's mouth twitched and the shadow of a smile etched her lips.

"Take care of her," Tristram rasped.

His voice was harsh with emotion as he jerked to his feet,

leaving Bella in the hands of the waiting women. He knew he could not remain in the room and watch dispassionately while they prepared her for the doctor. Helpless frustration rode him as he stormed into the hall.

A footman waited outside the room to tell him the doctor was with Colin. Tristram proceeded to his own rooms where his valet Demeritt was waiting with hot water and fresh clothing. Thus restored, he hastened along the hall to his son's room.

Colin, face white and tight with pain, was already in bed. His arm had been set and was resting on a lace-edged pillow. Lady Wyndham, her walking stick restored to her hand, was seated beside him. Tristram crossed the room and kissed his grandmother on her cheek.

"How goes our young hero?" he asked, reaching out to ruffle his son's curly head, still damp from washing.

"Much better now, sir." Colin's words came slowly, and from the half-shuttered lids, Tristram suspected the doctor had administered some narcotic for pain. "Did Todd give you a good ride?"

It took a moment for Tristram to remember the boy's new hunter. It seemed like at least a week had passed since they'd purchased the horse, and it amazed him it had only been earlier in the day.

"He has an excellent stride. You will be the envy of all at the next hunt season," Tristram said.

"Wizard, sir," Colin exclaimed.

Tristram turned to his grandmother, but she anticipated his question.

"The doctor has gone along to Bella's room," she said.

"And did he have any strong words for you, madam?"

"He suggested I might take to my bed for several days like some simpering debutante. The man's an old fusspot!" She tapped her walking stick on the floor to emphasize her disgust.

Since Dr. Danderfield was at least twenty years younger than his grandmother, Tristram had difficulty repressing a smile.

"Harker is pacing the hallway outside the door, madam," he said. "She is threatening to quit your service if you don't go along to your rooms."

"Humph. I shall not be browbeaten by my own abigail,"

sniffed Lady Wyndham, but she rose to her feet nonetheless. She leaned over Colin's bed and kissed the boy's forehead. "Sleep well, young man. I shall check on you in the morning. Perhaps I could read to you, if you like."

"That would be ever so nice, ma'am," the boy said, yawning sleepily.

She turned to Tristram. "You will send me word, after you have spoken to the doctor?" Her hand shook slightly as she placed it on his arm, and he covered it with his own.

"I will, madam," he promised.

Tristram led her to the door, handed her over to Harker, and watched in amusement as the abigail followed her, nattering and scolding, much like a dog herding sheep. He turned back to Colin, who was almost asleep. His face hardened at the pain evidenced by the tightness of the child's mouth, but he forced a smile to his lips as he leaned over the bed.

"Demeritt will remain with you for the night, in case you should need anything. I will also check on you later," he said.

"Thank you, Father." A yawn seemed to creep up on him and, when his mouth closed, he grinned. "I think I will sleep."

"I don't doubt it, after the excitement of the day." Tristram brushed the hair off the boy's forehead, grateful that there was no sign of fever. "I am very proud of you, Colin."

The boy tried to speak, but sleep was already taking possession of his body, and he settled for a smile of contentment before his eyes closed. Tristram remained by his bedside, his face harsh in the flickering candlelight. He felt the agony of all parents at the realization that they could not take away their children's pain. He listened to the soft breathing of the boy and, with a final caress, left the room. When the doctor was ushered into the library, Tristram handed him a snifter of brandy and indicated a chair beside the fire.

"Your son has a simple break. Nothing to worry about," Dr. Danderfield assured him. "There should be no permanent damage."

"Thank God," Tristram said. "And Lady Wyndham?"

"Your grandmother is a remarkable woman," the doctor continued. "I suspect she will be rather stiff from her shaking up, but aside from that she is miraculously uninjured. Her disposition is as always."

Despite Tristram's urgency to hear about Bella, he grinned

across at the man. "She's a right crusty tartar, Nigel, as I am well aware."

"She is forever calling me an old fusspot, and yet she treats me as if I were four and ten." He rolled his eyes in chagrin.

"And Lady Mallory?" Tristram asked, unable to contain his eagerness.

"I believe the young lady, apart from a headache, will be fine in the morning."

At the news, Tristram sagged in his chair, swallowing with difficulty as a lump rose in his throat. "Has she awakened?"

"She did for a moment or two. She was lucid and spoke a few words, so I do not fear for any affliction of her mind. I have examined her quite thoroughly and, aside from some bumps and bruises, can find nothing of consequence outside the cut on her head. Even that will heal quite naturally. A small scar perhaps, but nothing disfiguring."

Tristram felt giddy at the realization that he had not lost Bella. He questioned the doctor further as to the proper care of his invalid household, but was grateful when the man finally took his leave. Alone, he finished his brandy, then reported to his grandmother. As he had expected, she, too, was delighted with the news. He bid her good night, and then walked down the hall to Bella's room. He was just about to scratch on the door when it opened and the maid hurried into the hall.

"Oh, Lord Wyndham," she gasped. "I was just coming to get you. My mistress is calling for you and is ever so restless. She won't take the laudanum the doctor left."

Tristram hurried across the threshold to the bed. He was oblivious to Bella's maid who hovered at his shoulder as he leaned closer. Bella lay beneath the bedclothes. She was dressed now in a muslin night rail, buttoned modestly at her throat. Her brown hair was freshly washed, the golden strands catching and holding the light from the candles. There was only a small bandage at her temple, partially covered by her hair but shining stark white against her pale skin. Her face held more color now, and there was only one bruise, high on her cheek, to detract from the beauty of her features. Sitting down on the edge of the bed when his knees began to tremble, he felt tears in his eyes as he lifted her soft hand in his.

Looking at her now, he was amazed that he had ever mistaken his feelings for her. It seemed that he had always loved her from the first moment he had seen her. He understood why he had been unable to leave her in the woods, why he had been furious when she said she would not marry him. Unless she was part of his life, his existence would have little meaning. He needed her with the same intensity that flowers needed the light of the sun. Without her, he would wither and die.

"Bella? Can you hear me?" he whispered.

She moved her head restlessly from side to side and her mouth worked, but she did not respond.

"Bella, it's Tristram." This time he spoke louder, and her head ceased its frenzied motion. "It's Tristram," he repeated.

For a moment he thought she had not heard him, but suddenly he felt the slightest movement of her hand in his. He raised it to his mouth and lightly kissed the tips of her fingers.

"Wake up, Bella," he commanded.

He waited patiently, watching her face, and was finally rewarded when her eyelashes fluttered against her cheek and the lids began to rise. He moved his head so that he would be in the circle of candlelight. Her eyes opened fully, but it was a moment before she seemed able to recognize him.

"Tristram," she sighed.

"I am here, my love."

"Colin," she said, her fingers tightening on his in rising agitation.

"Never fear, we have found him. The doctor has seen to his arm. It is broken, but otherwise the boy is fine. Both he and Lady Wyndham are tucked up in bed. Everyone is safe in the Keep."

Bella lay quiet as if her mind were slow to take in all this information, but finally she relaxed the grip on his hand.

"How do you feel?"

"Very old and stiff."

The humor in her voice heartened him, and he grinned down at her. Her brown eyes were less cloudy now, as if the effort of talking had somehow cleared her mind. He was so close to her that her scent seemed to surround him, a clean, flowery aroma that always made him think of a field of wildflowers.

"I was coming to get you after the accident," she continued. "I bumped my head again when I mounted the horse. I remember starting back to the Keep, but I cannot remember anything else."

She raised her free hand to her forehead, rubbing it as if to jog her memory. Tristram pressed her fingers and she relaxed against the pillows.

"You must have fallen off, but the horse returned to the stables. Whitcombe sent for me, and we raced to your rescue like true knights in armor."

A low chuckle rose from the bed. Tristram stroked the back of her hand, listening to the gentle sighing of her breath. He thought she had gone back to sleep, and was afraid to move for fear of waking her. He was content to sit by her side, holding her hand and caressing her lovely face with his eyes.

Bella dozed, sinking back into the fuzzy world of dreams to keep her from dwelling on the aches and pains of her body. She sensed Tristram's presence and wondered if she had imagined it. She peeked through her lashes, almost afraid to discover herself alone, but in the light from the candles she saw him poised above her. His hair was disheveled, black curls falling forward onto his forehead as if he had been running his hands through his hair. It gave him a boyish look, and for the first time she saw a resemblance to Colin.

Colin! Her body jerked at the thought of the boy, and her fingers tightened around Tristram's hand.

"Colin," she said aloud, struggling to rise from the bed.

Tristram's eyes opened wide at her words. She could tell he was confused. He pressed her back against the pillows, speaking firmly, as though to a child of four.

"Colin is fine. He is safe, Bella," he said.

"I know," she said, her voice slightly peevish. She stopped fighting the pressure of his hands, but her body was tense with her need to tell him her news. "Are we alone?" she said, trying to see beyond the circle of light.

"I am here, miss," Sarah piped up. Tristram jumped, as if he had forgotten the maid's presence.

"Leave us," Bella said. "I wish to speak to Lord Wyndham alone."

Sarah was clearly shocked by the suggestion, and looked to her employer for direction. Tristram hesitated, his eyes flickering back and forth between the maid and Bella. Finally he conceded and, at his curt nod of dismissal, Sarah dipped a curtsy and left the room. Bella listened for the click of the door before she turned her face up to Tristram's.

"I must tell you what I have discovered," she said.

"Can't it wait until morning?"

"No!" she cried. "It truly cannot wait. I should have told you yesterday, but there was no opportunity. I've almost left it too late. Just imagine what would have happened if I had died."

"Please, Bella, don't even say that. You must remain calm. The doctor warned me you might become feverish." It was apparent to Bella that Tristram thought her mind was wandering. His eyes searched the room, and he sighed when he spotted the waiting medication on the table beside the bed. "Let me pour you a dose of laudanum. You will sleep peacefully and will feel much better in the morning."

Bella fought back the urge to scream at his patronizing tone. She felt physically weak and knew she did not have the strength to continue the battle for long. She reached out her hand to grasp the sleeve of his jacket and tugged until she had his attention. Her voice shook in her frustration, but she was determined to have her say.

"You must listen to me!" she cried.

Some quality of desperation in her tone penetrated his concern, and he paused in the act of rising. He frowned down at her, then nodded his head, subsiding on the edge of the bed. He once more captured her hand and stroked it soothingly. "All right, Bella," he said. "I will listen."

She shuddered in her relief, almost too overcome to speak. She swallowed several times and waited for the pounding of her heart to return to normal.

"It's about Colin. You must go to Millicent Heathrow-Finchley. You must ask her to tell you what she told me yesterday over tea."

"Of course, my dear," he said. "I shall drop by tomorrow."

"Oh, Tristram, this is important. Don't treat me like a child. You must swear to me you will go to Millicent first thing in the morning."

"But why?" he said, his forehead wrinkled in puzzlement at her request.

"Because you will believe her. And she can prove to you that Colin is not Henry Addison's child. Colin is your son."

Chapter Fourteen

"Colin is really your son," Bella repeated more firmly as she saw Tristram's face harden to granite.

"Don't, Bella."

There was a note of pleading in his voice that indicated his fear at reopening such a painful subject. Tristram released her hand and started to rise, but she caught the hem of his coat and held him in place. Cognizant of the fact that if she had not survived the carriage accident he would not know his son's true parentage, Bella was filled with an urgency to tell him what she had discovered. She could not permit such a misunderstanding to continue.

Using his coat for leverage, she pulled herself to a sitting position. She was light-headed and swayed against him as the room spun dizzily before her eyes. Almost without volition, his arms closed around her. He sat back down, cradling her head against his chest. Slowly the room came back into focus, and she pushed herself away from the security of his body until she could look into his face.

"Listen to me, Tristram. I am not out of my head, although I will admit, it pounds like the very devil," she said.

Even the small moue of annoyance pulled at the skin around the bandage. She waited a moment until the worst of the throbbing had passed, then tried to order her thoughts. Tristram sat very still, his eyes trained on her face in concern, but there was a tension to his body that spoke much for his resistance to anything she might say. She sighed and forced herself to continue.

"Even when you told me about Colin, I did not believe it. I realize he does not look much like you, but curiously enough he bears a striking resemblance to Lady Wyndham."

Tristram shook his head, rejecting her words. "I told you, Bella. He is Henry Addison's son. Addison had the same curly brown hair," he said, as if offering irrefutable evidence.

A bubble of amusement rose in Bella's breast, but she knew this was no occasion for laughter. She suspected that Tristram's refusal to give much credence to her words was to protect himself from wishful thinking. Although he loved Colin, there must be some portion of his mind and heart that wanted nothing more than to believe the boy was his natural son. She stared up into his steady blue eyes, now tinged with pain.

She spoke slowly and firmly, so that he would not mistake a word. "Colin is your son for the simple reason that Johanna was already pregnant when she met Henry Addison."

For a moment she wondered if her words had penetrated Tristram's brain. He remained perfectly still, his face wiped clean of any expression. His eyes were unfocused and looked flat in the candlelight. When he spoke, his voice was harsh.

"How do you know?"

"Millicent told me. We began to talk about your wife, and she told me that Johanna was in despair when she discovered she was going to bear a child. She was afraid she would have to remain at the Keep instead of returning to London. Millicent planned a party to cheer her up, and it was there that she met Henry Addison."

Bella reached up to stroke his cheek, as if she could soothe away nine years of pain. Silence clamped down over the room, and she held her breath, waiting for some reaction from Tristram. He had withdrawn inside his mind, putting her at a distance, mentally if not physically. Her hand remained on his cheek, a reminder of her presence. Suddenly she felt a nerve jump beneath her fingers and, as if the involuntary movement had broken the dam of reserve in which he held himself, Tristram sagged against her.

"Dear God in heaven," he whispered into her hair.

There was such anguish in his voice that tears rose to Bella's eyes, rolling silently down her cheeks to soak into the shoulder of his coat against which her head rested. Relief washed over her as she realized that Tristram believed her. When he released her, there was an expression of wonder on his face that tore at her heart. She sniffed to hold back her tears, but cried harder when he pulled out a handkerchief to blot her damp cheeks. It was several minutes before she could control herself, and by that time she had exhausted all her reserves.

He seemed to understand and, holding her gently, he placed her back against the pillows, tucking the covers around her with much care. Afterwards he stood beside the bed, staring down at her with an expression she could not read. She reached out a hand and he took it, raising it to his lips.

"Thank you, Bella," he said, his voice muffled as he kissed the back of her hand. "I will go to Millicent at first light, but I already am convinced that what you heard is the truth. Sleep well, my dear. I shall talk to you tomorrow when you are feeling stronger."

Without another word, he placed her hand beneath the covers and left the room. Sarah bustled in, fussing around the bed to be sure that her charge was comfortable. Happiness surrounded Bella and cushioned her from the aches and pains of her injuries. Her eyes closed, and she gave in to the cottony feeling of sleep that crept around the edges of her mind.

It was late in the day when Bella woke. For a moment she lay quiet, listening to the faraway sounds of activity. Then she moved and, at the first twinge from abused muscles, all the events of the day before returned in a flood. Strangely enough for all her adventures, she felt only an occasional bruise and some stiffness in her joints. She threw back the covers and swung her feet to the side of the bed. Even her dizziness of the night before was gone, replaced by a slight throbbing beneath the bandage on her head. She was just about to place her foot on the floor when the door opened, and she heard Sarah screech.

"You can't get out of bed, miss," she cried, running across the room. "The doctor said you should stay quiet for several days."

"Nonsense, Sarah. I am perfectly fine." She slid out of bed but winced as her legs tightened under her weight. "Well, perhaps perfect is not the correct word, but I shall not stay in bed like some dyspeptic spinster."

Despite her effort to remain stern, Sarah giggled. "I cannot approve, but I can see you are determined to have your own way."

"Then at last we are in agreement," Bella said, moving stiffly across to the washstand. "And besides, I am starving."

"I could bring you a tray," the maid offered. "Just think how nice it would be to pile the pillows at your back with all of Cook's delicacies spread out before you."

Bella grinned over her shoulder at the suggestion. "Much better to sit up, fully dressed, beside the window."

Sarah sniffed that her clever strategy had not worked. "Whatever you say, miss," she said.

Once the maid had helped her dress and brush her hair, Bella sat on the window seat, slightly breathless from her exertions but triumphant. Outside the passing storm had left the grounds a verdant green. She cranked open the window and sniffed the earthy odors rising from below. By the time Sarah returned with the laden tray, she felt recovered from her adventures of the previous night.

"How is Colin?" she asked between bites of thin slices of ham and dainty cucumber sandwiches.

"Word in the kitchen is that he is much recovered. But wait until you hear the news." Sarah's face was flushed with excitement. "Lady Wyndham went to his room this morning and read him a story."

"What?" Bella said, almost spilling her tea in her surprise.

"No one here at the Keep can ever recall such a happening. Even when he was a wee tyke, she never gave him any mind."

It was clear that the servants were stunned by such a turnaround, no more so than Bella. She did not believe that Tristram would have had time to tell his grandmother the momentous discovery. She hurried through the rest of her meal, anxious now to see how Colin was faring and to find out what had caused such a change in Lady Wyndham's behavior. Colin's door was open when she arrived at his room, and she poked her head around the doorframe, peering at the figure on the bed.

"What ho, young man," she called.

"Oh, Bella, I'm so glad you've come."

Colin pushed himself up against the pillows, looking much like a tiny potentate in regal splendor. His face was flushed with pleasure, and she could not resist hugging him, mindful of his bandaged arm.

"You seem none the worse for wear," she said, eyeing the happiness that bloomed in his face.

His expression sobered when he noticed the bandage on her head. "Are you all right?" he asked.

"Much improved, my dear. Just a touch of headache and some bruises in an area no lady would mention," she said. This brought the smile back to his face, and she pulled a chair close to his bed, easing herself into the soft seat. "Now you must tell me about your adventures and the exciting rescue. Although your father explained, I fear I am rather fuzzy as to the details."

She sat beside his bed as Colin launched into his story. As he told her about making tea for Lady Wyndham, she thought her heart would burst with happiness. She felt compassion for the dowager who had held herself aloof from the boy for nine years, only to discover what a wonderful child he was. Love had conquered her stubbornness and pride. Bella had always hoped that Lady Wyndham would acknowledge the boy before she discovered his birthright and was stunned to find that just such a miracle had taken place. Bella could just imagine how wonderful it would be once the woman realized that Colin truly was Tristram's son.

Colin's voice interrupted her joyous thoughts. "You're not listening, Bella."

"I'm sorry, dear. I was just woolgathering."

"I was telling you how well my new horse did on Father's return to the Keep. He said Todd jumped every wall and downed tree. I'm sure he'll be a blistering good hunter."

"I shudder to think what havoc you will wreak on the fox population," Bella teased.

"Just wait until hunting season," he crowed.

"In actual fact, I am not sure that I shall be here at that time," she ventured hesitantly. "I am thinking of taking a little trip."

"But I thought you were going to marry Father," he said, his voice accusing. "At least that's what Father said. He asked me if I approved and I did. That way you would always be here."

"I see. I didn't know whether your father had spoken to you. You didn't mention it."

"He talked to me when we first came back to the Keep. He said it wasn't settled yet. Said I shouldn't go nattering at you until you'd made up your mind," Colin explained succinctly.

Now that the discussion had started, Bella wasn't sure how to continue. "Well, he did talk to me about marrying him but I am not sure it would be a very good idea."

"Don't you like Father?" he asked, his forehead wrinkled in concern. "I know sometimes he can be ever so stiff, but he is really a very good fellow."

"Yes, Colin, he is. And I do like him very much." She paused, choosing her words carefully. "You see, dear, your father only offered to marry me to save me from a very embarrassing situation. I have a wicked uncle, and your father was trying to protect me from this man. He told my uncle that we were to be married, but it was not exactly true. It was very kind of your father, but I am not sure that I can accept such a sacrifice."

"I don't think it would be all that much of a sacrifice," Colin said. "You are smashing with a fishing rod and have an excellent seat."

Bella chuckled at the boy's criterion for a wife. "I have the feeling your father might require more stringent qualifications. You must understand, Colin, that your father does not want to marry."

"I didn't *want* a governess," Colin argued in his own logical way.

"Ah yes, I remember so well. And you were kindness itself to take me on for such a lofty position." She winked at him, and he lost his petulant look as a grin stole across his face. "We have become friends, haven't we?"

"Yes. Very good friends, and I should not like it if you went away." His voice shook slightly on the final words.

"Nor should I," she admitted.

She rose from her chair and put her arms around the boy. He snuggled against her, and she found her resolve weakening. How could she consider leaving this child who had stolen her heart?

"You will stay until my arm is better, won't you?" he asked when she released him.

"I will try," she hedged.

"Then at least you can see me on Todd. It's going to be ever so awkward with my arm all wrapped up." He glared down at the offending limb.

"I doubt if that will hold you back," Bella said dryly.

She remained for a while in his rooms, telling him stories and listening to him while he described a hunt his father had taken him to last fall. Finally he appeared to be tiring, and she suggested a nap. It was evident that his adventures had taken a toll because he did not even argue but snuggled beneath the covers.

After discovering that Lady Wyndham was also abed, Bella returned to her room, curling up on the window seat and staring disconsolately outside.

Despite her words to Colin, she knew she would have to immediately make plans to leave Dragon's Keep. She had wanted to plant the idea that she was planning a trip in the boy's head so that her leaving would not be such a jolt. In time, he would get over her absence. More to the point, would she? For a moment she wavered, wondering if she might remain, but in an instant she knew the answer. She could not stay indefinitely as a guest of either Tristram or Lady Wyndham.

Colin's legitimacy changed much. Tristram had refused to marry for fear another wife might balk at Colin's inheriting. That was no longer in question, and now Tristram was free to find a woman he could love. He had only offered for her to save her from Derwent, and in his conversation with Lady Wyndham that she had overheard, he had made his position very clear. He had only agreed to go through with the wedding in the face of his grandmother's threats. For the sake of her personal integrity, Bella could not accept marriage on such terms.

Even Lady Wyndham could no longer be counted on to champion the marriage. Originally the dowager had been insistent that Tristram marry for the sake of the line. Once she understood that Colin was the true heir, she would not be so eager. She would not press him with the threat of blackmail now that there was no need for a new heir. Granted, she liked Bella well enough, but she would not demand Tristram marry her.

All in all, her usefulness to the Wyndham household was

quite at an end. The only reason for her to continue to remain was the painful awareness that she was in love with Tristram. But if she held him to his pledge to marry her, she would keep him from establishing a loving relationship with someone he would desire to make his bride. He would grow to hate her in time, and that she could not bear.

She pressed her hands to her chest, feeling the pain of heartbreak as if it were real. She knew she must leave, but did not know how she would find the strength to survive the lonely years ahead.

Tristram stood with his back to the mantel in the Danforth study. His face was stiff with anger as he glared at the bowed head of the woman sobbing in the chair. Eden sat immobile in a leather chair behind the desk, his normally half-shuttered lids wide open, displaying eyes glazed with shock. The crying continued, and his mouth pursed with distaste as he raised his head and gazed at his wife.

"Stop that caterwauling, Glynis," he snapped.

A gasp followed his words but, to the relief of the two men, the sobbing ceased. The woman sniffled into a handkerchief, raising a face blotched with red and swollen from crying. Tristram hardened his heart to the ravaged face, wondering if she had truly aged before his very eyes. Gone was the bright, brittle prettiness that had always been present. Glynis Danforth looked every day of her forty years.

"You will go to your room and remain there until I come to speak with you," Eden said. She opened her mouth but he cut her off, his tone implacable. "Listen to me well, Glynis. You will go immediately to your room."

She seemed to shrivel at his harsh words. She sniffed again, then rose from her chair. Crossing the room, she shuffled her feet much like an old woman. Neither man spoke as she opened the door and exited the room. The air was heavy with tension, and Tristram stared down at his boots to avoid making eye contact with his cousin. Finally Eden broke the silence, his voice quivering with emotion.

"I am so dreadfully sorry, Tristram. I had no idea. Believe me."

"I understand that. The groom said it was Glynis who hired him."

"She must have lost her mind!" Eden appeared totally undone by the realization that his own wife had connived at killing Tristram. "And all for the title!"

Until Colin was born, Eden had been Tristram's heir. Over the years Glynis had begun to think that Tristram would never marry and that eventually the title would fall to Eden. When Tristram married Johanna and produced an heir, Glynis, by some incredible piece of logic, believed that the title had been stolen from Eden. Apparently the anger festered over the years, but the woman held her hand on the belief that Prudence would marry a titled gentleman.

It was only in the last year that Glynis realized this hope was in vain. Prudence was not interested and almost rebellious when she was introduced to an eligible titled gentleman. In some twisted way Glynis blamed Tristram, and he became the reason for her inability to reach the upper strata of society. With Tristram out of the way, she was convinced everything would work out for the best.

To give Glynis the benefit of the doubt, Tristram suspected that she had never really considered the fact that once he was gone Colin would still prevent Eden from inheriting. Tristram had become the focus of her obsession and beyond that she had not considered.

Now that the puzzle of the attacks had been resolved, Tristram could almost feel sorry for his cousin. It had been apparent from the moment he entered the study and told his story to Eden that the man had had no part in the nefarious business. He had blustered at first, but when Glynis was confronted with the groom's story, she had crumbled. She confessed to hiring the groom, and admitted that he had been behind both shootings and the carriage accident. Eden's horror at such complicity was so evident that Tristram cleared him of any knowledge of the plot.

"Dear God, Tristram, Lady Wyndham and Colin might have been killed if the carriage had overturned!"

"I am well aware of that. From what Glynis said she had a change of heart before the carriage left, but by that time it was too late. And perhaps that's true. I cannot judge."

"What do you intend to do?"

"Nothing," Tristram snapped. "She is your wife, and as such it is your responsibility to deal with her. Perhaps if you explain to the local magistrate, he will be willing to handle the punishment of the groom without creating a scandal. Although personally I would prefer to see him hung, you might suggest transportation. Naturally, I will demand restitution for the family of the coachman. Davis was a good man, and he leaves behind a wife and two grown children."

"I will take care of them, never fear. For the rest, I do not know how to make it up to you. You must know that I would never wish harm to you or any of the family. I realize there is nothing I can say or do that will lessen this dreadful situation. I can only think that Glynis's greed drove her to the point of insanity. But I give you my word, Tristram, that you will never again have to fear for yourself or your family."

Tristram raised his eyes to study Eden's face. He had always considered the man a pompous weakling, but there was a new resolve that gave a certain air of character to the balding man. Perhaps some good might come out of this, after all.

"I will take your word and will fault you for nothing except an inability to control your wife. My household will always be open to you and Prue, but I tell you truly I cannot say the same for Glynis. I have no desire to see her ever again."

Eden bowed his head, accepting the verdict. Tristram's last view of him was hunched over the desk, his hands clenched on the tooled leather surface. He closed the study door, grateful only that the situation had been resolved. The whole thing had left a bad taste in his mouth. Outside he sniffed the air, wanting to wash the stench of fear and guilt from his nostrils. He placed his beaver hat on his head and climbed into the curricle for the return to Dragon's Keep.

Once the Danforth estate was far behind him, his heart began to lift. It had been a busy day, and he had covered the gamut of emotions from jubilation to despair. At first light he had ridden to Neddy's and in the quiet of the salon he had listened to Millicent's story. There was no question that Colin was his son. Now that he thought back to the events of Johanna's elopement, he realized he should have come to the same conclusion. He still could not believe that his wife had hated him so much that she would condemn her own child to the stain of illegitimacy just for the sake of revenge.

After he had heard Millicent's story, he told his old friends all the circumstances surrounding Colin's birth. Only then did they understand why he had been so adamant against remarriage. They rejoiced with the knowledge that they had been instrumental in resolving the question of Colin's parentage, but Millicent was inconsolable that she had not spoken sooner. Tristram disabused her of any feeling of guilt, reminding her that she had tried to speak to him but he had refused to listen.

The rest of the visit had gone well. With the privilege of friendship, he twitted Millicent on her impressive figure, which indicated she would soon add to Neddy's brood of mischievous-eyed girls. When Tristram turned the subject to his engagement to Bella, they had begged him to permit them to plan a party after the arrival of the new baby. He was so filled with well-being that he gladly accepted the offer.

Riding back to the Keep, Tristram kept the pace slow. He was enjoying the fresh air after feeling so confined in Eden's study. His eyes acknowledged the beauty of the scenery, and he cast off the remainder of his blue-deviled mood. Eden would take control of his household, and Tristram could close the dark chapters concerning Glynis. He had all of his life ahead of him, and with Bella he would make a wonderful new beginning.

Just the thought of her brought a headiness to him. His chest expanded with happiness as he looked out over the horses's heads for his first view of Wyndham land. He was anxious to see her, eager to feel the rush of joy in her presence. He wondered how quickly he could convince her to marry. They could get a special license and be married this day.

He felt like a young man, coming to love for the first time. There was a depth to his emotions for Bella that there had not been when he had met and married Johanna. He realized that his love for his wife had been a chimera, created out of his desire to be in love. It was a feeling more akin to lust than to love, but in his youth he had not known the difference. He and Johanna had never been friends; in fact, he had been stunned to discover he did not much like her. They had made love, but had never been lovers.

His relationship with Bella was entirely different. He thought of her as a friend and companion, a woman he enjoyed talking with or just sitting quietly beside. He knew her as a real person with ideas of her own and a sense of self that he was eager to plumb. It would be years before he would know her more fully, but there would be a joy in the search for understanding that would never bore him. She had character and an honesty he treasured, but perhaps it was her sense of humor that he especially enjoyed. There had been little laughter in his life since his disastrous marriage, and he reveled in how Bella embraced the joyfulness of life.

He clucked to the horses and snapped the reins, eager to be home and confide to Bella the depth of his love. At his own thoughts, a warning bell sounded in his mind. Would Bella be delighted by such a declaration?

In his arrogance he had only been thinking of his emotions. He had been so caught up in his dreams that he had not considered the possibility that she might not welcome his love and devotion. She had already voiced an objection to the marriage, but he had assumed that it was out of fairness that she was giving him an opportunity to cry off. What if her objections were personal? What if she really did not want to marry him?

He pulled back on the reins, bringing the horses to a walk. He blinked his eyes in bewilderment as he looked around at the landscape. The day seemed darker now, no longer aglow with sunshine. He could feel his heart pounding, but the beat was ponderous, a fitting echo to his thoughts.

In his concentration on his own emotions, he had failed to consider that Bella might not return his passion. He searched his mind, trying to remember every occasion when he had been with her and what he could deduce from her reactions. It was true that she treated him with a certain fondness, but he had put it down to the fact she had never considered him in the role of suitor. He knew she enjoyed his company; she was far too open in her expressions to fabricate pleasure where none existed.

He recalled their kiss in the library and winced when he remembered her shock and horror at his rough handling. While it was true she had been repelled by his behavior, she had trusted him enough to let him kiss her the second time, and there had been no question that she had enjoyed that embrace.

But all of these ruminations did not answer the one question that needed to be asked. Could Bella love him?

Although he wanted to return to the Keep and sweep her into his arms and declare undying love, he realized glumly that he would have to restrain his ardor. He knew enough of her history to realize she was frightened by the thought of male domination, and she was inexperienced enough to not understand that true love involved personal freedom and a shared trust in each other.

He ground his teeth, knowing he would have to move slowly. He would woo Bella with a tenderness and control that would not frighten her. And if in the end she could not love him, he loved her enough to set her free.

Chapter Fifteen

In the shadow of the trees Tristram's face took on a feral cast, eyes narrowed in concentration as he watched Bella pick her way along the path on her return to the Keep. He felt the elation of a hunter who has stalked his prey to its lair and waits, biding his time to have the advantage in the coming attack. There was a smirk of satisfaction on his face as the petite figure disappeared from view.

He pushed away from the rough bark of the tree. He moved slowly, his face set in concentration as he walked the short distance to the little clearing that Bella had just left. He stopped at the edge of the trees, staring around the space, struck by an instant recognition. Suddenly his eyes lit up, and his mouth spread in a grin of unhallowed delight.

He remembered an identical spot. It had lived in his memory, magically invested with a golden light which was the way he had first seen it. It was morning light, and he had wakened with a terrible headache and had looked around to see a fairy maiden washing at a stream. The maiden brushed her golden brown curls and turned, showing an adorable face to his bemused vision. This little clearing was similar to the place where he had first met Bella, the place of safety she had brought him to after he had been shot.

Tristram's blue eyes glittered in the late afternoon light as he scanned the area. It was not far from the Keep, and yet he could not recall ever being here. Cutting along one side of the clearing there was a vagrant spring-fed trickle of water which eventually wound its way down the hillside to join the trout stream at the base of the home woods. The resemblance to that other wooded bower was striking and, for the first time in two weeks, elation bloomed in his heart.

He walked across the grass to the edge of the water, his boots sinking into the soft, mossy ground. Picking a broad leaf, he held it over the water. He dropped it and watched it float along, to be picked up by the invisible current and borne away. He spotted a fallen log and sat down. He sat motionless, letting the silence of the woods surround him, and took heart.

For two agonizing weeks he had tried to woo Bella, but the exasperating chit had proved curiously elusive. He never seemed able to catch her alone, and the presence of others had inhibited any progress in his suit. At the rate he was going, he would be old and infirm before he was able to speak to her and unburden his heart. He gravitated between an angry frustration and a wry amusement which covered his real fear that when he did approach her, Bella might not return his feelings. Eventually it dawned on him that the contrary girl was deliberately avoiding him.

At first he was aghast, assuming it meant she didn't want him to speak. He was plunged into despair at this indication that she did not have strong feelings for him and did not want to hurt him by telling him so. But occasionally he would catch her watching him, and there was an expression of warmth in her eyes that gave him reason to hope.

It was then he turned crafty, spying on Bella to discover her whereabouts so that he might approach her at a time and place that would be most advantageous for his declaration. He had noticed that she disappeared every day right before tea. By the simple expedient of following her, it had taken him only two days to discover where she went. The first day he had let her get too far ahead and had lost her among the trees. But the next day, he had been successful and followed her to the little clearing in the woods. Today confirmed the fact that she was visiting the spot on a regular basis.

Just the look of the place had given Tristram some hope that his suit might not be in vain. Bella could not have come to this spot without seeing the resemblance to the place where she had nursed him, and if she came here often it must be because she enjoyed remembering that time. The more he thought on it, the more he realized that this would make the perfect setting for his talk with her. He would use her memories of the day they met to rekindle the companionship of that occasion.

Tristram rose to his feet and, after one more glance around, he started back to the Keep. He needed to stop to talk to Whitcombe, and as he neared the stables, he spotted Colin, arm supported by a black sling, sitting on the top rail of the paddock fence. Todd pranced beside the fence, his head occasionally nuzzling the boy's shoulder. Tristram quickened his pace as he noticed the somber expression on his son's face.

"Is something amiss with Todd?" Tristram asked as he approached the fence.

Colin's face cleared in an instant. "Oh no, sir. He's doing wondrous well. He jumped an oxer today, but still shies a bit on the water jump."

"He'll get used to that in time," Tristram said, patting the hunter's neck. As if the horse realized he would no longer have Colin's full attention, he trotted across the field, his tail flicking in disdain. "Well, if Todd is not the problem, there must be something else on your mind. Anything I can help you with?"

He was much struck by the concentrated stare Colin bent on him. The boy's head was cocked to the side and his eyes were narrowed as if viewing his father in a strange light. Finally Colin nodded and, despite the fact he only had the use of one arm, scrambled down from his perch on the fence.

"Could we walk a bit, Father?" he said.

Although amused by the gravity of his son's voice, Tristram kept his face expressionless. "We could walk toward the lake, if that would be acceptable?"

For answer, Colin merely nodded. Tristram shortened his stride as they walked together, keeping silent until the boy was ready to speak. They reached the shore of the small lake and, as was their habit, picked up small stones and began to skip them across the water. Once again the broken arm did not seem to interfere with Colin's aim. The rhythm of motion had a soothing effect for Tristram, and finally his patience was rewarded.

"Bella is a very nice lady, isn't she?" Colin asked, eyes intent on the stone skipping on the water.

"Yes, she is. I think there is no one at the Keep who wouldn't say the same."

"She's awfully pretty." His head was down as he concentrated on choosing another stone. "Do you think so, Father?"

Now that Tristram understood the topic of conversation, his eyes began to crinkle at the corners and he felt a definite urge to laugh. If he was correct in his assumption, it appeared that Colin was up to some sort of matchmaking scheme. He flipped his last stone expertly and then seated himself on the grass where he stared gravely up at his son.

"Well, I don't know if I would say Bella was pretty." At this remark, Colin jerked his head in surprise, his face a picture of confusion. Tristram took pity on him. "I do not think pretty is a strong enough word. I would have to say, Colin, that Bella is as beautiful as an angel."

"Do you really think so?" the boy asked in relief.

"Yes, I do. I can honestly say I have never met a woman I have liked better."

"That's excellent, Father!" His teeth flashed in a wide grin of happiness, but suddenly his eyebrows lowered and he stared at his father accusingly. "Then why don't you want to marry her?" he asked.

"But I do want to marry her."

"You do?"

The boy looked so astonished that for a moment Tristram wondered if he had misread the situation. "Would you be upset if I did want to marry Bella?"

"Oh, no, sir!" he cried. He gave up all pretense of an interest in skipping stones and, oblivious to his broken arm, threw himself down beside his father. "I would be ever so pleased if you would marry Bella. She is great fun to be with, and we have such jolly times when we are together. Even when she hugs me it is different. She doesn't go all sticky sweet. She treats me more like I am grown up. And, besides, I love her very much."

"I love her very much, too," Tristram said quietly.

"Oh, I say, sir, that's smashing!" Colin's face, which was wreathed in smiles, made one of those lightning changes and was once again very serious. "I don't suppose you could marry her immediately, Father?"

"Well, I think it might be polite to get Bella's consent first. Is there some reason for this urgency?"

"Yes, sir. At least, I believe so," Colin said. "You see, I think Bella is planning to leave the Keep."

"Ah," sighed Tristram in understanding. "Do you have any actual information that might lead to such a conclusion?"

"I'm not really certain, but right after the accident she told me she was thinking about taking a trip. And yesterday, when we were out riding, she asked if I would take care of Fortune if she went away for a while."

"Devil you say!" Tristram clucked his tongue while Colin stared at him in concern. "Well, old son, it looks as though we may have to take drastic measures to convince Bella that it is her duty to remain at the Keep and marry me. Are you game?"

"Oh yes, Father!"

Colin threw himself at his father, hugging him with all the enthusiasm of his youthful heart and one good arm. Tristram cuddled the boy against him and wondered at the happiness that had been given him in this small bundle of energy. Finally he settled the boy beside him, checking to make sure the sling was back in position and then, heads together, they began to make their plans.

Before setting out on the flagstone path, Bella looked carefully around the garden to be certain she was alone. It had been an exasperating day and she wanted to get away undetected. Colin had been unusually clinging, wanting her attention most of the day. First thing in the morning, he had badgered her into visiting one of the outlying farms to see, as he put it, a "special litter of pigs." Although she had enjoyed the ride and the visit with the tenants, she had found nothing exceptional about the piglets.

Even Lady Wyndham had demanded her presence to discuss at great length the layout of a canvas she was planning to work in needlepoint. For what seemed like hours, they had pored over a series of floral designs that at any other time would have left the old woman bilious. Since Bella had rarely seen the dowager with a needle in her hand, she found the whole exercise curious. When Lady Wyndham had suggested tea, she had politely excused herself and quickly escaped out of doors.

Before she entered the woods, Bella peeked over her shoulder, feeling ridiculous for such furtive behavior. However, since she had begun visiting the clearing in the woods, she had treasured the privacy and was reluctant to share it with anyone. She would sit beside the stream, away from the temptations offered by the presence of Colin, Lady Wyndham, and most especially Tristram. In the quiet of the woods, she was able to analyze her situation and make plans for her future.

Under cover of the trees, Bella slowed her pace, her half-boots kicking up little puffs of dust on the well-trodden path. She looked around as she walked, trying to store up memories for the time when she would be gone from this beautiful spot. She knew the scenery in the north of England was much harsher than she was used to, and she suspected she would miss the Keep as well as its inhabitants.

She pushed away the vision of Tristram that rose to her mind. She refused to dwell on him, knowing that it only brought her more heartache. Instead, she turned her mind to thoughts of Colin and Lady Wyndham.

It was incredible how their relationship had changed in just two short weeks. Once the dowager had accepted the child the night of the accident, she did not settle for half-measures. Each day Colin visited with Lady Wyndham, and their activities ranged from reading to playing chess and, on one startling occasion, a demonstration of marble shooting. Colin was thriving under the dowager's loving attention. For all intents and purposes, there might never have been an estrangement between them.

Bella had not been present when Tristram told his grandmother the real story surrounding Colin's birth. He had told Bella that Lady Wyndham had listened without expression, her face paling to an alarming degree. At the conclusion, she had closed her eyes, all evidence of her interior struggle invisible, except for the whitening of her knuckles as her hands gripped her ever-present walking stick. When she opened her eyes, she merely nodded her head and requested Tristram to notify her solicitor so that Colin could be included in her will.

Just the thought of the indomitable old woman brought a smile to Bella's lips. Her pace quickened as she neared the clearing, and as she cut through the woods she waited eagerly for the first glimpse of her favorite spot. She broke through the last line of trees and skidded to a halt at the scene before her. She closed her eyes to clear her vision, but when she opened them again everything remained the same.

Violet grazed beside the spring water, and she raised her head to whicker in welcome. On the ground behind the mare was a pile which consisted of Violet's saddle, Bella's portmanteau, and a canvas bag she had used for her escape from her uncle. In the center of the clearing the grass had been cut away to form a bare space on which a fire was ready laid. The dented metal teapot and mugs she had brought with her from Mallory were nestled on the ground next to the pile of kindling. A large hamper was near at hand beside a smaller, cloth-covered woven basket.

Time slipped away, and Bella was transported back to the afternoon of the day she had run away from home. The only thing missing was the sound of a shot and Tristram's bloodied body.

Her heart was pounding so loudly in her ears that at first she didn't hear the sounds emerging from the hamper. Eventually she noticed the angry shaking of the wicker, and then identified the sharp yipping. She shook her head in disbelief, but she crossed the grass and knelt beside the hamper to unlatch the top. As she folded back the top, Beau's head popped up, and he sprang out, bounding around in ecstasy at his release. He leaped up to lick her face, and she buried her own flushed cheeks in his fur.

"Well, my fine friend," Bella said, "where is your master? I must have a word with him for treating you so shabbily."

Beau bounded a few steps away, staring into the woods until a small figure stepped out onto the trail. Colin, his eyes alight with laughter, walked silently toward Bella. He stopped in front of her, leaned down to kiss her cheek, and then, without a word, walked to Violet. With his good hand, he reached up to the mare's halter and led her out of the clearing, while Beau frisked happily about his feet.

Bella sat motionless, waiting for the next scene of this meticulously crafted play. She could feel her heart thundering within her chest, but it was not an ominous beat; it sent a message of excitement through her body. Twigs crackled underfoot, and she swung her head toward the sound.

Tristram stood at the edge of the clearing. He was wearing

buckskins and boots, and looked quite at home in the woods. There was a tension in his body and a wariness in his expression that Bella had never seen before. He looked as if he were poised on the edge of flight, and she wondered if she blinked if he would disappear. When he moved toward her, she licked her lips to ease their dryness.

"I am Wyndham. Lord Tristram Wyndham. At your service."

The repetition of the words he had spoken the night he was wounded jolted Bella, and she sucked in her breath. Without hesitation, she responded, "I am Arabella."

His eyes crinkled at the corners, but he did not smile. His features were somber, almost grim as he knelt down before the cloth-covered basket. Without paying her any attention, he removed the cloth and spread it before her, then he proceeded to lay out a picnic of ham, cheese, and bread. When he finished, he sat down across from her. Only then did he lift his eyes to hers.

Despite the soberness of his expression, there was a wealth of emotion in the glitter of his blue eyes. For all her life was worth, Bella could not turn away from the magnetism of his glance. She felt light-headed at the sensations that were racing through her body. Since she entered the clearing, she had felt a sense of magic, but it had been a dreamlike feeling that had no reality. From the moment she looked into his eyes, she began to understand the fiery passion that Tristram was holding in check, and her heart sang with happiness.

"And where are you bound for on this fine day?" he asked, once more reminding her of their first conversation.

"I am going to the north of England," she answered quietly.

"Not London this time? Perhaps a wise choice, all things considered." He nodded as if in approval. "Of course, it is a long trip. No doubt fraught with many uncomfortable nights on the road, not to mention dangers. And what do you plan to do once you reach the north of England?"

"I will look for work," she answered, fighting to keep her voice steady.

She was amazed that Tristram had strong enough nerves for such a game. His words were drawled as if he didn't have the least care in the world, while all the time she felt as if she might scream with the rising tension of their word play. Then her eyes dropped to his hands, fingers bunched into fists. She was pleased that he, too, was so caught up in the charged atmosphere that he needed to restrain himself.

"I can understand that you would need to find a position." He was silent for a moment. He raised one tanned hand and tapped his cheek, his eyes narrowed in thought. "It is a strange coincidence, but I am seeking to fill a position in my household."

"Oh," she said. "A governess?"

"No. No." He shook his head, his expression grave. "We had one once, but she did not work out."

She had been almost too afraid to hope, but now her heart lifted in anticipation. Tension tightened every muscle in her body, and she had to clear her throat before she could speak. "Why not?"

"It was very sad really. My son was quite contented with her, and even my grandmother found her to be respectable. The servants, both here and in London, fair doted on the woman. Whitcombe, my head groom, who has never been very fond of females, thought she was a singular young lady. I myself was the one at fault. You see—" Tristram raised his head and his eyes blazed with feeling. "I fell in love with her."

"Oh."

The single syllable sounded loud in the silence of the woods. Its utterance tore away any semblance of calm that Tristram had fought to maintain. He leaped to his feet to glare down at Bella. "Is that all you have to say, you contrary chit!"

In exasperation, he ran his hands through his hair, although by the harassed expression on his face, it seemed to her he would rather have his fingers around her throat. The numbness that had held her frozen at his words dissipated, and a slow smile pulled at her mouth.

"Would it help if I told you that I love you, too?"

Tristram groaned and reached down to pull her to her feet. He swept her into the circle of his arms, holding her against his chest where she could hear the pounding of his heart beneath her ear. He held her with a fierce gentleness that she found endearing. Finally he loosened his grip until she could look up into his handsome face. There was such passion in his gaze that for a moment she was frightened, but immediately he sensed her panic.

"I love you, Bella," he said. "If there were no other way, I would adore you from afar with a knightly chastity that would not frighten you. But if you marry me, you will have to give me your trust. You will have to believe that I would never abuse you or hurt you intentionally. Can you give me that trust?"

"Yes," she whispered, but there was a tremble of apprehension in her voice.

"There is a power in passion, but you need not fear it. You are a loving person, and it is only ignorance of true love that makes you afraid. My love for you will kindle the passion I sense within you. Then you will discover that love brings not only glory to your heart and mind, but to your body, as well."

He stared down at her, his eyes intent. He seemed to be waiting for something, and then she realized what he wanted. She reached her hand up to circle his neck. As she rose on tiptoes, she pulled his head down until her lips touched his.

His kiss was gentle, the merest brush of his lips. She could feel herself relax as his mouth moved over hers, lightly whispering salutations that stirred a feeling deep within her body. Beneath her hands the muscles of his body trembled as he restrained his emotions. That very restraint convinced her that she had nothing to fear from this man. She would always be safe with Tristram, and in that safety she would find the glory of passion.

When his kiss deepened, she was not afraid. She felt a rush of sensation when his tongue touched hers, and she reveled in the experience. She was almost swooning when he groaned and released her.

"We will marry immediately!" His voice was hoarse as he glared down at her.

She blinked several times to recover, then grinned up at him saucily. "But I have not said I would marry you."

"You have to marry me," he snapped, taking her hand and dragging her toward the woods.

"Why?"

"Because you have compromised me, you hussy."

At this outrageous bit of nonsense, Bella burst out laughing. "*I* have compromised *you?*"

"May I remind you, my girl, that I spent the night alone with you in the woods. My reputation would be in tatters should the least word of that leak to the gossiping old tabbies. Why, I would be scorned by society, a man of easy virtue with never a woman to make an honest man of me."

"Oh, Tristram, I adore you," Bella said. "And since I have been the author of your tale of degradation, I will most properly do the honorable thing."

For answer, Tristram scooped her up in his arms. From the moment he had opened his eyes and found her staring down at him, he had loved her. He carried her in his arms, just as he always would carry her in his heart.